Martha Roddy transports the
with romance, espionage, and
prevails. A captivating book i
to romantics.

e
v
.... purls

Cherri Taylor, Storyteller, Contributor, *Chicken Soup for the Soul*
Author, *Wake Me When I'm Skinny*

Where else can a reader find salvation, sweet romance, espionage, and World War II tidbits that both intrigue and satisfy? Martha Roddy has managed to mix her plot in just the right combination! The Sleeper is a not-to-be-easily-put-down read.

Melanie Stiles, Life Coach, Author, and Speaker

When Martha Roddy penned THE SLEEPER, she hit a home run. Her novel skillfully combines intrigue, romance, and love with the realities of World War II, all in a capsule of spiritual truth and conviction. It makes a lasting impression of an era that should never be forgotten and would be a meaningful addition to any library.

Robert E Driver, PhD
Professor of Finance and Business Ethics
LeTourneau University

In her novel, Martha creates a unique spy story of suspense and intrigue, keeping the readers' attention to the last page. She travels back in time to a college campus during World War Two which makes the story more and more intriguing. The suspense keeps the reader's attention to the point it is hard to stop reading until the very end.

Martha pays great attention to detail, which helps the reader vividly picture the next turn of events in the lives of the main characters. Her story of suspense, spying, and romance is wonderfully written. The Sleeper is a must-read book.

Jeff Campbell, PhD. Author,and Speaker
Hidden in Plain Sight
The Little Girl Without a Name

THE
SLEEPER

* * *

MARTHA RODDY

WESTBOW
PRESS®
A DIVISION OF THOMAS NELSON
& ZONDERVAN

This is a work of fiction. Names, characters, places, and incidents are a product of the authors' imagination, and any the resemblance to actual persons, living or dead, business establishments, events or locale are entirely coincidental

WestBow Press books may be ordered through booksellers or by contacting:

WestBow Press
A Division of Thomas Nelson & Zondervan
1663 Liberty Drive
Bloomington, IN 47403
www.westbowpress.com
1 (866) 928-1240

Because of the dynamic nature of the Internet, any web addresses or links contained in this book may have changed since publication and may no longer be valid. The views expressed in this work are solely those of the author and do not necessarily reflect the views of the publisher, and the publisher hereby disclaims any responsibility for them.

Any people depicted in stock imagery provided by Getty Images are models, and such images are being used for illustrative purposes only. Certain stock imagery © Getty Images.

Scripture taken from the King James Version of the Bible.

ISBN: 978-1-9736-9011-5 (sc)
ISBN: 978-1-9736-9010-8 (hc)
ISBN: 978-1-9736-9012-2 (e)

Library of Congress Control Number: 2020906883

Print information available on the last page.

WestBow Press rev. date: 6/3/2020

In memory of
my husband,
Stephen Robert Roddy, MD,
WWII Cadet, US Army Air Corps,
Lieutenant Colonel, US Air Force Reserve.

Acknowledgments

*M*y husband, Stephen R. Roddy, a WWII veteran and a surgeon, and Marge Roddy were my first critics. Other early critics included Linda Leschek, Society of Children's Book Writers and Illustrators, and Marion Donahoe, both deceased, as well as Patricia Kougar-Melton, deceased, NW Houston Inspirational Writers Alive! (IWA!) webmaster who created a work-in-progress cover for my novel.

I gratefully acknowledge Stephen H. Roddy, artistic director of Houston Children's Chorus, for help with music and songs included in *The Sleeper*, and Walter A. Aue, professor of chemistry, Dalhousie University, for his translation of "I am the captain of my soul" from Henley's poem "Invictus," and Mason Rook for his bequest of humor.

I am deeply grateful for the valuable assistance of members of critique groups.

Melanie Stiles and others in DiAnn Mills's group, Diane Batista and Martha Rogers, members of Central Houston IWA!, Lois Harris, Bronwen Spindle, Jeff Campbell, Cherri Taylor, Marie Riffle, Debbie Sapp, Linda Slate, Connie McWilliams, and others in NW Houston IWA!.

Connie McWilliams kept me motivated with emailed prayer and scripture. The critique skills of SCWBI members who met at my home motivated me to continue work on *The Sleeper*. Thank you, Kathleen Endler, Julie Herman, Heather Walters, and Vicki Chapman. I'm thankful for Carolyn Lacy, Carrie Roddy, and Bronwen Spindle, who read selected chapters and offered encouragement.

My thanks to CompuSolutionX's CEO, Kenneth Akiri, who solved my computer hang-ups with alacrity.

I am forever indebted to each person who guided me along the way with my work in progress. In spite of efforts to keep up with those who critiqued my work in progress, I failed. If I omitted your name, please forgive me.

Part I

*Y*outh is the first victim of war; the first fruit of peace.
It takes 20 years or more of peace to make a
man; it takes only 20 seconds of war to destroy him.
—King Baudouin of Belgium (September
7, 1930–July 31, 1993)

* * *

CHAPTER I

Winning WWII

Washington, DC
July 29, 1944

ieutenant Colonel Edward Matthews hopped out of a taxi on E Street, NW, and walked a block to a cluster of obscure buildings housing the Office of Strategic Services (OSS), the United States WWII intelligence agency.

At the administrative building, the colonel handed his identification to a door sentry and said, "I have an appointment."

The soldier saluted and said, "Yes, sir. Mike Ward, the director's assistant, expects you. Follow me."

In his office, Ward said, "Colonel, after the Normandy invasion on June 6, D-Day, US carpet-bombing cracked the enemy line, but our ground fighting troops have moved only eighty square miles into France. You're our most fluent German-speaking OSS agent. We've brought you from the battlefields in Europe to interrogate recently captured German officers held at Camp Clinton in Mississippi.

"Where did you learn to speak German so well?"

"Tradition snagged me. My family's 1800 German emigrants sparked a desire to learn the German language."

"Beginning with your first assignment in North Africa, you have an exemplary record of interrogating captured Germans."

"I considered my service in North Africa a failure."

"Why?"

"Guilt burns deep in my soul for the bloodshed at Kasserine Pass. Hans Schiller, Germany's star saboteur, outsmarted me."

"Army investigators criticized every facet of the North African invasion except American Intelligence. No one held you responsible for US casualties at the pass. Allied forces regrouped and crushed Germany's Afrika Korps, and many captured German soldiers ended up in US prisoner of war camps. Schiller's name hasn't popped up since North Africa. He's probably dead, Colonel."

"I doubt it. Schiller's clever and slick. I've promised myself he'll never outsmart me again."

* * *

Norway
July 29, 1944

Hans Schiller read and mulled over his orders:

> Following the Normandy invasion, Allies destroyed the German submarine pens in France. Early in the war, Germany captured and converted Norway naval bases for submarines—a brilliant takeover and perfect for your mission. Report to the German submarine base in Bergen, Norway.

Within hours, the handsome saboteur boarded a U-boat, *unterseeboot* (undersea boat), in a Bergen pen. Twenty-eight days later, the boat surfaced in the Gulf of Mexico off the Louisiana coast. Hans climbed out on the deck and grinned, then patted fellow sailors on the back and said,

"Thanks for the ride."

In seconds, skilled crewmen launched the renowned saboteur in a small vessel into choppy Gulf waters. Bucking gusts of wind, Hans maneuvered the small craft into West Bay, a marshy inlet west of the Mississippi River, and docked at an old pier. He cut the craft's motor and hoisted a waterproof satchel, valise, and bag onto the decaying boards. Resetting the boat's motor speed, Hans removed plugs from the floorboard, pulled himself up onto the rotten deck, and shoved the tiny boat toward the Gulf.

Heavy weights under the floorboard guaranteed the expendable dinghy would sink. The saboteur listened to the hum of the little motor until it sputtered, then sputtered no more. Less than two months after the Normandy invasion, he'd made a brazen, surreptitious entry into the United States. His mission? Sabotage American military might on the home front.

After German espionage agents lost bicycles from a raft in rough waters off the coast of Ireland, engineers designed a bike-in-a-bag for Schiller's use. Blindfolded, Hans practiced putting the cycle together in Berlin. On the creaky Louisiana dock, he quickly assembled the bike and propped it on the kickstand. Removing American-made angler pants, a shirt, shoes, and socks from the valise, Hans changed clothes and yanked on a brunette wig and beret. The satchel he'd thrown on the deck held everything he needed to continue his journey. He stuffed a flashlight, tools, and a Lugar into zipper pockets on the fisherman pants, then slipped a telescopic fishing rod under clips on the bike frame. Submarine-worn clothes were stashed in the waterproof satchel to be destroyed later.

While seated on the bike, Hans leaned over to pull on socks and shoes and felt something brush against his pants. Imagining a hungry alligator snapping off his legs, he grabbed his flashlight and shined the light about him. He saw nothing. After he switched off the light, he felt a slither across his bare feet. He'd read about Louisiana's deadly cottonmouth, a venomous black water moccasin, and the fatal harlequin, a coral snake. In a panic, he put both feet on the pedals and slung the satchel across his back.

"I may run over a snake, but I won't step on one."

Barefooted, he hunched over the bike handles and departed the alligator and snake-infested marshland. At the intersection of a hard surface road, he paused to put on socks and shoes and fastened the satchel onto the bike rack.

German Intelligence had filled secret pockets in his jacket with American items and his bike journey printed out on a silk map. He checked out hidden pockets for food packets, a water flask, compass, and booklets of ration stamps. In one pocket, he found the American 4-F card issued to men physically unfit for the military service, folding money, and coins. Confident with the fake papers and his Monsieur Jacques Herbert fisherman disguise, he pedaled off in the darkness.

US coastal cities were under blackout orders, and he biked several miles on the hard surface road before he saw the outlines of houses against the dawn's light. Dismounting the bike, he walked it through the town. At Louisiana SR 23, a superior state highway, he jumped on the bike and pumped hard on the pedals toward his destination, Algiers on the

Mississippi River and the New Orleans ferry. A Schutzstaffel, the SS contact, awaited him in the crescent city.

A good biker averaged about sixty miles a day, but Hans biked seventy-five grueling miles to the Canal Street ferry at Algiers. Breathing hard, he stood on the ferry deck and looked across and up and down the Mississippi River. He bristled with anger at the sight of American industrial plants churning out war equipment and freighters weighted low in the water with trucks and tanks destined for battlefields in Germany. The war had paralyzed German factories and crippled Germany's military might.

In the setting sun, the Mississippi River appeared blood red, German blood red. Powerless, he gripped the handlebars of the bike and vowed he'd return and destroy the Port of New Orleans.

When the ferry docked at the city pier, he rolled the bike onto Canal Street's wide sidewalk and stared at Americans living in peace on the home front. Office workers streamed out of buildings along Canal Street, a 170-foot-wide thoroughfare, and crossed the medium to board streetcars where passengers sat by open windows. Conductors clanged friendly warning bells and maneuvered the long vehicles out of downtown. While he attended Tulane, he rode in the vintage green cars trimmed in red.

Shrugging his shoulders, he lifted the bike off the broad sidewalk and pedaled on Decatur Street to Jackson Square in the French Quarter. At the famed triple-steeple St. Louis Cathedral, he followed Berlin orders and sat on an outside bench. On a nearby bench, a man who appeared to be dozing, squeezed the thumb on his left hand three times, tipped his fedora, and walked away.

Masked as Monsieur Herbert, Hans remounted the bicycle and followed the SS contact until he disappeared. At the spot where the man vanished, Hans halted the bike, looked about him, then pedaled onto a long brick alley. The narrow walkway led to a wrought iron gate, slightly ajar. He dismounted the bike and rolled it through the gate into a beautiful courtyard.

Across the quadrant, he saw the man he sought standing inside French doors. Walking the bicycle through the double doors, he recognized Arnost Kluge from Abwehr's, German Intelligence, espionage school. The old German American agent greeted him warmly and took the bike.

"Herzlich Willkommen. Schön, dass Sie Wieder zu sehen, alter Freund." ("Welcome. Nice to see you again, old friend.")

"Gut dich auch zu sehen, Arnost," said Monsieur Jacques Herbert. ("So good to see you as well, Arnost.")

Arnost stored the bicycle in a closet and turned to him. "Please address me as Arnold, Arnold Keller, my name on naturalized American citizenship papers." The name Arnold brought Benedict Arnold to Hans's mind. The elderly agent's names suited him well. In German, Arnost meant "a battle to the death," and Kluge, "clever one." Arnold meant "to rule," and Keller, "keeper or master of the cellar" or supplier of all materials needed for sabotage.

CHAPTER 2

Satan's Suit

*T*he senior German agent, a naturalized American traitor who engineered and dictated every second of the saboteur's journey to America, directed Hans upstairs to a bedroom.

"Schiller, German Intelligence owns the apartment complex with exits for a hurried departure."

Hans laughed. "Thanks to German ingenuity, I'll sleep well."

"Yes, my apartment is a haven and provides basic needs. The armoire holds clothes and shoes for you. You'll find a hamper in the bathroom for your dirty clothes," said Arnold. "And everything needed for a bath. Dinner will be ready in one hour."

"Thank you. I'll dress and be down shortly. I'm hungry."

Arnold gave a knowing smile and left the room.

Always mindful of capture, Hans looked out the bedroom window and sized up his escape options. From the balcony, he saw two courtyard exits and multiple apartment doors, exits for a breakaway, and relaxed. Gazing at the inviting four-poster bed covered with a white canopy and linens, he put aside the temptation for a nap. Standing in front of a full-length oval mirror mounted on a pedestal, he stared at Monsieur Jacques Herbert for the last time.

In the bathroom, he yanked off the beret and wig, peeled off the sour-smelling fisherman clothes, tossed them into the hamper, and closed the lid on the foul odor. Eager for a hot bath, he turned on the faucets in a massive cast-iron, claw-footed tub, breathed over a soap basket, and chose two bars of soap.

With the red Lifebuoy soap, he scrubbed his aching body and washed his hair until dirt and grunge turned the bathwater a brownish yellow and left a grimy, gummy circle on the porcelain-lined bathtub. He crawled out the tub, drained the dirty water, scoured away the telltale ring, and refilled the tub with clean water. Lathering his body and hair with Ivory soap, he drained the sudsy water and rinsed himself with a hand sprayer. After rubbing dry with a thick white towel, he scrubbed the *die badewanne* (bathtub) until sparkling, cognizant of his mania for cleanliness related to his dirty saboteur work.

He glanced again toward the bed, but the smell of German food overcame his desire for sleep. Pulling on underwear and socks from neat stacks on armoire shelves, he took a civilian shirt, trousers, and jacket hanging on the left side of the wardrobe and finished dressing for dinner. The full-length mirror allowed for self-aggrandizement in his new clothes. He liked his new image. Moving the swinging mirror back and forth, he said, "Who am I?"

* * *

In the dining room, Hans smacked his lips over the platters and tureens of German food on Arnold's table.

"A German woman true to our homeland used all her food stamps preparing the food before you," said his host.

"Please thank her for me. People in our homeland are starving."

"I know. Hungry Germans grieve me. You've had a long day, Hans. Enjoy the food before you." Hans ladled Rouladen—thin beef slices filled with bacon, onions, and pickles—onto his plate and poured Bratensaft (gravy) over the food. Seconds included *döppekuchen* (potato flan), Wiener schnitzel (veal cutlet), bratwurst (German sausage), sauerbraten (roast), red cabbage, and boiled potatoes.

While Arnost Kluge pressed for news about their homeland, Hans sampled Bienenstich, Bee Sting cake filled with creamy vanilla custard, topped with caramelized almonds, and his favorite sweet, *welfenspeise*, a vanilla and wine pudding.

"Thank you for the German food my first illegal night in New Orleans."

"You've visited New Orleans before, Hans?"

"Twice legally," Hans said and grinned. "When I learned to speak the English language, my uncle rewarded me with a two-month trip to the US. We visited Mississippi relatives, who drove us to New Orleans. While in international studies at Universtät Heidelberg, I became an exchange student at Tulane University. I have fond memories of rumbling about town in swaying green streetcars and passing by Creole cottages in New Orleans's Historic District and the magnificent oak trees on St. Charles Avenue."

"An avenue of grand homes surrounded by lush gardens," said Arnold.

"Indeed. In the Garden District, I'd stop off at the Pontchartrain Hotel for their tangy shrimp remoulade appetizer and pompano en papillote."

"Ah, on occasion, I've enjoyed the pompano filets swimming in seafood sauce and baked in parchment paper. Knowing your way about New Orleans will be helpful in your work here. On the streetcar to Tulane, you passed Loyola University, synagogues, and St. Charles Avenue Baptist, the church with wrought iron stairways leading up to dual entrances. Like Jackson Square, perfect outdoor sites for quick meetings in the future."

"No more meetings in the French Quarter?"

"Exactly. You won't come back here ever. We will not meet again."

The German food relaxed Hans's tired body. Only a German woman in love with Arnost Kluge could cook the food he'd eaten. Drowsy from overeating and the long bike ride, the majestic bed upstairs awaited him, and he bid the old spy, "Gute Nacht."

"Good night." Arnold reminded him, "No longer speak in the language of our homeland. You are now James G. Waters. The G is for Grant, after Ulysses S. Grant, the American Civil War general."

"I know. I am a student of the Civil War," said Hans.

Arnold unlocked a desk drawer, handed Hans an envelope, and said, "Here is your birth certificate, driver's license, more identifications, and extra food stamps. You now have every possible American citizen ID. In the morning, we'll go over Berlin orders."

* * *

The next morning, Arnold pushed back from the breakfast table. "It's time to go to work in the US, James G. Waters.

"Since the Normandy invasion, stateside US soldiers deploy daily to fight across Europe. Your orders: sabotage US factories and refineries producing war equipment and aircraft fuel and destroy US troops before they deploy for Europe."

Arnold dropped the papers on the table and said, "The US sabotage correlates with a massive German assault planned in Europe."

"Why postpone the sabotage in the US for a massive assault in Europe?"

"Chaos. Chaos on the home front and battlefront simultaneously buys time for the launching of Hitler's secret weapon and ultimate Axis victory. Your orders include spying for Japan."

"Spy for the Japanese? My expertise is sabotage, not surveillance."

"Japan depends on German intelligence for victory in the Pacific and ultimate Axis victory. This morning, you will walk to a nearby bank and open bank accounts for The Café, the restaurant purchased by the SS. The bank opens at nine o'clock." Arnold handed him a card. "Ask for this banker. Bank accounts are set up for your signature under the name of James G. Waters. Sign for the accounts. Walk out of the bank and to the right. You'll see a parking garage on the left side of the street. Give the garage attendant this receipt for a Ford coupe.

"This is a map marked with the best route to your headquarters, the restaurant in southwest Mississippi. We made reservations for you at the only hotel in town."

"You will supply everything needed for the restaurant and sabotage?" asked Hans.

"Yes. After you install the radio and microphones in The Café, we'll deliver kitchen and food supplies for the restaurant and the sabotage operation, but never call or try to get in touch with me. I am no longer a part of your life."

* * *

Disguised as Jim Waters, Hans walked into the New Orleans bank with two certified checks. After a pleasant conversation with Arnold's banker friend, who he suspected was a German American in covert operations in the US, Hans deposited the checks in commercial and personal accounts under his alias, James G. Waters.

At the garage, Hans spoke to the attendant. "Good morning. I'm here to pick up my car."

"Yes, sir. Your Ford coupe has a full tank of gas, ready to go."

Less than forty-eight hours after leaving the U-boat, Hans drove a new 1942 Ford two-seater onto Canal Street toward Metairie Road and Airline Highway, then drove to Baton Rouge, the capital of the state of Louisiana.

In Baton Rouge, Hans drove onto the Louisiana State University (LSU) campus, parked by the Campanile, and listened to the bells chiming. He was stunned by a sign with red, white, and blue bulbs flashing dot-dot-dot-dash, the Morse code and universal symbol for American and Allied victory, "Victoire" in French, "Vitezsti" in Czech for victory, "Vryheid" for freedom in Dutch, and "Vitesto" for a hero in Serbian.

He'd scorned the victory symbol in Europe and ignored New Orleans drivers honking the Morse code for Allied victory, and now he sneered in anger at LSU's American flag pulsating the V signaling Germany was losing the war.

In North Baton Rouge, unbelievable multi-industrial plant smoke billowing and swirling high in the sky proclaimed Allied victory. "Nothing in New Orleans or Baton Rouge points to German victory," said Hans in the confines of his car.

Driving north on SR 19, he crossed the Mississippi state line and found himself in a hilly region heavily forested with a mixture of trees and towering pines—loblollies, he learned later.

Hans lowered the car window and breathed in the distinctive and refreshing pine scent, a fragrance that reminded him of the Black Forest in his beloved Germany. Putting his hand on his belly, he pushed down on his body and sucked pine air into his lungs.

Tension drained from his body, and he relaxed his hands on the steering wheel and whispered, "My US sleeper agent role, far from German battlefields, provides for massive sabotage, wiping out American power and Allied victory."

Thrusting his right arm in the air with a straightened hand, he shouted, "Heil, Hitler!

Heil, Mein Führer!"

CHAPTER 3

A Choice

Middleton College
December 8, 1944—4:30 a.m.

A breaking heart tore Lucinda Reed apart. Her chest hurt, and she gasped for air. David hadn't called in two nights. Why? Was David shipping out for war today? Would she ever see him again? The thought of forced separation from her sweetheart brought on deep despair, and the misery physicians labeled a WWII malady.

Usually, she prayed and lived confidently under the Lord's guidance but not this morning. A strategy flashed through her mind, and she made a choice. Leaping from her warm bed, she ripped off her pajamas, snatched on underclothes, a blouse, sweater, and jodhpurs, and grabbed sneakers from under her bed.

Lamplight flooded the room. "Lucinda, what are you doing?"

"I'm on my way to the stable, Jean."

"At four thirty in the morning?" her roommate said and switched off the lamp.

At the door of the room, Lucinda threw a crimson scarf around her neck and pulled a black beret over her ears. With a boot tucked under each arm, she tiptoed downstairs. In the darkest hour before dawn, she slipped out the side door of the dormitory and hid her riding boots behind a side bush.

The thrill of first love and the cold night air exhilarated Lucinda as she sprinted across the wet grass toward a forest, a camouflage for her secret trek. Hesitating at the tree line, she took a deep breath before she plunged into the woodland, dense with hardwoods and pines.

Racing to reach her destination and find answers to ease her pain, Lucinda bumped into tree trunks and thrashed about in an understory of small trees and creeping plants. In a lurch forward, she fell on the forest floor. Turning and tugging, she grappled with a massive vine that held her ankles captive. With nothing to cut nature's rope, she gave a mighty heave and plummeted headfirst into a rock-filled ravine. The fall bashed every wisp of air from her lungs, and Lucinda Reed lay facedown in forest rubble, dazed and concealed from human eyes.

The crack of a nearby lightning strike startled Lucinda to full consciousness. An owl screech from somewhere above and a wolf howl in a reply sent shivers down her spine. Lucinda rubbed her aching head, and salty tears ran down her face. "I've fallen into a pit," she murmured and struggled against vines strapped across her legs.

Drenched and freezing, Lucinda turned onto her side and fingered sticky clay and foliage. Hesitantly, she explored the earthy cradle in which she lay and found her beret tucked under her left shoulder. Easing into a sitting position, Lucinda clutched her arms across her chest and rubbed her forearms. With gloved fingers, she combed wet leaves from her long, curly hair, shook the dirt from her beret, and pulled it over her ears. Images of David Atherton deploying bounced about in her mind. *If I'm ever to see my sweetheart again, I have to get up and move on.*

Tugging at the vines pinning her down, she pulled her feet free, leaned forward, and clawed for a hold in wet clay. Inch by inch, she ascended a steep incline until she touched the rough edge of asphalt on the narrow paved lane that connected the women's campus to the men's college grounds. Pushing hard, she pulled herself onto the hard pathway and lay exhausted on the firm surface until she stretched her legs and stood.

Halfway up the winding hill, the staccato of reveille shattered the predawn quiet. *Why?* The first call to assembly sounded every morning at five thirty. "It's not even five o'clock in the morning," she said.

The urgency of the bugle's short, clear notes made her more uneasy about David. Breathing heavily, she forced herself to run faster. A command crackled in the cold, damp air, and she recognized David's deep voice. "Forward march. Left, left, left."

In quick response to the sharp order, stout seamen's shoes hit the pavement. The cadence of sailors' boots pounded in her ears and reverberated through her heart. Was David's V-12 unit answering their call to arms?

Until last week, David wore civilian shoes. His long, narrow, hard-to-fit feet were a problem, and the Navy Supply Corps special-ordered David's footgear from the Florsheim Company, the manufacturer of sailors' regulation shoes.

"Shoes to hit the deck of a warship." Lucinda grimaced, her face twisting in agony.

At the edge of the college campus, the college girl crossed a road barricaded by a wooden horse with a sign: Keep Out—US Navy. She walked around the barricade and hurried until she reached a faintly lighted warning on a ten-foot Cyclone fence.

No Trespassing
By Order
United States Navy
United States War Department

Ignoring the formidable warning, Lucinda yanked off her gloves, stuffed them into her coat pockets, climbed the metal fence, scaled over the top, and fell. Hitting the hard earth with a jolt, she muttered, "Ugh."

After catching her breath from the free fall, Lucinda turned over on her knees and arched her back. On her hands and feet, she cat-walked to the thick holly hedge surrounding the former Middleton football field, now a US Navy parade ground.

Hidden in a prickly hedge, she peered through branches thick with leaves and leaned against hedge branches for a better look at the parade grounds. The weight of her body snapped a twig and pulled her beret askew. Lucinda yanked the wool headgear off and crammed it inside her jacket.

The platoons continued marching toward her, and Lucinda heard David shout, "Left, left, left." David's high forehead and stern jaw attracted her; his smile and indigo eyes captivated her heart, and she loved him. David was her world, and all her interests revolved around her sailor. Lucinda wanted to reach out, touch his wrist, and entwine her slender fingers in his strong ones. She yearned for the pressure of his firm grip sending tingles throughout her body.

David never complained that the war interrupted his college life in Texas; he found the rigid training regulations a challenge, not a sacrifice. Lucinda marveled at his bravery and courage. Filled with gloom, she remained motionless against the hedge. *I fill a small role in David Atherton's life—in contrast to his role in mine.*

"Left, left, left." David was nearer to her, and his deep voice carried an unsinkable spirit that washed away her dreary feelings.

In the muffled light at the corner of the hedge, David emerged through the mist. He commanded the sharp-looking platoons of sailors in naval officer training. Lucinda stared in awe at her sweetheart, who stood tall above the others. In dress blues with bell-bottoms, he wore the dark navy, wool peacoat and wool pancake cap with a headband monogrammed US Navy. Lucinda's heart soared with pride at the sight of him and sank when she realized the dress uniform signaled a journey.

She crunched her shoulders and remembered another day David wore the double-breasted, eight-button coat. Intrigued with six black buttons hand-sewn in a Z pattern onto his jacket, she had moved closer to him. With her index finger on the first button, she'd traced the embossed image of an anchor and chain. David pulled her to him, took her cold hands, and slipped them into the warm peacoat pockets, pockets lined with corduroy soft as velvet.

"A tradition," whispered David, "dating way back."

"Warm pockets?"

"Fouled anchors," he said, grinning. David tightened his arms around her and teased her with an astute explanation about the peacoat buttons. "The navy adopted the buttons with the chained anchor symbol from an emblem that began with Lord Howard of Effingham, Lord Admiral, when the British defeated the Spanish Armada in 1588." She wanted to be in David's arms forever.

"Left. Left, left, to the rear. March!" David shouted.

Her sad feelings vanished at the grave tone of David's voice, but she gasped at the platoons turning and marching in the opposite direction and crouched back into the hedge. *Did David see me peeking from behind the bush?* She squeezed her eyes closed and pressed both hands against her hot face.

The platoon marching ceased. Lucinda heard the motors of weighty conveyances on the college circular driveway, looked, and saw the outlines of buses stopping in front of the navy headquarters. The coaches confirmed her worse fear. "David is shipping out, out of my life," she moaned under her breath.

A bird fluttered from the hedge. Startled, Lucinda pivoted on one foot and gaped wide-eyed at a naval officer who stood inches from her. In the dim corner light, her skin crawled as the officer's eyes roamed over her from head to foot. After he sized her up, his icy-blue eyes peered into hers.

"What are you doing here?"

Quivering but angered by the tone of his voice, she stood her ground and looked him straight in the eyes. "I am an MC student."

"You're off-limits on the restricted military ground with trespassing strictly prohibited under federal law. Penalties for violations include monetary fines and imprisonment. Report to the dean of women immediately, young lady," the officer ordered, then turned and walked away.

Lucinda watched the officer's dark form disappear in the mist. She had expected the officer to escort her to naval headquarters. Why didn't he?

She was on the student council. The consequences hit her for students who broke Middleton rules and ignored posted War Department laws for trespassing on the military area.

Easing back into the hedge, she deliberated her options: risk climbing the fence or creep inside the enclosed, restricted area to the main campus? She crawled out of the hedge, and her coat snagged on the tips of the holly leaves. She jerked free, and with her head down, she crept inside the fence toward the main campus. Voices sounded in the direction of the naval headquarters building. She didn't want to run into another officer and walked away from the clatter.

Military authorities ordered campus blackouts months ago, but Lucinda didn't need streetlights to find her way to a hiding place. She crossed College Drive toward the sanctuary with an inscription she knew by heart.

Chancellery
1828

Walking stealthily up slick, marble steps and across the colonnade of the chancellery, she reached the front entrance and brushed her fingers across brass escutcheon plates and locks on massive mahogany doors.

"Please, God." She gingerly pressed on the right door handle. The heavy door opened without a squeak.

Lucinda slipped into the familiar hallway. Shadowy lights mounted in magnificent brass chandeliers threw a pale glow on oil portraits of scholarly men who gazed down upon her, and Lucinda shuddered under their penetrating eyes.

On a massive library table, a large Holy Bible, heralding the mission of Middleton College, lay open to the fifteenth chapter of John, verse 16:

"Ye have not chosen me, but I have chosen you, and ordained you, that ye should go and bring forth fruit, and that your fruit should remain: that whatsoever ye ask of the Father in my name, he may give to you." She ran her fingers down the maroon velvet ribbon in the center of the large Bible and over the four columns of printed verse on the open pages. Apprehensive she had lost the privilege to ask for His assistance, she murmured, "Forgive my behavior tonight, Lord. Please help me."

Double doors appeared at the end of the hallway. Thankful her sneakers softened her footsteps on the wide-planked, walnut floor, Lucinda moved down the vast hall. At the rear doors, she pressed her palms together, raised her hands to her lips, and whispered, "Please, dear God." She pushed down on the latch, and the heavy door opened. Slipping out of the chancellery, she ran across the parking lot toward the girls' campus.

* * *

Hans Schiller sauntered by the chapel, one of the most excellent examples of neo-Grecian architecture in America. Military history fascinated him. During the Civil War, Union soldiers had occupied the college town. General Grant quartered horses on the ground floor of the historic chapel and used the upper level for a hospital.

"I never expected to spend the night here or walk into someone who could identify me."

He was under orders to kill anyone who could identify him in a court of law. He should have killed the girl on the spot. Why didn't he? He'd figure that out after he exited the campus.

In the chapel parking lot, he hastened toward a sedan, stenciled US Navy. Unlocking the car door, he slipped behind the steering wheel, turned the key in the ignition, shifted into first gear, and drove without headlights onto College Drive.

Near the college entrance, he whistled a sigh of relief. The large wrought iron gates were open. Last night, he drove through the archway with the sedan's lights off, and he couldn't read the caption incised on the front side of the arch. He recalled a Berlin photograph of the imposing gateway's worthy inscription, "Enter to Grow in Wisdom, Knowledge, and Stature."

Exiting under the entrance archway, he said, "Depart to share my knowledge with German and Japanese intelligence." On the highway, he raised his right arm above his head and bellowed, "Heil, Hitler."

CHAPTER 4

The Puzzle

December 8, 1944—5:00 a.m.

*H*ans switched on the sedan's dimmer lights and, at the sight of a figure in the road, slammed on the brakes. "The girl," he said. He wheeled the car onto the forest lane and caught sight of the girl's red coat.

After jumping out of the car, he caught up with her and grabbed the sleeve of the coat, but she twisted and sprinted ahead of him. He couldn't believe the speed with which she ran as he chased after her. "You'll never outrun me," he muttered and closed the distance between them.

The girl reached her dormitory and dove beneath a bush, then reappeared on the steps. Hans grabbed at her coat sleeve, but she turned, struck him with something on the head, and slipped in the door. Dazed, Hans stumbled for cover in the forest and made his way back to the sedan. He'd lost his chance to kill her.

Bristling with anger, Hans cursed his spying for the Japanese. "Fraulein, I'll get you on my next trip to Middleton."

* * *

David Atherton halted the platoons at the buses parked in front of the ROTC V-12 headquarters. "Load the duffel bags in the underneath compartments." Sailors grabbed their bags, threw them below the bus, and hopped on board the Greyhound buses.

The platoon leader saluted the reviewing officers and requested permission to report to Commander Kemp.

"Permission granted," said the ranking officer and saluted.

David returned the salute and ran up the steps of the building. At the entrance, he saluted the sentry and asked to speak with the commander. An aide escorted him into the senior officer's reception room and introduced him to the chief petty officer, a yeoman, in charge of the commander's clerical work.

David took deep breaths and pondered his reporting of the unidentified officer. An officer popping from behind the hedge and jumping back behind it didn't make sense to him. Was Peek-a-Boo a planted officer evaluating platoons? Or was a Peek-at-You assessing his seaman leadership competence and ability?

The yeoman opened the door and signaled for David to enter the commanding officer's office.

"At ease, seaman. All buses loaded?" asked Commander Kemp.

"Yes, sir. There was an incident."

"An incident?" said the surprised skipper.

"Yes, sir," David said. "A naval officer jumped from behind and back into the hedges bordering the far side of the drill field. The officer was unfamiliar to me, sir."

"That area is in the military off-limit zone."

"An unidentified officer was there, sir."

"Rank? Nameplate?"

"Too dark to read the nameplate. The officer wore the dark dress uniform and hat. There were service ribbons on the coat and two wide stripes on the sleeve."

"Are you reporting a navy lieutenant jumped from behind the hedge and back behind it again?"

"Yes, sir. That's my best description. Dawn and the early-morning mist limited the visibility. We marched to the shielded light pole at the break of the hedges. The officer jumped to his left into the dim light and skipped back to his right behind the hedge."

"Was he alone?"

"I didn't see anyone else." David pinched his eyebrows together. "But I don't know. The hedge is thick. In the daytime, you see red berries all over the bushes."

"The incident, as you called it, has to be reported and recounted in detail to Navy Intelligence." The commander buzzed for his aide. "Come and bring the stenograph machine with you."

"Yes, sir."

Lieutenant Commander L.M. Kemp dictated his rank and said, "To US Navy Intelligence. An unknown officer sighted in the restricted area at Middleton College. Sighting by ROTC Seaman David Atherton, Middleton, December 8, 1944."

David marveled at the yeoman's rapid typing on the shorthand machine. The chief petty officer rank indicated top security clearance with Navy Intelligence.

"Send the dictated report immediately," ordered the commander. He turned to David and said, "Seaman, remain in my office. If the Intelligence officer releases you, your departure remains as expected." The commander stood and walked toward the door.

David swallowed, jumped to his feet, and stepped forward.

"As you were, sailor. Remain seated."

"Yes, sir." David saluted.

The commander walked into the petty officer's office. David sat down and slid back on the wooden seat with his calves against the chair's front crosspiece. Stymied and tense, he waited for—what? Navy recruiters recommended him for the ROTC V-12 officer training. He was only days from receiving a commission. He'd outworked everyone in the unit and sailed through every test hurled at him. Now, thanks to Peek-a-Boo, he waited for authorization to leave Middleton. What a mess. He wanted to be on that train when it steamed out of Jackson.

The holdup overwhelmed and disgusted the seaman. He puckered his brow, inhaled, exhaled, and grasped the chair armrests. Sitting erect, he placed his hands on his thighs and kept his feet flat on the floor. He boiled and gritted his teeth over the delay. Commander Kemp's crisp manner triggered questions in his mind. Sitting at attention, he calmed his stomach and cooled his anxiety about the future.

Was the unknown navy officer judging his performance? Did the commanding officer know or not know who was behind the hedge?

CHAPTER 5

Shame

Adalia Hall
December 8, 1944—6:00 a.m.

ucinda's heart pounded from fright. She didn't see the car until the driver switched on the dimmers, and the vehicle almost hit and killed her. *Why would anyone drive without the dim lights on?* she wondered.

She'd heard the car stop and saw someone running after her but didn't know who until she slung her riding boots at the pursuer and hit the navy officer who had ordered her to report to the dean. Scooting in the back door, she slid the rod in the security bolt and locked the officer out of the dorm. The officer didn't know her name.

Tiptoeing down the shadowy corridor, Lucinda passed by war posters tacked on the wall. Her heart skipped a beat at the image of a torpedoed ship's bow thrust straight up out of the sea. The caption cried out ominously, "A Slip of the Lip May Sink a Ship." The tune and words of Duke Ellington's song "A Slip of the Lip" swirled through her head.

She clutched her throat at the next poster showing an American sailor sprawled lifeless on a beach. The poster sent shivers down her spine. In a few weeks, David would be at sea. She vowed never to tell anyone that David's V-12 unit shipped out today because the slip of her lip might sink his ship.

In the dark hall, the light showed under the dean's office door. Dean Wright was at her desk. Lucinda darted up the steps to the second floor and her room and heard her roommate's voice behind her.

"Lucinda, I just signed out. You left here early. Did you ride?"

"No, it was too wet."

"You're all wet. If you didn't ride, where have you been?" said Jean.

"Shh," said Lucinda. "Promise not to tell?"

"I guess so. But why?"

"I'm in love. David hasn't called in two days. I've been miserable. I wanted to see him," she said, crying. "You promised not to tell."

"You left the dorm without signing out?"

"It was too early."

"It sure was at four thirty in the morning. Where did you go? David is in the navy. Surely you didn't trespass on the US Navy base?"

"Yes, but I didn't talk to David. I saw him from a distance. Jean, you promised not to tell on me."

"I didn't know you'd been off-limits. I'm not going to lie for you, Lucinda. Did anyone see you?"

"An officer, but don't worry. He didn't ask for my name. He followed me but didn't come into the dorm. I locked the door."

"But he will call Dean Wright and find out who you are. Lucinda, you could be shipped from Middleton for sneaking out of the dorm. What else did you do besides locking the officer out of the dorm? Lucinda, you could be in all kinds of trouble with the navy."

"Well, Jean, I guess you could say I defended myself, but I didn't know who was chasing me until—"

"Until what?" Jean said, putting her hands on her hips.

"Until nothing. The navy is not a problem. It's Middleton and our being under the old Oak Hill Female Institute rules." She wiped her face on the bedsheet and snuffled up her nose.

"Except for attending classes on the boys' campus, there are few changes for girls living on the girls' campus. At home, boys and girls sat together in church. Here, girls walk two-and-two to church services and sit with chaperones in church, one of Middleton's laws, not God's. David and I never sat together in the church here, a no-no. I believe in freedom of religion, and I know God does too. There is no freedom here."

"Well, it's not that bad here. You've never broken a rule until now. I'm afraid you are in trouble. My sister came early for me, and Dean Wright signed me out. I only came back to the room for my things. I'm worried about you."

"Don't worry. I told you the officer doesn't know my name."

"But he can find out. You may be in trouble, Lucinda."

"I'm not in trouble. Don't worry, Jean."

"Well, I will worry. Before the war, we had three weeks for Christmas. With the navy's accelerated semesters, we get four weeks off. I won't know for a month whether you are in trouble or not. My sister is waiting for me. I have to go. I hope the officer forgets about you."

"He'll have to. He doesn't know my name. Nothing will happen. I'll be okay. Go on, Jean," she said, then hugged her roommate and closed the door.

Shivering, Lucinda kicked off her sneakers, yanked off her socks and scarf, and spread them under the heating vent. Jerking off her clothes, she hung them on hangers spaced wide apart on the closet rod and draped underclothes over a spooled-back chair. The puddles on the closet floor from waterlogged clothes soaked her conscience with disgrace. Exhausted, she snuggled into flannel pajamas, slipped under the bed covers, and closed her eyes, but an emotional upheaval raged within her. She couldn't sleep, punched her pillow, and tossed in depths of despair like a boat pitching up and down in a stormy sea.

She had run blindly from the dormitory, fractured the trust others held for her, and hit a US Navy officer on the head with her riding boots. She mulled over the reality of her situation and the looming consequences, and gloom consumed her.

A friendship with David brought on love and a possessive closeness to him. He'd never really kissed her. He did brush his lips across her forehead once.

What was she thinking? She scrapped her integrity when she left the dorm. She lay in a fetal position and wished she could disappear within the cocoon of dishonor in which she had wrapped herself. "What happened to me?"

Morning light filtered in the room. Overcome with shame, her heart accelerated, and her face flushed. Her stomach hurt, her body ached all over, and she sweated over the degradation and disgust others would see in her. Grasping her hair, she pressed her thumbs against her temples and wept bitterly. "Heavenly Father, forgive me."

Joseph Peek's music and Howard Walters's lyrics from "I Would Be True" rang in her head. *I would be true, for there are those who trust me.* Humiliation in her mother's eyes and the hard stares of her grandfather emerged in her mind. In anguish, the prodigal daughter got back in her bed and drew the covers tighter over her face. She'd failed her parents' trust and her commitment to her Lord and Savior.

The Middleton manual for girls listed strict dorm rules for females. The navy posted off-limit signs throughout buildings all over the campus. When she'd vaulted over the fence into the restricted area, military repercussions never entered her mind. She hit a navy officer in the head. If the officer identified her, would the navy send her to prison for trespassing and assaulting an officer?

The image of living behind bars blotted out feelings of shame and anguish and restored a sense of self-preservation within her. Why should she worry? The officer didn't know her name. Chewing over that possibility boosted her spirits.

Other issues gnawed at her mind. If caught, unauthorized dormitory leave resulted in the termination of studies and residential living. Could she get out of a charge of sneaking out of the dormitory? "No" rang in her head. The faculty emphasized honesty and integrity with zero tolerance for violation of rigid academic and residence rules. Lucinda envisioned the dean's surprise and shock at an honor student's disobedience.

She trembled, remembering a conversation between her parents and her grandfather.

"I don't like it. I'm opposed to your sending Lucinda off to school with the United States Navy," said her grandfather. "The church established Middleton in the 1820s for males and Oak Hill for females before 1860 and the Civil War."

"Papa, most male professors and students at Middleton College were drafted or volunteered after Pearl Harbor. Loss of faculty and students and the lack of money forced the church to combine Oak Hill with Middleton. The US lacks enlisted men and officers to win this war. The navy selected Middleton College for training officers. After one or two six-week terms at Middleton, an ROTC V-12 seaman ships out. Following another few weeks of training, the ROTC seaman acquires a commission. In a matter of weeks, a V-12 trainee finds himself a commissioned officer at sea on a battleship.

"V-12 sailors are Lucinda's age," said her father. "They are the best of the best volunteers and conscripts from colleges and the fleet. Recruits who qualified for the V-12 passed rigorous academic, physical, and mental tests. If Lucinda were a boy, she could enroll in the officer-training program. In England, we train boys her age to fly planes over enemy territory," said her father, a commercial pilot serving in the US Army Air Force.

"She is not a boy. She is a girl," said her grandfather, looking at his granddaughter.

"Some girls volunteer for service, Granddaddy," she'd said.

"Not my granddaughter," he said, giving her a stern look.

"Lucinda, you are going to college," said her mother. "Papa, girls will continue to board on the Oak Hill campus and only go to classes on the Middleton campus."

"Our country does not have a minute to waste to win this war. We have to train men to fight and men to lead them. V-12 recruits will not have time for girls," said her father.

"Granddaddy, the navy area is off-limits. I doubt I'll ever see a sailor at Middleton."

"Stephen, Louisa, don't forget my service in WWI. No one or Cox's army will keep those sailors and girls apart at Middleton," countered her grandfather.

Lucinda pulled the covers off her face. Her grandfather was right. She fell in love with David the first time she saw him. Her eyes filled with tears as she thought about her grandfather's prayer that same night.

"Lord, give us strength and courage during this war. Keep Lucinda from harm and evil at Middleton. Help Louisa with her war efforts and protect Stephen at airfields in England and in the air over enemy territory. We commit the souls of our soldiers and sailors and souls of enemy soldiers and sailors to Thee. Bless young men on whose shoulders the war will be won or lost. In Thy will, we pray. In Jesus's name. Amen."

Filled with bitterness, she said, "Lord, boys my age are dying in waters and countries I never knew existed until Pearl Harbor." Except for attending classes on the boys' campus, there were few changes for girls at Oak Hill. She stretched her thumb and forefinger over closed eyes.

"Dear Lord, You know everything. I do ask for Your forgiveness about this morning, but I had to find out the truth. You knew David was shipping out. I didn't. I wanted to see David and did *not* run how or when by You. I am sorry. You saw me sneak out of the dorm. I didn't have time to pray and wait for Your RSVP. If I had asked, You could have arranged for me to get a last peek at David without my bumping into you-know-who at the hedge. You knew the officer was there. I didn't. If only I had prayed first. You could have rerouted me away from the arrogant officer. I'm sorry I hit him overhead. If You arrange it for me, I'll apologize to him.

"I have gotten myself in a mess. If that conceited officer describes me to Dean Wright, my copper hair is not my fault either. You created me with red hair before there were clouds in the sky. Forgive me, Lord, for fretting over my red hair. I blame myself for my mistake before daylight. I dug this pit for myself. Please don't let that officer, a snake, identify me. I believe, and You promised if I believed, You wouldn't forsake me, and You'll help me whatever and wherever as far as east from west. Heavenly Father, put Your impenetrable hedge around me (Job 1:10; Hebrews 13:5). In Jesus's name. Amen."

CHAPTER 6

Interrogation

"Commander Kemp, an army colonel and his aide are in the reception room. The colonel asked to speak with you," said his aide.

"An army colonel?" said the navy commander. "Tell the sentry to escort the colonel and his aide to the office across the hall. Are there any changes in my schedule?"

"There are no changes in the schedule, sir."

The commander walked to the office across the hall. "Good morning. I am Commander Kemp of Middleton's ROTC V-12 unit."

"I'm Lieutenant Colonel Matthews. We're here to investigate the unknown person reported on base this morning." He and his aide, Lieutenant Harris, handed the commander their Office of Strategic Service (OSS) identifications.

Commander Kemp returned the IDs and said, "You are OSS officers. It hasn't been an hour since we reported the unknown to Navy Intelligence."

"OSS receives strategic information from all intelligence agencies. We were minutes away from Middleton, and OSS assigned your report to us."

"I appreciate the quick response. I contacted Navy Intelligence because no one on my staff was near the sighting. How can I help you?"

"We need an office for interrogations and evaluation of evidence."

"We have a vacant office adjacent to the rear door and out of sight of a passerby."

"Great. The least obvious our presence is on campus, the better."

"What about equipment?"

"Thank you. We have our equipment. We need a lockdown of the campus. No one in, no one out."

"I took care of the lockdown."

"Good. Lieutenant Harris, have agents place equipment in the office the commander provided. Search all buildings and grounds for witnesses and evidence. I'll join you in a few minutes."

The colonel turned to the ROTC commander. "What do you know about Seaman Atherton?"

"Atherton ranked first in his unit, academically, physically, and in leadership. He led the platoons on the parade field this morning. He'll receive a US Navy ensign commission shortly. His V-12 unit left Middleton ten minutes ago, but Seaman Atherton is in my office."

"Fine. Glad you kept Atherton here. Do you have anything to add to the naval intelligence report?"

"Nothing. The navy trains ROTC V-12 recruits to report unknown persons or objects on naval grounds. Atherton followed orders."

"Are navy and college vehicles on campus?"

"Yes, with drivers for each carpool."

"Our agents will take over both carpools. We are ready for interrogation of the seaman."

"He's waiting across the hall. Come with me."

* * *

"Seaman David Atherton, you will be under Colonel Matthews's command until he releases you."

"Yes, sir." David jumped up and saluted the army colonel.

"Your commander arranged an office for us. Let's take a walk," Ed Matthews said in a pleasant voice and walked with David side by side.

"Where are you from, sailor?"

"West Texas, sir."

"Wide-open spaces and blue skies."

"Yes, sir."

"I've been on a few deer-hunting trips in West Texas. You have turkeys, hogs, antelope, elk, and sheep out there."

"Yes, sir. Mountain lions and bears too."

They exchanged a few more words about Texas before Lieutenant

Harris joined them in the OSS office. Ed Matthews introduced them and motioned for David and the lieutenant to sit in the chairs opposite his desk. David sat erect in an at-attention posture, and Harris leaned over the recorder in his hand.

"Relax, sailor. We are from the Office of Strategic Services. Lieutenant Harris, please turn on the recorder."

David knew he wasn't in trouble, but it was difficult to relax. All he wanted was to be on a bus with his men.

"Please give your rank, service, and serial number," said the colonel.

"David Atherton, US Navy V-12 ROTC, Middleton College," he said and gave his serial number.

"An unknown person in a restricted military area is always a crime, even more so during a war. OSS classified your sighting top secret. Confidentiality is essential. Do not discuss or disclose any part of this interrogation or investigation. Do you understand?"

"Yes, Colonel Matthews."

"You were leading the platoons this morning. What happened?"

"At 0500, facing the west goal post, we marched on the football field, now the parade grounds. A hedge surrounds the area. Hooded ground lights line the field. At the southwest corner, at a break in the hedge, a shielded pole light gives off feathery illumination. In that faint light, a sudden movement in my peripheral vision caught my attention. I turned and saw a navy officer. He had jumped from behind the hedge and hopped back to his right behind the hedge and out of my sight."

"How about his height and weight?"

"Less than six feet. Maybe five eleven. Weight about one ninety, with a shorter and heavier frame than mine, sir."

"What is your height?"

"Six three, sir."

"Did you see ... was he a blond or a brunette?"

"Happened fast, sir. I saw his face but blonder, in my opinion."

"Scars?"

"I don't think I was close enough to see markings on his face."

"Uniform? Insignias?"

"He wore the dark naval officer uniform with two stripes on the sleeve and hat."

"A full US Navy lieutenant?"

"Yes, sir."

"Did you see insignias on his coat?"

"Yes, sir. On the left side of the coat, two rows of battle ribbons."

"Identification badge?"

"I didn't see a name tag."

"Any other observations, son?" said Colonel Matthews with a fatherly tone.

David frowned. "No, sir, but something caused the officer to spring from behind that hedge and back. Come to think of it, sir, there was something else. It just occurred to me Middleton officers wear the white officer's hat. The officer I saw wore a darker hat."

"Dark blue or khaki?"

"The hat looked black, so the dark blue one."

"You did not see another person?"

"No, sir." David pinched his eyebrows together. "I couldn't see through the hedge covered with red berries."

Ed Matthews watched him for a moment before asking, "Nothing else unusual?"

"That is it, sir. I am sorry I did not observe more. All this happened in milliseconds. I gave the about-face order, spun around, and marched with the platoons toward the administration building for the platoons to board buses as ordered."

"Atherton, until we identify the officer in question, you are under OSS protective care. An OSS agent will be with you at all times. The investigation will not interrupt your schedule."

David sat up straighter. "Your orders are: rejoin unit and continue officer training. In a few minutes, a sedan, driver, and OSS agent will drive you to Jackson. We will try to get you on the same train with your unit. An OSS agent will travel with you. Remember, you are not to discuss our meeting with anyone. You are in the navy, but my orders override the navy orders. Understood?"

David stiffened his military stance. "Yes, sir."

"Lieutenant Harris will accompany you to the car."

David saluted the colonel and left with Lieutenant Harris.

* * *

Chief OSS Agent Matthews switched on the recorder and listened to the interrogation with Seaman Atherton. He stared at a scar on his hand from an injury in North Africa. The old wound sparked a hunch. Schiller had a slight scar along his right chin line. Atherton saw only the left side of the unknown's face. But the seaman's physical description of the unknown navy officer matched Hans Schiller's, a German saboteur agent woven into his psyche. Was it possible Schiller was in Mississippi? Yes. Why? The unknown spotted on navy parade grounds was within walking distance of thirty-five hundred German POWs housed at Camp Clinton.

In 1940, he would have laughed that any one man would forever dwell in his mind. But it happened. WWII broke out in Europe in 1939. In 1940, the year he finished law school, Congress passed the first peacetime conscription. Men didn't know when their draft number would be called up. It was a time of uncertainty. Edward Matthews, the esquire, decided to complete the compulsory military service before he became busier in his law practice.

If a man freely volunteered, US Army recruiters promised service equivalent to his civilian occupation. Ed volunteered. As promised, the army assigned him to the Office of Adjutant General in the judge advocate's office. Unless he had the weekend duty, he went home to be with his young children.

Former law colleagues who waited for the draft went into the infantry and became causalities, injured or killed on the battlefields. Ed was glad he volunteered early, but in a twist of fate, his life changed.

After Pearl Harbor, the United States unified all intelligence agencies into one, the Office of Strategic Services. The army transferred Ed to the newly formed OSS and shipped him out to Canada for espionage training with British Intelligence Secret Service, M16. The carefree weekends at home ended.

Fresh out of the UK M16 espionage training, assigned to the UK and US's Operation Torch, Ed landed in Algeria. Embedded with green US soldiers, Ed engaged in the United States' first overseas fight against Germany's professional troops. During the North African campaign, Ed encountered Hans Schiller, Germany's most seasoned espionage agent, and Schiller outwitted the American intelligence rookie.

At a gap in the Atlas Mountains and near a village in north Central Tunisia, Germany's Afrika Korps captured Allied troops and killed more than a thousand US soldiers. After the battle, Hans Schiller's name topped the OSS's most-wanted list. Ed had lived and fought with the men killed and injured at the breach in the mountains and winced at the memory of the crushing defeat in February 1943. Later, Allied troops defeated the Afrika Korps at the pass, but Ed never got over Schiller's crafty land mine planting, resulting in overwhelming American casualties at the mountain pass.

The possibility Hans Schiller operated in the US signaled danger. Ed wanted Schiller, dead or alive. He heard a rap on the door and squared his shoulders. "Come in."

"You sent for me?" said his lieutenant.

"Yes, get Mike Ward in Washington on the secure line and speaker. Listen in for orders."

Lieutenant Harris made the connection and said, "Chief Ward is on the line, sir."

"Mike, I believe the unknown reported at the Middleton ROTC V-12 parade grounds about an hour ago is the big fish at the top of our list."

"Hans Schiller? You are kidding. The renowned German espionage agent in Mississippi? Impossible."

"It's a gut feeling. The seaman's physical description of the unknown fits Schiller. We need roadblocks on all federal and state highways in Mississippi immediately."

"You've got it. As we speak, my aide will notify officials. You are positive?"

"Yes. The commander stated the naval officer in question was not on ROTC staff. The unknown's strange behavior, hopping from behind a hedge, attracted the sailor's attention."

"Fill me in with what you know and need, and we'll take care of it as we speak."

"Schiller, disguised as a navy officer loitering near Camp Clinton housing Africa Korps POWs is horrible news. That POW camp has over three thousand German prisoners, including thirty-five high-ranking German officers. There are over three hundred thousand German prisoners in the United States and more arriving weekly. Hitler doesn't have to invade the United States; he has a ready-made army of German POWs on the home front. Camp Clinton is within minutes of Middleton College, where a V-12 platoon leader spotted an unknown naval officer who, for some reason, jumped from his hideout behind a hedge.

"POWs at Camp Clinton are under lax security. They work on farms and cotton fields. The US Corps of Engineers have Camp Clinton POWs digging drainage ditches on a one-mile-square model of the Mississippi River Basin, an endeavor for studying flooding."

Ed took a breath. "You sent my team down here because some Camp Clinton POWs tried to escape. Most German POWs are glad to be out of the fighting, but the oppressive heat motivates escape. The possibility exists die-hard escaped POW Nazi officers could lead German POW soldiers and fight in the US.

"In the summer, POWS swelter in scorching barracks at POW camps located in the South, but no more than American soldiers who live in the same structures. At Camp Clinton, in keeping with his rank, the US provides a house and a car with driver for General Von Arnim."

Colonel Matthews laughed. "I discounted local rumors the well-known general survived Mississippi's hot summer by attending movies at the only air-conditioned theater in Jackson. The general never had it so well, but a disgruntled officer could easily escape," said Ed.

"Hans Schiller's helping POWs escape fits into the picture, and he'd get help from known German sympathizers who live in the US. And we know German agents spy for Japan," said Mike. "The Japanese stature and their features prevent Japan's sending intelligence agents to the United States. Japan pays Germany bundles for intelligence information."

"Yeah. Schiller speaks English fluently and passes for an American. The navy has a V-12 ROTC unit stationed at Middleton. Most seamen training to be officers will lead sailors in the Pacific. Japan would like to know how many officers the US is training and when they ship out. That would explain Schiller's presence on the Middleton campus. But Camp Clinton and the V-12 ROTC do not add up to Germany's foremost espionage agent's presence in the US. Something bigger is going on, Mike," said Ed.

"You are right. I haven't forgotten Operation Pastorius. Fortunately, the German saboteurs were captured before they blew up factories or troop trains," said Mike.

"There is a big difference in German Intelligence now. The admiral who previously headed German Intelligence supported the Geneva Convention mandates. He protected civilians, prisoners of war, and soldiers rendered incapable of fighting and befriended Jews seeking sanctuary from the Nazi government. Because the admiral had a heart, the SS arrested him and took command of German Intelligence. There is nothing humanitarian about the SS. They ignore Geneva Convention policies, encourage atrocities, and murder innocent civilians. If Germany has Hans Schiller with a saboteur team in the United States, we can project horrendous destruction and loss of life. The OSS Washington office stands by you 1,000 percent with agents and every requirement for Schiller's capture."

"We're going after him, Mike."

CHAPTER 7

Magnetics

At the secluded navy headquarters' back entrance, Lieutenant Philip Wiley opened the rear door of a navy Chevrolet sedan, and David crawled into the back seat. The driver shifted gears and drove the car out of the Middleton service entrance.

A sailor in the passenger seat turned to face David. "Good morning. I am Seaman Frank Miller, your OSS special agent. We'll call each other by our first names."

"Yes, sir," he said.

"Leave off the sir, sailor. We have the same rank."

"I understand," said David. The man in the front seat was his babysitter. His sighting of the officer at the hedge rated a top secret classification and confirmed Commander Kemp didn't have a clue of the officer's identity.

"Are you hungry, David?" Frank handed a sack over the seat.

"I am. And thank you." He reached for the sack. The heavy scent of bacon tickled his nose, and his stomach growled.

"The colonel takes care of his team. We ate while we waited for you." Frank handed a thermos bottle over the seat. "This is orange juice." He held up another thermos. "And this is coffee."

The boxed breakfast with bacon, scrambled eggs, buttered biscuits, sweet rolls, and jam eased David's hunger pangs. Texans ate sausage and potatoes for breakfast, but he enjoyed the grits provided by the colonel.

"When you finish, hand the trash up front. An admiral might check out this car next."

David smiled and handed him the sack and thermos jugs and settled back in the soft leather seat, a comfort he hadn't experienced since he'd joined the navy.

He patted a little black book in his pocket. In high school, he'd kept a little black book entitled "Qualifications for Dating," in which he wrote down his father's wisdom and his inklings about girls. An MD, his father had talked frankly with him about the biological and mental attributes of males and females and the discipline necessary for a boy when he considered friendships with girls.

His dad stressed the importance of dating girls who believed in God's Word. "God has a plan for your marriage. You will fall in love and want to marry her. In the meantime, behave like the man we've brought you up to be."

David pulled out his current little black book, titled "Marriage Essentials," with qualities desired in a wife listed as 1) religion/faith; 2) intellect/interests; 3) personality; 4) physically attractive; and 5) love.

Frank chided him. "It's too late for that little black book."

"But not a list of requirements for a wife."

"Are you getting married?"

"Not yet."

"Bet you met a girl here. How'd she measure up?"

David chuckled. "She failed four out of five." His guard and the driver laughed with him.

David closed his eyes with a smile on his face. The song he'd sung at the Oak Hill Sunday Tea whirled in his head. Lucinda's eyes locked into his as he belted out Harry James's version of "You made me love you, I didn't wanna do it. You made me want you." Lucinda turned his trait preferences for a wife upside down; the last item on the list became the first.

With every nerve in his body, he'd wanted to kiss Lucinda, and she knew it. Once, his lips brushed her forehead. He wanted to feel the warmth of her lips on his but backed away. His father's faraway voice reminded him to behave himself, to be honorable. Lucinda looked hurt; he was hurting. He'd resorted to his "Essentials for Marriage" list with first things first and confronted Lucinda about her faith, saying, "Lucinda, what do you believe, spiritually?"

"I believe what my church believes," she said and interlocked her fingers with his and coyly fluttered her eyelashes.

He stifled his desire for her and said, "What does your church believe?"

"We both believe the same thing. The church believes what I believe," she said.

"And what is that?"

She looked up, her eyes tempting him, and smiled. "Well, I am a Baptist enrolled in a Baptist college, David."

He wanted to smother her with kisses but controlled his behavior and said, "I didn't ask about your denomination, and college enrollment has nothing to do with my question. What do you believe?"

Lucinda gave him an alluring smile and did not answer his question. He squirmed and said, "We'll talk later."

"Hey, sailor, are you okay?" He opened his eyes and looked at Frank.

"Oh, yes. No problems. I'm fine."

But in truth, he wasn't at all okay with Lucinda on his mind. Why was he attracted to her? She failed religion, the first and most vital quality in the girl he desired for a wife. He wanted her to say she believed what he believed, John 3:16, "For God so loved the world, that he gave his only begotten Son, that whosoever believeth in him should not perish, but have everlasting life." The temptation to kiss her threw him. Later, he resumed the serious pursuit of the second trait he considered essential for the girl he married and the mother of his children: intelligence and intellectual interests.

If Lucinda had any brainy interests, she never spoke about them. He suspected she was smart, but as far as he knew, he was her only interest. He penciled a minus by Intelligence.

Her individuality captured his heart; she charmed him. Other girls appealed to him but no one like her. He wasn't sure her extroverted personality suited him. He entered the question mark by Personality, the third trait he desired in a wife.

In the little black book, under Physically Attractive, he'd written "a statuesque blonde-haired girl with creamy skin and dreamy blue eyes or a tall, elegant brunette with smooth, ivory skin and sparkling, deep brown eyes." Blonde or brunette, he'd envisioned a girl with a heart-shaped face, slender, willowy, and not too tall. Lucinda wasn't what he'd call slim, and she was taller than average. She had a round face and high cheekbones, not on his list. She had a small, often puckered mouth and a permanently turned-up nose, also unlisted. Neither had he listed a ruddy complexion, red hair, or eyes of traffic light–yellow sparkling with go-go-green.

He frowned. He'd forgotten to put "teeth" on his list. Lucinda had nice white ones, but overall, she failed essential number four and overall struck out on three essentials on his list, and one he questioned.

He groaned within. Nothing in Lucinda's coquettish looks warned him to slow down or stop. She urged him on, and he liked it. Was his desire for her real love? Or was it infatuation fueled by the life changes brought on by the war? No! What he felt was real.

What was magnetic about her? He'd studied magnetic and gravity in physics. Gravity pulled masses together. Magnetics pulled objects together and pushed them apart; opposite poles attract, while similar poles repel.

He and Lucinda were different; he never pushed her away. A magnet of greater strength pulled toward one of lesser power. He was stronger than she. He smiled. Forget gravity and magnetics. Whether she passed or failed, all his essentials for marriage didn't matter. She passed number five—love, the last item on his list. She was in love with him, and he loved her. He wanted to marry her, but he had a job to do before he could get serious about marriage.

"Okay, seaman. We are pulling into the station. Move it!"

CHAPTER 8

The Declaration

December 8, 1944—7:00 a.m.

*S*unlight broke through the heavy mist, and Hans glanced in the rearview mirror. No cars followed him, but he clenched the steering wheel until his knuckles turned white. He'd breached his cover at Middleton. "Why?" he asked himself out loud. But he knew why.

At Heidelberg, long a center of democracy, he'd thrived, studied hard, and lived a life with noble thoughts and hope. His linguistic ability and international experience attracted Abwehr, German Intelligence. With the stroke of a pen, Abwehr recruited him, and his espionage career began.

In espionage schools at Berlin and Hamburg, he became the protégé of Abwehr's commander in chief, an admiral, who abhorred persecution of the Jews. His sordid life in the craft of violence and the indiscriminate slaughter began when the SS took over Abwehr. He was under orders to liquidate any person who could trip up planned sabotage.

During the night, he hid in the Middleton chapel, and he heard the voices and laughter of young college students. He yearned for his peaceful college days, the days he laughed, sang, and strolled with his darling sweetheart. The sight of the Middleton girl overwhelmed him with desire. He wanted to stroke her hair, caress her.

For the first time in his illustrious sabotage career, he faltered and blew his cover. If either the sailor or girl reported him, US Intelligence would suspect he was spy and search, capture him, and execute him. He grasped his uniform lapel and fingered a hidden cyanide tablet but laughed at the dark thought. *As a sleeper in America, I live a pleasant life far removed from past atrocities.*

At US 51, he exited State Highway 8, turned south toward Operation Heil's base, and rechecked the rearview mirror. No one was tailing him. He loosened his grip on the steering wheel and wrinkled his nose at the sheepish, wool smell of the wet uniform he wore.

Unbuttoning the jacket, he brushed his hand over the wet shirt that clung to his body. His physical discomfort paled in comparison to capture. He had no intention of being executed. Therefore, he had no scruples over killing a person who could identify him. He had to eliminate the sailor and the girl. He'd order an agent under his command to track the sailor and eliminate him. He pondered taking out the girl.

He held every detail of the girl in his mind, average build, five foot six or so, round, apple cheeks, and an oval jawline. Silly, hiding out in a red coat. If she was a student, it wouldn't be difficult to locate her. Was it possible she was an American Intelligence agent assigned to the campus? *Nein.* (No.)

He mopped his brow and breathed in and out deeply. In Berlin, he'd checked out a map of the campus. Middleton College had separate grounds for males and females. The girl had accessed the military area by the private road connecting the female dormitories to the main campus. She had to be a female student spying on her boyfriend. He should forget about her and let her go on with her life, but he could not do so.

His eyes narrowed. The girl had a sixth sense. Intuitively, she had whirled around with composure befitting a German saboteur. She hadn't screamed. She pursed her lips, tilted her turned-up nose and chin, and glared with nerves of steel at him. In the lamp pole's faint glow, her amber eyes sparkled with fire. He suspected she had German genes. If she were at Universität Heidelberg, the SS would snap her up for espionage training.

Disgusted with himself over the senseless encounter with the girl, he shook his head in an attempt to erase his blunder. Sweat broke out on his forehead. German Intelligence warned espionage agents about females, and a pretty girl had throttled him. Girls talked. Miss Turned-Up-Nose was a greater risk than the sailor. She jeopardized German strategy in America. And he, a German saboteur, rendered death to witnesses, even unarmed civilians, male and female. He slipped up. He should have killed the girl on the spot.

He pressed his lips together and sneered, and his mouth turned up in a cynical smile. He'd ordered the girl to report to the dean of women. If she was smart enough to sneak out of the dormitory, she could reenter the building undetected. Unless caught, the girl wouldn't report her offense. But she could identify him. The SS advocated "wink not, gamble not"; liquidate risks. She had to go.

Military honor prevailed in the soul of a principled soldier. On a brutal battlefield, it was a warrior against warrior. Military combatants honored the white flag, the signal of surrender by an enemy. There was no military honor in his sneaky work, no white flag to raise. He'd killed civilians. He sharpened a double-edge dagger every day, carried it daily, and in the past, never failed to use it. This morning, his hand relaxed on the knife when he saw the girl. Was living a life intermingled with civilians, his enemies, interfering with his mission? Was he getting soft?

Hans slammed his left hand on the steering wheel, then pressed his fingers into his temples. By the grace of God, he'd never deliberately murdered a female or child. And now he had to kill an innocent girl. He was under orders to stop factory and military power on US soil. He and his team had explosives to blow up factories, bridges, and troop convoys and trains.

Spying for Japan was not his first surveillance at Middleton College, adjacent to Camp Clinton. He communicated with a Camp Clinton informer who'd help POWs lucky enough to escape. At the edge of the college campus, he and the informer buried American identification papers, civilian clothes, and weapons. And at Middleton, he'd spied for Japan.

Although German men appeared as large, hairy barbarians to the Japanese, Japan prized and depended on German Intelligence.

"I can be a secret agent for Japan, but a Japanese agent cannot be German me."

He pounded his thigh with his fist. Surveillance for Japan and helping POWs escape jeopardized Operation Heil's prime mission. He commanded Operation Heil's demolition experts in the US. The destruction and carnage Germany planned on the American mainland would exceed Japan's surprise attack at Pearl Harbor.

Handpicked by German Intelligence, every saboteur on his team had worked in the US, spoke fluent English, and understood the ethnicity of American people. His men lived as sleepers and mingled daily with civilians. He prided himself on a repertoire of masquerades and a metamorphosis of identities. Masked as a businessman, he blended in with friendly, gracious southerners and enjoyed pleasant days in a small town. But he was Germany's foremost saboteur. He cast out the admiral's code of ethics and banished all thoughts of sparing the girl.

He relished his brand of espionage, a world of secrecy and deception and killing. The poetry he heard at his mother's knee flashed through his mind.

Ich bin der Meister meines: Schicksals Ich bin der Kapitän meiner Seele. He swallowed hard, and quoted from "Invictus" by William Ernest Henley, "'I am the master of my fate: I am the captain of my soul.'" He shouted to the wind, "'Invictus! Unconquerable!'"

CHAPTER 9

A Rendezvous

*H*ans exited US 51 onto a secluded logging road. Cutting through forested rolling hills and descending to the Bogue Chitto River, the backwoods road served as an excellent site for a rendezvous with two agents on his team. And the river was a planned escape route, should his team need one.

An overhead canopy of trees shielded the road from the rising sun's rays. Avoiding exposure, he drove without headlights along the shadowed gravel side road. He swerved around menacing curves until sweat broke out on his forehead. After harrowing minutes, he saw a dim, flashing light and slowed the sedan. He followed his agent's signals and turned the car back toward the main highway. After he cut the motor, another agent stepped from behind trees.

"I did not come here to play Hansel and Gretel," Hans said, getting out of the sedan.

"Entschuldigung," said the agent and smiled at Hans's dry humor. ("Sorry.") "Guten Morgen." ("Good Morning.")

"Guten Morgen."

The experienced electronics agent tuned the radio while the other agent removed US Navy insignia from the sedan doors and pulled vines off a circa late 1930s' Ford coupe.

As they worked, Hans cleaned himself up and changed into civilian clothing. He pushed dirty, navy-regulation shoes under the front seat of the sedan, folded the damp American uniform into a laundry bag, and shoved the officer's hat on top of it. The cap fell back onto the car floor. In a glint of morning light, the keen eye of the American eagle on the hat seemed to mock him. Gnashing his teeth, Hans jammed the intimidating enemy symbol underneath the laundry bag and blamed his irritability on lack of sleep.

Dressed out in American civilian clothes and a dark brown Stetson porkpie hat, Hans crossed the narrow strip of gravel, pulled out a map, and spread it out on the hood of the car. "Here is a map of Middleton College; here is Adalia Hall, a female dormitory." He handed over a roll of film and said, "Get this film developed. There is an image of a girl on it. She lives at Adalia Hall. Watch for her and eliminate her."

"Kill her?" said an agent, astonished.

"Is there any other way to liquidate her?" said their commander.

"Nein. Nein," said his agents and rolled up the map before Hans started the coupe.

Tipping his porkpie hat, Hans said, "Danke Sehr, Auf Wiesderschen." ("Thank you very much. Goodbye.")

Keeping the automobile in low gear, Hans maneuvered along the gravel road. The sun had burned off moisture in the air, and sunlight shined through skyscraper-high trees. He marveled at the magical sight of green, magenta, and gold leaves dancing in the breeze and laughed at his fear of driving without headlights on the slippery, loose-gravel road. After emerging from the fairy-tale forest, he drove south on US 51, closer every mile to his command base. The agent now driving the sedan turned north on the highway toward Middleton.

CHAPTER 10

The Predicament

December 8, 1944—7:15 a.m.

ucinda railed over the arrogant naval officer with service ribbons embellished on his chest. She did not care where he fought.

Her fury didn't stem from the fact he caught her off-limits but the conceited look in his eyes. She could feel his breath steaming on her face. He stood close enough to, well, kiss her. She blushed as she remembered the goose bumps that crept around her neck when he boldly looked into her eyes. She did not want to see him ever again.

Why was the officer behind that hedge? What was he thinking when he told her to report to the dean? Did the officer think she would walk straight into Dean Wright's office and say to Dean Wright that she, Lucinda Reed, a trusted honor student, snuck out of the dorm and trespassed onto military property? Well, he had a preposterous idea. She had no intention of telling on herself.

At the thought of lying to Dean Wright, Lucinda grasped her wet hair at the roots and pulled upward until her scalp ached. Her record at Middleton was spotless. If the officer reported her, would the dean believe his account of her shameful behavior?

She sighed and wrapped her fingers around the pre–Civil War wrought iron headboard, a relic bought by the college in 1840. Middleton updated the male dormitories with twin beds. She shared a double bed with Jean, her roommate. *Why did I tell Jean about the officer?* Thankfully, Jean left the dorm first for the Christmas holidays.

"Never put yourself in a position for anyone to say evil of you," her father had said to her many times. Jean, her parents, and grandfather would never understand why she left the dorm. Lucinda ran her fingers through her hair and breathed in and out several times to relieve her pain.

Glancing at the morning light filtering into her room, she checked the clock on the bedside table. "Seven thirty, and finally, I'm warm," she murmured, snuggled under the cover, and continued thinking about her dilemma.

WWII changed everything in America except Oak Hill. At tables for twelve, a faculty member sat with eleven girls and continuously upbraided them. "Sit up straight. Keep one hand in your lap. Use your napkin. Do not stab at your food and shovel it in your mouth. Do not slurp. Cut one piece of your food at a time. Break your bread with your fingers. Eat with your mouth closed."

Her favorite was "Lucinda, you paused your fork in midair." At every meal, she heard, "Girls, when you have finished eating, please place the fork with tines up and the knife with the blade on the left side of the plate at the 4:20 position on the right side of your plate. Remember, if we were in Europe, we'd place the fork with tines down." We weren't in Europe, so why bother reminding girls about Europe?

When her grandfather attended Middleton, Oak Hill forbade girls being in a buggy with a boy. In 1944, Oak Hill didn't allow female students in a car with a boy.

Disgusted with the rules she lived under, Lucinda threw her arms on top of the comforter, crossed her eyes, and gritted her teeth. Faculty supervised study hours, seven until nine thirty in the evening, and never let up on female students' social training. College teachers chaperoned Friday and Saturday nights during visiting hours from six to eight, and Sunday tea, from two to five in the afternoon. "Weird rules," Lucinda said and sighed.

Lucinda relaxed in bed and smiled about Sunday tea. For more than a hundred years, under the supervision of the head cook, Oak Hill girls baked cookies for Middleton College boys who visited for Sunday tea. Now, V-12 sailors came for tea on Sunday.

At first, only a few curious, somewhat amused sailors ventured to the girls' campus for the Sunday tea. In time, more and more sailors invaded the parlors for the Sunday social event, and more and more girls baked more and more batches of cookies in the college kitchen. Under the duress of wartime sugar and butter rationing, war-challenged school cooks struggled over having enough ingredients for the tea tradition.

"We never served more than a few batches of cookies at Sunday tea before this war, World War I, or the Civil War either," said Miss Susie, the chief cook.

"You weren't even born before the Civil War, were you?" said one sassy girl.

"No, but I heard about it. My mother and grandmother had been in food service at Oak Hill for generations. In this war, all the sugar we're allowed comes from your ration books. Not enough sugar, flour, or lard, much less butter, to run this kitchen with all these cookies ya'll bake for those boys. And you are making candy too."

"They're not boys," said another impudent Oak Hill student. "They are the United States of America Navy recruits."

"They look like boys to me. Boys gobbling up our sugar."

"They don't gobble. They're seamen training to be officers in the United States Navy," chorused several girls.

"Officers in no army or navy gobble up cookies the way they do. Officers have manners. I've served those navy officers up at Middleton and plenty polite people at teas too. They take no more than two cookies, one cup of punch. That's all. That's southern manners, what you're supposed to learn living at Oak Hill. You girls should know better, but you urge those sailors to come for tea, and they grab cookies by the handful and swallow punch by the gallons. Food and drink that's coming out of this kitchen."

"Well, the navy recruits are not southern. They're from all over the United States, and the navy doesn't serve them delicious cookies and drinks."

"The cooks at Middleton cafeteria work under me," chortled the head cook. "Those navy boys don't eat rationed food. They feast like kings every day. They drink milk by the quarts and eat plenty of cake, pie, and cookies baked in men's cafeteria. That's why we're short here. Everything's rationed and going to the military. This war changed everything here, baking all these cookies. Girls in classes at the Middleton campus is no good. You are long-legged babies, and you play up to sailors from who knows where."

Lucinda had heard enough. "We are not playing up to them."

"That's what you're doing, playing up to them. I'm gonna talk to the dean about your playing up to sailors you don't know, your sassy manners, and all these cookies and candy and everything else coming out of this kitchen."

"Oh, don't do that, please! The sailors will be disappointed!" the girls chorused.

"Excuse me. Who'll be disappointed? Those boys won't come down here without batches and batches of cookies and batches and batches of divinity and fudge."

The cook shook her head as she waved a towel in the air. "You make Jesus weep when you talk ugly to me. I don't like it, and I am ready to talk to the dean. She needs to know about the cookies, candy, and bad manners. You board here. You supposed to act nice and talk nicely to everyone."

"Please, don't talk to the dean, Miss Susie," girls pleaded.

"We are sorry. We didn't mean to be disrespectful. Please, please don't tell the dean. She'll give us demerits, and we won't even be able to go to Sunday tea."

"You are im-pu-dent. You need to get demerits for your sassy talk." Miss Susie filled a pot with water and placed it on the stove. "You sure aren't gettin' desserts with all the sugar you're using, and don't come around here complainin' there're no biscuits for breakfast. All the flour is going out of here for Sunday tea cookies."

"Oh, we don't mind." A couple of the girls hugged Miss Susie, hoping to soothe her feelings.

Lucinda bit her lip. The administration held Miss Susie in high regard, and Miss Susie knew it. Miss Susie had full authority to reprimand students for nonconformance to Oak Hill's high standards. Respect for college employees at every level of employment topped the list of rules at Oak Hill.

In truth, all the girls loved Miss Susie, and she loved them, but she never let up on southern manners and being polite to everyone.

Lucinda grinned. Miss Susie's rationing concerns didn't last long. Watkins Town Ladies for Victory watched a growing Sunday parade of sailors on their way to Oak Hill. Zealous to assist in any war effort, the ladies pooled food ration stamps and catered the Sunday teas.

The town takeover of Sunday tea pleased Miss Susie. That first Sunday, the WTLV women brought in hearty meat sandwiches and cheese straws on sterling silver trays. There were also luscious caramel, chocolate, and coconut cakes on crystal cake pedestals. Dressed in their prettiest Sunday clothes, girls cut and served ample slices of cake to sailors and ladled thirst-quenching punch from heirloom silver bowls into crystal cups held out for refills by boys in navy blue.

In parlors with ceiling-to-floor windows and draperies heaped in puddles on hardwood floors, sailors sat side by side with Oak Hill girls on green or rose moiré velvet Victorian love seats and ate sugared pecans, divinity, and fudge from crystal bowls conveniently placed on marble-topped side tables.

In the Green Parlor, on the grand piano donated by the Woman's Missionary Union (WMU) for playing sacred music, a pianist played never-before-allowed popular music. Girls and sailors gathered around the piano and sang romantic, sentimental melodies from arrangements by Harry James, Glenn Miller, and Artie Shaw and jazz music that lifted their morale.

The sound of Harry James's trumpet whirled through her head with a song popularized by Glenn Miller. Lucinda hugged her shoulders and remembered David's deep baritone voice belting out, "Don't sit under the apple tree with anyone else but me," lyrics by Lew Brown and Charles Tobias.

With the navy's rigid schedule and Oak Hill's strict rules, she and David had never officially dated. Once, David treated her to a Coke at the Blue Jay, the snack shop off campus. Rubbing the spot where David's lips touched her forehead, she hummed the James V. Monaco melody and remembered Harry James's version that topped the charts in 1941. She knew David loved her when he looked into her eyes and sang Joseph McCarthy's lyrics, "You made me love you. I didn't want to do it."

"Sunday tea time was the most fun I ever had in my life," she whispered.

Father had been right. Reveille at 5:30 a.m., "Taps" at dusk, and study hours at night left V-12 sailors little free time for girls, but she'd fallen in love with David anyway.

She looked at the clock again and jumped out of bed to shower, dress, and sign out for the Christmas holidays. She'd board the train for Vicksburg and never come back to Oak Hill. Rolling up her sleeve, she drew up the muscle in her upper arm like she'd seen in Rosie the Riveter poster. She'd become a riveter and work near David's base and be with him before he shipped out to sea.

Half an hour later, she stood in the doorway to her room and took a deep breath. She dreaded the face-to-face meeting with Dean Wright and shuddered on her way to sign out with the kind, well-liked woman of authority.

Timidly, she tapped on the dean's door.

"Come in, please." She slowly opened the door and entered the dean's office.

The tastefully dressed, well-bred woman reflected the qualities of honesty and trust. Respected by her students and peers, she did not seek popularity. She was just who she was and was admired by those with whom she worked.

"Good morning, Lucinda. Ready to sign out?"

The dean's poise unnerved her. "Yes, ma'am," she said and hoped her voice sounded natural.

"You requested a lift to the train station this morning. The driver will be ready for you with enough time to load your luggage in his car, unload at the station, and for you to buy a ticket to Vicksburg. At the dorm meeting, you shared you planned to be in New Orleans over the holidays."

"Yes, ma'am."

Dean Wright smiled. "New Orleans is a wonderful city. Have a merry Christmas, Lucinda."

"Thank you." Her knees shook, and she worried they might give way under her. "Merry Christmas."

Dean Wright nodded and waved her off. She walked out of the office and gasped a deep breath. The dean didn't know she'd left the dorm in the middle of the night. The officer hadn't reported her.

Hunger pangs struck like a knife across her midriff. She circled her tongue in her mouth. She could taste Miss Susie's hot buttered biscuits and honey. If she hurried, she could grab a couple of them and race out of the dining hall, but she'd never get away with it. Mrs. Farr would scold her and make her sit down at the table and eat slowly. She was not up to dealing with the former dean of women.

The college ruled all rooms had to be empty because maintenance cleaned and painted the dorms during holidays. No one would be suspicious that Lucinda had removed all personal items from the room. She'd never return to Adalia Hall.

At 8:30 a.m., she carried two suitcases downstairs to the doorway she'd slipped out of before dawn. On the second trip downstairs, she dragged a massive box of books to the side door. Lucinda returned to the room for the suitcase. She opened it and kissed David's picture before she snapped her suitcase shut.

After scanning the room for anything she missed, she picked up the suitcase and walked down the stairs in Adalia Hall for the last time. She dropped the suitcase by the side door but held the wet laundry bag up off the floor. Someone knocked, and she opened the door.

"Good morning, Miss Reed. My name is Frank Harris. I am your driver this morning. Is this your luggage?"

She expected old Mr. Simmons to drive her in the station wagon. This driver was in street clothes. Most men were in the service and wore uniforms on the street. He didn't look disabled, a 4-F, and appeared as healthy as David. Why wasn't the driver in service?

"Is this all the luggage?" He reached down and picked up the box of books.

Startled from her thoughts, she responded, "Yes. Three suitcases, the box, and a laundry bag."

"The laundry bag is damp. We don't want to put that near the box."

Lucinda's heart thumped at his discovery. She'd crammed the wet red coat in the bag and hoped it wouldn't bleed through the sack.

After loading her items into the back of the station wagon, Frank Harris opened the rear door and motioned to the back seat. Lucinda slid across the seat, and Harris gently closed the door.

Mr. Simmons always talked on the way to the station, but the new driver didn't say a word. At the station, he stood discreetly aside while she bought her ticket and then waited with her in the dingy little depot. At the sound of the approaching train, he jumped up and moved all her paraphernalia outside to the platform.

Before the train came to a complete stop, two soldiers leaped off the train. "Sir, we will help with the luggage for the young lady."

Harris stared at them with tongue in cheek. "Don't put that damp laundry bag on the box," he said before he turned to Lucinda. "Have a good trip, Miss Reed."

"Thank you for helping me."

CHAPTER 11

Life Changes

Friday
December 8, 1944—8:00 a.m.

After Lucinda left her office, Dean Helen Wright checked the student roster. Only two girls had not signed out for the holidays. The quiet and almost-empty dormitory brought on suppressed memories of the sparkle and energy of other young girls.

Helen walked over to a bookcase, stroked the spine of an album labeled England 1939–1940, and removed it. A letter fell from the book. She picked up the unfolded letter and read:

Dear Helen,

My heart goes out to you for the loss of your parents and your fiancé. You are all alone in London. You have friends in New York who love you. We want you to come home, so we can hug you and comfort you.

The day England declared war against Germany, a German U-boat torpedoed the SS *Athenia*, a ship sailing between Britain and Canada. Three hundred American passengers were aboard the ill-fated British passenger liner sailing for Montreal. My oldest daughter was on a college tour in the United Kingdom when England declared war. She found a passage in Ireland on a freighter from another neutral country and arrived in New York via Argentina. We know of another group of American students who left

England on ships from neutral Ireland bound for neutral ports and ultimately docked in America.

I mention the plight of my daughter and her friends, praying you will book passage soon on a freighter sailing to a neutral country and on to New York. Come home for a great welcome and lots of hugs.

Dorothy Hirsch
January 1940

"Dorothy's letter initiated my coming home to America," Helen said to herself and lay the unfolded letter on her desk. Looking over pages of photographs, she choked up at the sight of the images made in England.

At a tap on the door, she heard, "It's Dora." Helen opened the door and hugged Dora Farr. She and the older woman enjoyed each other's company. The college honored the retired dean with a lifetime apartment in Adalia Hall. Grateful for the lodging as long as lived, Dora insisted on hosting a table for twelve students at each meal served in the dining hall.

"Most students signed out for the holidays. I won't be hosting a table. We can eat together this morning, and Miss Susie is cooking breakfast to order. Are you ready for a hearty meal?"

"Yes, that would be nice," Helen said with her voice breaking.

"Helen, what is the matter?"

Helen placed her hand on the open album and brushed her hand over a photograph. "My parents. The images in this album mirror happy days and tumultuous changes in my life. I've been strong and never allowed myself to give in to my grief. Signing out girls for the Christmas holidays opened up wounds healed long ago."

"Sharing the pain may help," said Dora.

"You are very wise, my mentor, and my best friend. Before the war, I was a dean of girls at a boarding school in Switzerland. A few days before the Christmas school holidays began, I chaperoned school girls dressed in smart uniforms on an outing in the picturesque village of Gstaad. We walked along the cobblestone way, and my students shopped in chic boutiques stocked with luxury items with prices appropriate for their purses. The teenagers I supervised came from wealthy homes and the homes of leaders from all over Europe. Undaunted by world-renowned individuals, some of the girls dared to approach vacationing celebrities for autographs.

"Across the lane, I noticed an amused RAF officer watching them. He walked over and said, 'I saw you with your charges on the slopes this morning. Do you ever get a reprieve from them?'

"'Never,' I answered.

"'Never?' he asked playfully, and I said 'never' again.

"'Do you mind if I walk along to help keep an eye on your students?'

"'Yes. I do,' I said, glowering at the flirtatious stranger in uniform.

"Several girls overheard the officer and chorused, 'Please, Dean Wright.'

"The officer laughed. 'May I help chaperone, Dean Wright?'

"'Please. Please,' said the young students. Delighted by attention from the handsome RAF's pilot's escort, they asked, 'May we have your autograph?'

"'A worthless X?' he said. 'How about Swiss chocolates instead?' Of course, the girls chorused, 'Yes.'"

"I can believe that. What happened next?" said Dora, her eyes sparkling with mirth.

"While I looked on impatiently, he bought the chocolates and then wrote his treasured signature in their autograph books. His interference infuriated me. I hustled my students back to the train station for a short ride back to the school, glad to get rid of the cocky pilot."

"I have a feeling that was not the end of the story," said the retired dean.

"It wasn't. When we arrived on campus, the headmaster called me into his study. 'Dean Wright, a fine-looking RAF officer just presented impeccable credentials and requested my consent to call on you'. Dora, I was dumbfounded.

"The headmaster chuckled. 'You are not on duty, Dean Wright. My friend John Carlton is waiting for you in the reception area.'"

Dora giggled. "And you were delighted?"

"And very angry. I confronted the officer with, 'This is unbelievable. You asked the headmaster's permission to call on me. You don't even know me.'

"'Not so,' said the RAF officer. 'We met in the village of Gstaad an hour ago. Remember? I asked you a question, to which you replied, 'Never,' twice. 'Never' is not in my vocabulary. My casual tactics with you did not succeed, but the girls' uniforms revealed your address. Jack Marsh, the headmaster of this exclusive school, is a lifelong friend. His parents and my parents own chalets side by side near Gstaad. Upon my request, Jack graciously assisted me with the means of an introduction.'

"'So I heard. You are ridiculous,' I said and crossed my arms, emphasizing my anger.

"'Seeking a formal introduction from my closest friend was polite, not ridiculous,' he said.

"'Formal introduction?' I countered.

"'The headmaster is in his office.' He motioned toward the door and said, 'If you insist, I will fetch him.'"

"His sense of humor amazes me," said Dora

"John had a great sense of absurdity. 'Idiotic' was my reply to him. I remember every word of our altercation.

"'Nothing rash about it at all,' he said. 'My buddies and I sky-hopped over to Gstaad to ski. While headed downhill on skis, I saw you for the first time. The second time, I saw you in the village. After you gave me a cobblestone brush off, I resorted to help from your—'

"'My employer,' I said.

"'Nonetheless, we are now well acquainted. Will you join me for dinner tonight at my parents' home? My flying friends will be there with girls they met on the slopes,' he said.

"'The girls they met this morning on the slopes?'"

Dora grinned at Helen's sarcastic response.

"'The girls and my fellow fliers met the weekend before last. You need not worry. Your employer will be there.'

"I melted inside, fought a smile, and asked him one question. 'Will your parents be there?'"

The young dean's resistance to the RAF officer brought on a hearty laugh from Dora.

"He laughed too, Dora, and said, 'Most assuredly. What time may I pick you up?'

"I gave into him. And so began the love of my life," said Helen. She touched the string of pearls about her neck, and tears filled her eyes. "John bought my necklace in a village shop before he left Gstaad. His peacetime RAF schedule allowed frequent trips to Switzerland, and our whirlwind courtship continued on alternate weekends. Before he proposed, I knew the answer. Yes!"

"I want to hear the rest of your love story, Helen, while we eat breakfast."

"And I want to share it with you." Helen shelved the album and reached for the register she kept at her fingertips. "Lucinda Reed signed out for the morning train. The last two girls won't sign out until it's time for the afternoon train. We'll have plenty of time to talk in the dining hall."

CHAPTER 12

The Unexpected

*M*iss Susie greeted Dean Farr and Dean Wright, "Good morning, ladies. If you are tired of scrambled eggs, this morning we are serving eggs, soft-boiled, sunny-side up, over easy, or over medium."

"Miss Susie, sunny-side up sounds good to me," said Dora. Helen agreed with the choice.

Miss Susie poured steaming cups of coffee for them and said, "Sit back and enjoy a nice, quiet breakfast for a change." They looked around the empty dining room and laughed with her.

"Helen, tell me more about John Carlton."

"John's voice and my father's ring in my ears with thoughts of our official engagement day.

"John said, 'Mr. Wright, the first time I saw your daughter, I fell in love with her. I've been courting Helen since my longtime friend, and headmaster of her school, formally introduced us.'

"John grinned, cut his eyes to me, and said, 'Sir, I come to ask for your daughter's hand in marriage. Your consent to marry her will make me the happiest man on earth.'"

"How romantic, Helen."

"Oh, it was Dora. And Dad said something I never knew: 'Since Helen's birth, her mother and I have prayed for the finest man in the world for her. You are that man, John Carlton. Helen loves you, and we couldn't be happier you've found each other. You have our wholehearted consent to marry our daughter. Welcome to our family, son.'"

"Your love story brings tears to my eyes, Helen."

"And to mine. John's commander granted him a week's leave during the Christmas holidays, and we chose Christmas Day 1939 for our wedding date. John's RAF base was near London. At the end of the school year, I resigned from the boarding school and spent a lovely summer in London planning our wedding. Mother and I shopped for my trousseau and wedding dress, chose floral arrangements, and tasted wedding cake and food for the reception. John's parents included me with plans for the rehearsal dinner, and John and I spent days together selecting our china, crystal, and silver patterns.

"Mother and Dad gave an engagement party for us in their home, and the next day left London for a long-planned vacation in Wales. On their way back to London, a tragic automobile accident claimed their lives."

"The engagement photo of your parents captured their joy for you and your sweetheart."

"I treasure the image, but at Christmastime, their images bring on sadness."

"I hope sharing your sorrow with me helps you this year," said Dora.

"And it has, Dora. You understand. Adalia girls mentioned your husband died in WWI, but we've never discussed your loss."

"Grief overwhelmed me, but the blissful days my husband and I spent together overruled the unhappiness."

"At times, I've sensed you'd lost the one you loved and wondered about it. Until now, I've never been close enough with anyone to share my sorrow. You are very dear to me, Dora, and will understand my Christmas melancholy. John wanted to marry me the week after my parents died and said, 'You have no siblings. You are living over three thousand miles from distant relatives. You cannot live alone in the London house. Marry me now in the cathedral or at my parents' home in Gloucester.'

"I put him off, but John was persuasive, and we planned an early-September wedding at his parents' home. John managed to get a long weekend off." Helen ran her fingers through her hair. "The last day of August 1939, we drove to Gloucester and visited the magnificent Gloucester Cathedral. Sunrays streaming through cloistered windows enhanced the sacredness of God's love. We knelt in a carrel and prayed. His holy presence filtered through the grief over my parents and enveloped me with thanksgiving about our marriage.

"But God had other plans. The next day, September 1, 1939, Germany invaded Poland. Two days later, on Sunday, England and France declared war on Germany. Within hours, the RAF ordered all pilots to report to their bases.

"John insisted I stay with his parents in Gloucester and said, 'The first leave the RAF gives me, we will be married.' He wrapped his arms around me and kissed me goodbye. I had an ominous feeling. In a few days, the dark emotion became real. Over France, enemy fire riddled the Spitfire he piloted.

"Miraculously, John flew the plane back over the English Channel and landed it at an airbase. At the base hospital, we found John conscious but fatally injured. He held my hand and whispered, 'I will love you always,'" Helen said.

"Helen, I wish I had known earlier how you have suffered."

"Oh, Dora, those were wretched days for me. I stayed with John's parents in Gloucester for several weeks before I returned to London."

"And you lived in London for some time after 1939?"

"Yes, I had no other place to go. My father's company offered me a job. Working with people who knew my father and mother comforted me during the day. At night, I walked until exhausted enough to crash into bed.

"The afternoon of September 7, 1940, Germany bombed London, a blitz that lasted fifty-seven straight days and nights, and people sought shelter in the basements of commercial buildings. One day, a woman supervising several young children sat nearby me in an air raid shelter. At the all-clear signal, the lady led the children to a house near my home.

"Many London parents sent their children to the country for safety. Curious about the young children in the air raid shelter, I made inquiries about an underground movement rescuing orphaned children and smuggling them into England. Eager to work with children again, I offered to work with the war orphans, and the inheritance from my parents allowed my volunteering full-time at the war orphan refugee center."

"And with your educational background and expertise in languages, they welcomed you at the center."

"Yes, very well. We had adolescents, young children, toddlers, and baby refugees speaking different languages." Helen closed her eyes and said, "Frightened, hungry children with gaunt faces and bony bodies in tattered clothes arrived at the center day and night. Until the starving children could tolerate a regular diet, volunteer physicians ordered gruel for their shrunken tummies."

"Hearing your firsthand account of the children's shameful suffering makes my heart ache," said Dora.

"Their faces and emaciated bodies are etched in my heart and mind forever. The United Kingdom imported twenty million long tons of food a year for a population of fifty million, and Hitler planned to starve them. Britain prioritized rationed food for those most in need—the elderly, expectant mothers, and children. British citizens cultivated every available inch of ground for food. Baskets of vegetables and fruits in season from the gardens of caring Londoners arrived for the emaciated young refugees.

"Rabbis advised about kosher food and brought provisions for their children. Jewish and Christian people exchanged rationed food allowances to meet the dietary needs of Jewish children. Food for the soul accomplished more than table food. The children brightened up from the words and prayers of visiting Anglican ministers and rabbis.

"All the children needed clothes. Friends of my mother used their clothing and handmade underwear, blouses, and shirts to tailor pants, skirts, and coats for the orphans.

"How long did children stay in the center?" said Dora.

"Most children left the center within a few days."

"How long did you work with the refugee children, Helen?"

"Until 1942, the year I became dean—"

"Excuse me for interrupting your conversation, ladies. Your breakfast, compliments of all the kitchen staff."

"Oh, my goodness. Quite a spread, isn't it, Helen?"

"Yes. Thank you, Miss Susie, for a wonderful breakfast."

"Yes, ma'am. We're happy to serve you," said Susie and left.

"The war is not over, and children are starving, and I feel guilty eating."

"I know. I do too," said Helen.

Miss Susie came in with a second plate of hot biscuits. "Your secretary is on the kitchen phone about something urgent." The call came at the right time for Helen. She'd said enough about the London orphan center. *I can never tell Dora or anyone how the refugee organization managed to relocate four little Jewish children.*

The young dean walked to the kitchen phone and asked her secretary, "What is the problem?"

"An army officer is waiting in the reception room. He said his visit was urgent."

Perplexed by the call, Helen raised her eyebrows and said, "An army officer? Have him wait in my office and serve him coffee. I will be right over."

On her way out, she paused and said to Dora, "I have to go back to my office."

"You haven't finished your breakfast."

"I've had plenty. I'll call you later."

CHAPTER 13

The Search

December 8, 1944—10:00 a.m.

he OSS Washington office checked out every Middleton College employee for a record of illegal cooperation or conspiracy and found a file on one employee. An aide handed Colonel Matthews the intelligence report.

"Thank you. I have an interview," the colonel said and slipped the confidential information in his inside coat pocket. While he waited for Dean Wright, the intelligence agent opened the OSS report. He was astounded. Helen Wright's name appeared on the cover sheet.

Flipping to the first page in the file, he read:

> Helen Wright arrived in England when her father's company transferred him from New York to London. After attending a private elementary school, she received secondary education at a boarding school in Switzerland.
>
> Miss Wright graduated with honors with a master's in education from the University of London. After graduation, the accomplished multilingual woman became dean of girls at a costly Switzerland school for secondary level students from wealthy homes worldwide, including state leaders.

Ed's eyes opened wide with amazement. He recalled Hans Schiller's first Abwehr assignment was the bodyguard for a top Nazi general. Was it possible the Middleton dean of women knew Hans Schiller? Yes. As dean

60

of girls at the Swiss boarding school, Helen Wright met German parents, including Nazi military leaders and their bodyguards.

Would Hans dare communicate with Helen Wright in the United States? Yes. Like the devil, Hans could be anywhere.

Ed turned to the next page of the album and found a clipping from a London newspaper's society section. He stared at the photo of a gorgeous woman, Helen Wright, and RAF Wing Commander John Carlton at their engagement party.

Additional news about the Wright family appeared in another society article.

> At every opportunity, London society favorites, Americans Malcolm and Judith Wright, explore Great Britain's historical sites. After the beautiful engagement party given for their daughter, Helen, and John Carlton, the Wrights left for a vacation at Tenby, the lovely walled seaside town in Pembrokeshire, southwest Wales.

Ed turned a page and frowned as he read an obituary notice.

> On a leisurely drive back to London from Tenby, the American oil executive Malcolm Wright, and his wife, Judith, died from injuries sustained in a head-on automobile crash.
> Survivors: Helen Wright, their daughter.

Ed drew his eyebrows together at a second obituary.

> On a flight over France, Wing Commander John Carlton's plane took a hit. The heroic RAF pilot flew the heavily damaged aircraft back to England. Three days later, Commander Carlton died from injuries sustained on the flight. Immediate survivors include his parents, Raymond and Roberta Carlton; his fiancée, Helen Wright; paternal and maternal uncles, aunts, and cousins. Date and time for memorial service at Gloucester Cathedral to be announced.

Ed's mouth gaped open at the next entry in Helen Wright's file.

Subject: Helen Wright /Illegal Activity/ Refugees/1942

Strict US law limits immigrant admission into the US. In 1939, the United States Congress refused to raise immigration quotas for the admittance of twenty thousand Jewish children fleeing Nazi oppression.

Following her fiancé's death (see clipping in the file), Helen Wright, an American citizen, worked at a refugee center for children in London. A minister and a rabbi who volunteered at the center and an American woman, Dorothy Hirsch, from New York City, arranged circuitous passage for four minor refugees from the center on a freighter that sailed from the neutral country of Ireland to neutral Uruguay, and Helen Wright sailed on the same ship. In the port of Uruguay, Helen Wright booked passage on a boat sailing to the port of New York. When the ship docked in New York, Dorothy Hirsch boarded the ship and disembarked with four minor children, one in her arms. Later and alone, Helen Wright came ashore. Although no American Intelligence agent saw Miss Wright with the refugee children, agents suspected Miss Wright accompanied the children from Ireland via Uruguay to the Port of New York.

With the US at war and no known living relatives in Europe or documentation on their heritage, no attempt was taken to deport the four minor children. The three toddlers and the baby, technically Jewish refugees, entered the United States and remained under Mrs. Hirsch's care until legally adopted by three Jewish families. One couple took two siblings, a boy, and a baby girl. (See court report in the file for adoption proceedings.)

The last entry dated September 1942 stated Miss Wright accepted the position as dean of women, Middleton College, Mississippi.

The colonel stroked his brow. After reading the report, he had serious concerns. Helen Wright grew up in England and worked in Switzerland with the children of Nazi leaders. She ignored sovereign laws of her own country, outwitted US agents, and helped Jewish children illegally enter the United States. Ed ran his hand over his head, down the side of his neck, and under his chin. Where did Helen Wright's loyalties lie?

Schiller had a record of conspiracy with beautiful women. Possibly, Hans Schiller, a bodyguard for a Nazi general, knew Helen Wright before the war? Ed's nose flared in anger. He'd envisioned the espionage agent's philandering would trip him up, and he did not like the coincidence of Schiller being in the proximity of Middleton College and Helen Wright.

There were two sets of footprints behind the hedge. Could Helen Wright have been with Schiller on the Middleton Campus this morning? He stood with his back to the office door and squeezed his eyes shut. Turning around, he looked down at the dean's desk and saw an album opened to a letter signed by Dorothy Hirsch.

"The army officer is in your office, Dean Wright."

Ed moved away from the dean's desk and slipped the intelligence packet in his coat pocket. With a solemn expression on his face, he looked into the eyes of the loveliest woman he had seen in a long, long time.

"My secretary said you needed to see me?"

"Dean Wright, Colonel Edward Matthews, OSS Intelligence agent. He handed her his credentials. My purpose for being here is confidential."

She looked at the identifications and handed them back to him. "I understand. Please be seated. How may I be of help to you?" Was her courtesy suggestive of a cover-up? The dean motioned to the chair opposite her desk.

Ed set his coffee cup in the coaster on a side table by the chair. Trained to spot a liar, he leaned forward and scrutinized her face. Even the best liars could not suppress slight muscle contractions or lowering their eyes down to the left.

"An investigation at Middleton College indicates someone from Adalia Hall trespassed in Middleton's off-limit area."

Not a single muscle flinched on her face. She looked her visitor in the face and said, "It is hard to believe one of my girls left here and trespassed on the restricted military area."

With a quick, polite smile, she shifted blame from herself to "one of my girls," a pathological liar's tactic.

Ed patted the report hidden within his coat and said, "Do you live on campus?"

"Yes." He detected a slight involuntary twitch of a muscle on the right side of the dean's face. "The college provides an apartment for me."

"Where?"

"Adalia Hall."

"You live here?" He raised his eyebrows. "How many students live here?"

"Twenty. Adalia is one of our cottage-type dormitories. Most resident students left for the holiday after their last classes yesterday."

"How many students were in Adalia Hall last night?"

"Four."

"May I have their files?"

"Yes, of course. Two students left early this morning, and two students remain in Adalia Hall."

The dean walked across the tastefully furnished office to the file cabinets. She wore a brown tweed suit he assumed had been tailored in London. Intelligence reported her height as five foot seven and her weight as 110 pounds. She was, indeed, slender and graceful, not precisely the athletic figure for vaulting a ten-foot fence.

He glanced at her shapely legs and feet. She wore pointed-toe pumps. He'd found male and female footprints at the hedge. Her small feet ruled out a match for what had appeared long, narrow female footprints at the fence and hedge. Mentally, he lowered his red flag of suspicion about the dean to half-mast, but with her international background, her small feet didn't rule out she was a liar and possible acquaintance of Hans Schiller.

At the parade field corner, he'd examined the holly hedges. Amid clusters of berries, he'd discovered tiny wisps of red threads snagged on the prickled edges of the dark green holly leaves. He sent the leathery holly bush leaves and footprints for OSS laboratory analysis and expected the results shortly.

Dean Wright handed him four files. Before he opened them, he asked, "Do you know any girl in Adalia who wears a red coat or jacket?"

"There are different shades of red," She said, a tight smile indicative of a secret. She was withholding the truth. She knew the answer to his question.

"Holly red," he said impatiently and tapped the files.

"In the files before you, there is one girl who wears a red coat, a jacket. She's one of our most trusted students."

"Her name?"

Helen hesitated.

He looked directly into her eyes. "Her name is?"

"Lucinda Reed."

"Please call Miss Reed to your office, Miss, ah, Dean Wright."

"Our driver drove Lucinda to the railroad station for the ten o'clock morning train."

He looked at the clock on the wall. It was after ten. His first order at Middleton put agents in charge of all college-owned vehicles.

He didn't blink an eye. "Where is Miss Reed from?"

"Myrtle, Mississippi."

"May I use your phone?" He motioned to the phone on her desk.

"Yes, you may. I will leave the room."

"No. That is not necessary." He stood, dialed, and spoke to the person who answered. "I'll be in our office in a few minutes. Meet me there."

Turning to face Dean Wright, he said, "Thank you for the phone call and your assistance with the files, which we will return shortly. We may need more assistance from you. Where can you be reached over the next day or two?"

Helen handed him her card. "At this number, Colonel, I—"

Her downcast eyes and chin reflected genuine disappointment, and the dejected expression on her face disarmed him. *She feels guilty she implicated Lucinda Reed.* "This is distressing for you," he said in a warmer tone.

"Yes, it is. MC employed me in September 1942, the same year Lucinda entered as a freshman. Her record is exemplary."

Dean Wright's sincerity reflected concern for Miss Reed. The beautiful, sweet woman who stood before him was innocent of collaborating with Hans Schiller. He lowered and removed his red flag of suspicions about her.

"Dean Wright, Lucinda Reed may or may not be a suspect. During wartime, trespassing in a restricted military area is as serious as it gets. Our investigation of Lucinda is top secret. Do not discuss our conversation with anyone."

"You have my word, Colonel."

"Thank you. The investigation has the highest OSS priority," he said and rushed out of her office.

* * *

Colonel Matthews entered the temporary OSS office in Middleton's Moore Hall, and Lieutenant Harris snapped to attention.

"You drove a girl to the station. Did you see her board the train?"

"Yes, and I waited until the train left the station."

"The footprints we found at the hedge may belong to that girl. Give me a physical description of her.

"She was tall, five six or seven, not thin, not fat."

"Did she have long feet?"

"I didn't look at her feet. I thought she was an attractive, nice girl."

"Did you hear the destination she gave when she bought the train ticket?"

"No, but she boarded a train the stationmaster announced for Vicksburg."

"Tell me everything, every word spoken while you were with her."

"Except for 'thank you,' nothing significant. The young lady was well mannered, polite, and very pleasant. Sir, it is hard to believe what you said. I never met a more charming girl."

Ed ignored Harris's comment. The lieutenant was smitten with Lucinda Reed. "Change into your army uniform and check out Vicksburg trains bound for Myrtle, Mississippi.

"What about luggage? What did she have with her?"

"Three suitcases, a heavy box, and a laundry bag. The young lady said the heavy box held books because all personal items had to be out of the dorm over the holidays. The laundry bag was wet."

"On the triple, round up the team, and have them meet me with two car engines running at the back entrance." He dispatched Harris to the Vicksburg railroad station. "If you find Lucinda Reed, hold her and radio me."

Harris saluted and ran out the door. "The laundry bag was wet" rang in Ed's ears. He dialed the OSS phone on the desk.

"Mike, Ed. Do you have anything back on the footprints or red threads?"

"The lab concurred with your field assessment, a female shoe, sneaker, size ten and a half, narrow width. Red wool threads type used in heavy outerwear."

"Bull's-eye! The lab reports give us a lead on the female trespasser. If the lab report matches our field guess on the male footprints, about a ten double-E, they may belong to Hans Schiller, a big fish swimming about in navy regulation shoes."

"Another bull'-eye. The male shoeprints matched your field guess."

"Terrific. We're on the trail of the renowned man of shadows, Hans Schiller. To track him down, we'll need all the men you can spare and equipment we can get. That includes a couple of small planes down here, immediately."

Ed made notes and then said, "Thanks, Mike. I will be out of here shortly, on my way to the airport."

Was it possible Lucinda Reed was mixed up with Hans Schiller? Ed Matthews bowed his head and prayed, "Heavenly Father, we have mustard seed clues. I pray the young girl is not personally involved with Schiller, a snake who entices women to help carry out heinous sabotage. He will kill Lucinda Reed before he lets her disrupt a mission.

"Lord, you know Hans Schiller's whereabouts. Help us capture him. In Thy will, I pray. In Jesus's name. Amen."

Male footprints tracked to the chapel parking lot indicated the unknown naval officer had driven off the Middleton campus. His OSS team found no other signs of him.

* * *

At the small airport near Middleton, Colonel Matthews checked over evidence gathered at Middleton and waited for word from Lieutenant Harris on Lucinda Reed. The phone on a temporary OSS desk rang, and he reached for it.

"Sir, Harris speaking. We are at the Vicksburg railroad station, packed with military men. The stationmaster remembered the young girl who bought a ticket on a southbound train. The train will arrive in Myrtle at 6:30 p.m. and with a stop in Baton Rouge, over four hours to New Orleans, not counting on delays for troop trains."

"Drive to the Myrtle train station. If you arrive before we do, locate the Reed home. The rest of us will fly out of here for the nearest Myrtle airport."

At the sound of aircraft overhead, he grabbed his briefcase and ran across the tarmac with fellow agents toward two small airplanes with propellers spinning. He jumped into the first plane and said to the pilot, "Take off for the nearest airport to Myrtle, Mississippi. Every moment counts."

CHAPTER 14

Flight South

December 8, 1944—10:30 a.m.

fter the rendezvous with his agents, Hans Schiller drove south on US 51 toward Operation Heil's base. Gas rationing limited traffic off the highway cutting through the green, rolling hills of the countryside. Hans lowered the window and breathed in the crisp December air. He watched a farmer toil in a field.

Farmers, like saboteurs, worked alone, devised, improvised, and constantly labored for survival. Farm machinery, chemicals, unpredictable animals, and weather subjected farmers to severe and fatal injuries; risky equipment, explosives, unpredictable weather, and innocent bystanders brought about a high mortality rate among saboteurs.

After the US entered WWII, the admiral set up Operation Pastorius, a saboteur mission with eight German agents who snuck into the United States via submarines. US officials arrested all the saboteur agents.

In a military court, the eight Pastorious saboteurs received death sentences. President Franklin Roosevelt pardoned two agents who informed on their fellow Pastorius saboteurs.

"Yellow dogs," Hans growled. "They talked, and the Pastorius failure led to Operation Heil, another sabotage mission. He commanded Operation Heil, and he had a problem. He'd lost all contact with the admiral, his mentor and head of German Intelligence operations.

Initially, the admiral supported Hitler, but later, he became disturbed by Nazi Party actions. His mentor protected civilians, prisoners of war, and soldiers rendered hors de combat, mandates of the 1929–1931 Geneva Convention. Then the Gestapo's Sicherheitsdienst des Reichsführer (SS) took over Abwehr. The Gestapo carried out crimes against humanity, the SS directed Operation Heil, and his sabotage orders reeked of senseless killing and murder.

Each Operation Heil saboteur had lived in America, was familiar with the American culture, and spoke English fluently. Some of the German agents under his leadership had relatives in the US. As a boy, he'd visited distant family members in Mississippi. It riled him that, while his American cousins ate well, his precious *mutter and schwesterchen* (mother and sister) starved in Germany. Hans shifted about in the car seat and pondered his situation. Pending sabotage operations in the US bolstered his certainty of German victory and food for his mother and sister.

He'd escaped detection at Middleton but repeatedly checked the rearview mirror. No one followed him. He pounded his chest and proclaimed, "Hans Schiller, a.k.a. Monsieur Jacques Herbert, US naval officer, and James Waters will not fail. Operation Heil will succeed." Looking in the mirror at his James Waters image, he mentally patted himself on the back and continued driving south to the SS base.

Hans's covert accomplishments since leaving Berlin and boarding the U-boat in Trondheim, Norway, bolstered his ego. He'd entered the US undetected, and since that first night in America, he'd devised, improvised, and extemporized his way around America, and every moment tested his courage and confidence.

This morning, he had no qualms about murdering anyone who threatened the success of Operation Heil. Both the sailor and the girl had to go. The sailor, on his way to another naval base, would be an easy target for the experienced German agents on his team. If his agents failed to take out the girl on the college campus, he'd return to Middleton and eliminate her.

CHAPTER 15

The Train Ride

December 8, 1944—10:30 a.m.

he engineer switched the passenger train onto sidetracks, and a troop train whizzed by on the main tracks. Passengers waved to soldiers hanging out and waving from open windows on the fast-moving train.

A soldier across the aisle from Lucinda commented, "Look at those flatbeds loaded with tanks, trucks, and heavy guns. In a couple of weeks, those guys will be on a battlefield."

"Yeah, you're right," another serviceman said. "They'll clear tracks from here to a port of embarkation for that train."

Lucinda closed her eyes and sighed. David would soon be shipping out on a troop train headed to a port. The passenger train slowly moved onto the main tracks to Vicksburg, and a sailor said, "Here we go. Chug-chug again."

"Look, the Mississippi River!" another sailor said.

"Is this your first time seeing the muddy Mississippi?" his buddy asked.

"Yeah. Until drafted, I was never out of New York state. We are slowing down. The railroad station must be on the river."

Lucinda smiled. "It is. The Vicksburg station is a major hub for cross-country rail traffic, and unless passengers walk outside the front door, they never see the remarkable architecture of the building."

"What's remarkable about the front of the building?"

"The depot is colonial revival or neocolonial, a part of our American heritage. My grandfather attended the grand opening ceremony of it.

Daniel Burnham & Company, skyscraper architects from Chicago, drew up plans for the Y&MV station."

"Interesting. My father is an architect. He'd appreciate a photo of the railroad station." The sailor withdrew a camera from his knapsack. "I'll snap pictures of the building and send them to Dad."

"The station will be packed. You'll have to fight your way to the front of the building," said Lucinda and waved her hand toward hundreds of servicemen standing on the platform. Brakes screeched, and the train came to a stop.

The soldiers who escorted her onto the train gripped her luggage. "We'll handle these. You lead the way."

"Thank you. A porter will help me," said Lucinda.

"If there is a porter out there. We don't see one. We'll take care of your luggage," the taller soldier said and smiled.

"Thank you. The Y&MV station always has porters, but I don't see any today. I guess they are off to faraway places."

"In the military, just like us. My name is Allen. I'm from Pennsylvania. My buddy here is Larry from Indiana."

"What does Y&MV mean?"

"Yazoo and Mississippi Valley."

She needed the soldiers' help, but Lucinda hoped they wouldn't flirt with her. "I appreciate your help with my luggage. Maintenance cleans and paints dorm rooms during the Christmas holiday, and we have to empty our rooms. That's why I have so much," she said politely and waved her hand over her stuff.

"No problem," said Larry. The two of them reached for her things.

MPs walked among passengers boarding and leaving trains. In the waiting room, Allen and Larry scouted about and found a bench with enough space for Lucinda. She wanted to be by herself, but they dropped the luggage at her feet, stood, and talked to her. She sat primly, nodding and smiling at them. She wanted to sit by herself.

Conversation with her helpers lulled, and Lucinda overheard service wives or girlfriends share their wartime travel experiences.

"Troop trains have the right of way. I spent all day at the Dallas railroad station waiting for a connection to New Jersey. Here I am in Vicksburg, waiting again to be with my husband."

"I'm from Chicago. I missed my train in Memphis and waited for hours for a connection to my boyfriend's base near San Francisco."

"I'm from a small town in West Virginia. I've waited in several train stations, and now I'm waiting here for a train to New Orleans."

Lucinda realized college life isolated her from the real world. In the most challenging venture of their lives, traveling women, who roamed the country on trains to visit their sweethearts, banded together and shared the heart-wrenching goodbyes with their loved ones. Married girls chatted about allotments, a new term to her.

Crushed she never said goodbye to David, Lucinda listened to conversations of strangers grieving for their loved ones. She wanted to be a part of the traveling sisterhood. A young mother soothed her baby. Lucinda wished she and David were married and she could cuddle a baby who looked like David. Some girls held babies in one hand and smoked with the other. Lucinda's father detested cigarette smoke; she was her father's daughter and stared at cigarette smoke curling over a baby's face.

Long lines waited outside the men's and women's restrooms, inadequate necessities for people in the packed waiting room. Lucinda wondered how long she'd have to wait in line for the restroom. The soldier friends discretely suggested, "If you would like to walk around, we'll watch your things." Lucinda thanked them, joined the line of women standing outside the restroom, and talked to girls traveling to visit boyfriends or husbands before they shipped out. She joined in the conversation, saying, "I plan to meet my boyfriend at his new base."

A girl in uniform who stood next to her said, "As soon as I was eighteen, I enlisted in the WAVES.

"I'll soon be eighteen. When David, my sailor boyfriend, goes overseas, I'd loved to join the WAVES."

The WAVE smiled and said, "I like it. You would too."

In front of her, a weary young mother held a squirming baby boy. Lucinda grinned at the baby, and he wrenched toward her. "May I hold him?"

"Yes, you may," said the pretty girl. "My arms ache. Thank you for the rest." The girl rubbed her arms and bent close to Lucinda. "We're on our way to San Antonio," she whispered. "Deployments are secret. My husband is in the army air force. And he wants to see the baby before he ships out." In a normal voice tone, she said, "This is Andrew, and my name is Sue."

"Mine is Lucinda. Andrew is a beautiful baby."

"And strong for four months, but he's good-natured and seldom cries. So far, the trip has been easier than I expected."

They stepped into the restroom. "Finally, we're inside the door." Trash littered the floor around the waste cans. Sue pointed to a cubicle and clenched her teeth. I'm in such a hurry. Would you mind keeping Andrew?"

"I'll be happy to." Andrew squirmed when his mother disappeared from his sight, but Lucinda distracted him by wiggling her fingers before his face. It worked. He grabbed at her hand and cooed.

Moments later, Sue returned, and Lucinda passed the wiggly baby to his mother. "Thank you. Your turn, Lucinda. We'll wait for you."

Lucinda smiled at her new friend. "You're kind. Thank you."

At the grimy, stained counter, water trickled from faucets into discolored washbasins. There was no soap. On the wall, a rumpled, soiled cloth sagged down from the roller inside a hand towel dispenser.

"Use this." Sue handed Lucinda a small, pink, celluloid container.

Lucinda opened it and squealed with delight. "Camay, my favorite soap."

"And here is a clean hand cloth. My mother hates towel dispensers," she said, cutting her eyes to the towel box. "Mama claims the cloth goes round and round the roller."

"I know. I never use roller towels. Are you sure you won't need this towel for the baby?"

"I have plenty. Mother cut old towels into squares and stuffed these throwaway hand towels into the diaper bag, my purse, and luggage."

"That is a bright idea. Throwaway towels."

"Yes. Use 'em and toss 'em." Sue laughed and looked around the messy restroom. "There is no place to lay Andrew, and I need to bathe him. Would you mind helping me?"

Lucinda held Andrew while Sue lathered his body, shampooed his hair, and rinsed him with water squeezed from a wet towel. Andrew laughed at every squeeze. Sue dried her baby and dressed him in a clean baby garment appliquéd with a train.

"What a darling traveling outfit," said Lucinda. "Andrew, you are the only sweet-smelling person in this railroad station."

"Without soap, Mama's towels, and lots of baby clothes, Andrew would smell like me," Sue said.

"All aboard! All Aboard. Number fifteen arriving from Memphis and departing for New Orleans in fifteen minutes," shouted the trainmaster over a loudspeaker. "Number fifteen south, departing for New Orleans."

"That's my train, Sue! Great to meet you. Thanks for the Camay and towel." Lucinda pulled a notepad and pen from her purse. "I'll hold sweet Andrew while you write your name and address."

Her heart pounded as Sue scribbled down her information. Lucinda handed precious Andrew back to his mother and shoved the pen and pad into her purse. "It has been fun being with you. I'll write to you," she said and ran toward the trusty soldiers watching her belongings.

"Time to leave. My train is here." She reached for the laundry bag. There were soot marks on the dirty sack but no evidence of her wet red coat bleeding through it.

"We'll take care of all this," said Allen.

"Thank you. If I was alone in this shoulder-to-shoulder mob, I'd never get this stuff on the train."

Passengers scurried about them with arms full of luggage. Camaraderie prevailed among the wartime travelers. No one pushed or shoved in the crowded station. Strangers helped one another. Humorous servicemen who quipped "Give me air" or "Oxygen, oxygen," entertained the mass of travelers. A soldier played Glenn Miller's "Chattanooga Choo-Choo" on a harmonica, and passengers chimed in with "Pardon me, boys."

On the train, men in uniform crowded the passageways between passenger cars. Surprised Allen and Larry boarded the train with her luggage, Lucinda said, "You are traveling south too?"

"Yep," they answered in unison.

Inside the train, men in uniform occupied the seats, sat on the seat arms, and stood in the aisle. When Lucinda entered the car, soldiers, sailors, and marines jumped up and offered their places to her. Allen and Larry seated Lucinda next to a priest and stowed her belongings between plush, burgundy upholstered seats.

A soldier pushed aside other uniformed men in the aisle. "Excuse me, we offered the lady a seat."

"Sorry," Larry said. He and Allen didn't budge an inch from Lucinda's side.

Lucinda cupped her hand over her mouth, smothering laughter, and the priest smiled at the young serviceman vying for her company.

"We thought the two guys with you were your friends, but we decided they're not."

A second soldier added, "Since when friends?"

"Allen and Larry are my friends," Lucinda said, remaining loyal to the two who helped her all day.

"I am not convinced. Lifelong friends?"

"They are my friends."

The priest cleared his throat. "She is sitting with me, fellows. Are you comfortable, young lady?"

"Yes, sir. Thank you. Allen and Larry have helped me all day."

The complainer rolled his eyes and moved closer to her and the priest. Larry stepped next to the disgruntled soldier, who backed off.

"I am on my way home from school for Christmas," Lucinda said to the priest. Upon hearing she was a college student, the soldiers wanted to know how many civilian male students were on campus.

"Not many. Only 4-Fs, the guys who fail the physical."

"Where do you go to college?" Allen asked.

With the "Loose Lips Sink a Ship" and other WWII posters vivid in her mind, Lucinda avoided answering or asking about their destinations. Secrecy reigned with the military and with her too. Careless talk cost lives. Men in service were under orders not to divulge information. Lucinda did not utter one word about the V-12 unit located at her college or David, who was no longer at MC. She did not have David's address. How could she write to him? She had to find a way to write to David.

The train rolled south on tracks and cut through thick forests. Lucinda volunteered the information that bears roamed about in Homochitto National Forest, located near her hometown.

Her southern accent brought on laughter with the Yankee boys. "Do you mean large, shaggy, four-footed animals? Are there really 'baa-ahs' in the woods we are passing?"

"Yes, there are," she said and heard the laughs of soldiers near her. She didn't mind the laughter over her southern accent. She understood the ribbing and joking helped the sailors and soldiers push aside the dark days ahead of them.

The priest shared that after he became a military chaplain, he hoped he'd see some of the men standing around him. A serviceman asked, "Do chaplains go through basic training?"

"We go through basic training appropriate for our responsibilities."

"Weapon training?" said a soldier. "You'll be close to fighting whether on land or sea."

"That may be true," said the priest, "but chaplains are not armed."

The conversation about unarmed chaplains on battlefields and at sea and the increasing distance from David depressed her. She'd known David long enough to be his wife, but they weren't even engaged. She remembered his lips on her forehead, circled the spot with her fingertip, and felt a blush creeping over her face. Tucking her chin in the palm of her hand, she hid her red cheeks.

The conductor pushed his way down the aisle, collecting tickets. "It will be dark soon. We are under blackout orders. Please pull down the blackout shades." The dark passenger car brought on the harsh reality of war, and jovial sailors and soldiers became quiet.

Thoughts of David brought trickling tears on Lucinda's cheeks. She pulled a handkerchief from her purse, wiped the tears away, and closed her eyes. David, a person of obedience, virtue, and truth, had his life under control regardless of the circumstances. She did not.

Even if David had not seen her or Captain Steel Eyes had not seen her behind the hedge, God's eyes run to and fro, and God saw her. She sinned and broke the trusts of Dean Wright, her parents, and, more painfully, with Him. She couldn't stop tears that filled her eyes. Someone flicked a cigarette lighter. In the light, Lucinda's eyes met Larry's, and he patted her shoulder. She wished she could talk one-on-one with the priest about her problem.

Lucinda's aunt Rachel met her at the Carrollton Station in New Orleans, and Lucinda introduced them to the soldiers who held her luggage. "All of this is yours, Lucinda?" said her aunt, frowning.

"If your car is parked there by the curb, we'll load Lucinda's things for you."

"How very kind of you. My car is the black sedan." The soldiers rushed to her car with Lucinda's luggage.

"Allen and Larry have been helping me all day, Aunt Rachel. Hurry, guys, or you'll miss the train ride into town."

"Merry Christmas!" they shouted. They ran and hopped on the moving passenger train. Lucinda's aunt and cousin embraced her and said, "We're so glad to see you."

"And I'm happy to be here. Because of the Navy V-12 based at Middleton, we're out early for Christmas holidays, or I'd be in school. Before I left, I didn't have time to send anything out to the cleaners. Could we drop my good jacket off at a dry cleaner on the way to your house, Aunt Rachel?"

"Of course. Our neighborhood shopping center has Best Cleaners with a one-day service. You'll have your coat back tomorrow."

"That's great," said Lucinda, relieved she'd solved the wet, rumpled coat problem. At the house, Lucinda put on her bridesmaid dress and turned and twirled before her aunt and cousin.

"You're a lovely maid of honor in that shade of blue, Lucinda. We promised each other we'd be bridesmaids at our weddings. You are my bridesmaid, but I'll be your matron of honor. Are you serious about the David Atherton you met at Middleton?"

Lucinda placed her hand on her heart. "I won't see David Atherton for a long time. After he receives his officer's commission, he ships out to sea," she said sadly.

"Oh, I am so sorry for you, Lucinda. Paul and I were fearful he'd ship out before our wedding today."

"And now we know why you've seemed distressed, Lucinda," said her aunt. "I pray for Paul, and I'll pray for David Atherton."

"Thank you, Aunt Rachel. Your prayers mean everything to me."

CHAPTER 16

The Hunt

*I*n an office set up in Myrtle, Colonel Matthews said, "Lieutenant Harris, do we have an open-line phone ready to plug into Washington?"

"Yes, sir," he said and pointed to one of two phones. The other phone rang. The lieutenant answered it and said, "Colonel Matthews, a county sheriff's on the line."

"Hello, Sheriff. Colonel Matthews, OSS agent. What do you have for us?" His eyes widened, and he scribbled on a notepad. "Thank you, Sheriff. We'll be right on it. OSS agents will contact you immediately."

In a grave voice, the colonel spoke to fellow OSS agents standing about his desk. "We may have a lead on the unknown officer at Middleton."

Handing his notes to an agent, he said, "Contact the county sheriff at the number written down and interrogate the farmer who reported suspicious cars, two sets of tire treads, and footprints found on a logging road on his land. The farmer's wife spotted one car headed north on US 51, and the other vehicle headed south. Keep track of the details and follow up on everything with Washington."

The OSS Washington office had the most up-to-the-minute scoop on Schiller and German Intelligence agents. Hans Schiller had outfoxed him in Tunisia. Ed routinely requested top secret files to track down Germany's renowned espionage agent, but he didn't have time to wait on Washington files for new clues that would lead to Schiller.

If Schiller was in the United States, when and how did he get here?

Mike Ward would have the latest on Germany's espionage agents. He dialed Mike's private line in Washington.

"Hey, Mike. I need all clues possible on German espionage agents.

Could you run the most recent info on German agents by me? A few days ago, you mentioned Operation Pastorius. That operation failed, but it could throw light on what German Intelligence is up to now."

"An aide will have the Operation Pastorius file or other espionage files on my desk in a second. In the meantime, I'll tell you what I know.

"In OSS files, the newest entry came from the FBI. On December 3, 1944, a U-boat sank the *Cornwallis*, an unescorted Canadian freighter off the east coast of Maine, near Hancock Point. Alarmed, the U-boat launched enemy agents on US soil. The FBI searched for witnesses and found two residents suspicious of outsiders who wore light overcoats and carried suitcases. We're following up with the FBI on the Hancock Point lead, but nothing else was reported."

Ed whistled. "December 29—two weeks ago! There have been no sightings of Hans Schiller since Kasserine Pass. Is it possible a daring U-boat captain slipped by US naval ships guarding the US Gulf of Mexico and dumped Hans Schiller somewhere along the US Gulf Coast?"

"Could be. The US Navy patrols two oceans and all the seas and gulfs out there. That's a lot of water. Early in 1942, German U-boats in wolfpacks hit large ship convoys in the Atlantic, and U-boats patrolling the Gulf of Mexico blew up over fifty Allied oil tankers and supply vessels off Texas, Louisiana, Mississippi, and Florida coastlines. Now, the US Navy and Coast Guard accompany convoys in the Atlantic and ships in the Gulf."

"And anything is possible, Mike. The November entry, just days ago, confirms my suspicion. Hans Schiller entered the US from a U-boat loitering in the Gulf of Mexico, but when and where?"

"Figure it out, Ed," said Mike dryly.

"I will, and thanks."

* * *

Ed Matthews scrunched his fingers in his hair. In 1943, Allied troops defeated Rommel's Afrika Korps in Tunisia and held captured Axis prisoners in open-air stockades that lacked security. Captured soldiers suffered from the heat, sand, and a food shortage. The harsh and insecure POW open-air prisons did not meet the Geneva Convention's benchmark POW treatment, forcing Allied nations into transferring captured enemy soldiers to the United States. Ed Matthews's sixth sense told him Schiller remained near the North Africa stockades to help Afrika Korps POWs escape.

Did Schiller follow Afrika Korps POWs to the United States when Allied troops defeated Rommel's Afrika Korps in Tunisia? Or did Schiller follow Axis POWs to the US later in the war?

With captured soldiers and sailors coming into the US weekly, American POW camps held almost four hundred thousand Axis prisoners, and most of them were Germans. If enough German POWs escaped from American POW camps, Hitler had a ready-made army in the US.

A German agent had good reason to prowl in the vicinity of Camp Clinton, housing thirty-five hundred Afrika Korps soldiers and more than twenty-five German generals. General Hans-Jürgen von Arnim, who followed Rommel's command of the Afrika Korps, and General Ferdinand Neuling of the Wehrmacht, Nazi military army now lived at Camp Clinton.

Ed leaned back and drummed on the arms of his chair. Before the US entered WWII, he deep-sea fished off Louisiana's Gulf coast, a little more than a hundred miles south of New Orleans. Camp Clinton was two hundred miles more or less north of New Orleans. He slammed his fist on his desk. Hans Schiller could have entered the US on the Louisiana or Mississippi coast.

The OSS Washington office suspected a civilian worker helped the POWs who recently attempted an escape from Camp Clinton.

In the US, Axis prisoners lived under identical medical, food, and barracks accommodations as American soldiers. In the South, American soldiers and POWs sweltered in scorching hot barracks, and oppressive heat motivated POW escapes. Few POWs wanted to escape American camps, havens from the war, but with two or three die-hard Nazi POWs housed at Camp Clinton, another prisoner breakout existed. Ed's OSS Camp Clinton assignment, interrogating POW generals, included checking out an American civilian camp worker suspected of aiding prisoners in the attempted escape.

Camp Clinton POWs had a jazz band, theatrical group, and symphony orchestra. If prisoners didn't want to wear the prison uniform stamped POW on the back, they wore their uniforms, from which they easily ripped off German identification patches.

POWs worked by choice. At Camp Clinton, prisoners labored in cotton fields and on the Mississippi River flood prevention model, both easy escape sites. Prisoners were paid eighty cents a day, which was deposited into canteen accounts to buy soda drinks or snacks. A prisoner bent on escape could bargain for hard cash in canteen items with the civilian camp worker under suspicion. Any escaped German prisoner easily blended in with American civilians of German descent.

High-ranking POW officers were quartered in houses, and lower-ranking officers in apartments within the camp compound. During the summer, German POW officers lived comfortably in their cooler housing. The highest-ranking imprisoned general abided by POW rules and demanded the same of the POWs under his command at the camp.

The US military provided a driver for the commanding officer, and on occasion, the POW general visited the Middleton College library. Ed smiled. He nixed the rumor circulated in town that the captured general attended the flickers at the only air-conditioned movie house in Jackson, fifteen miles from the camp.

Hans Schiller, Germany's shining star saboteur, was another story. Schiller commanded himself and did as he pleased on sabotage missions. *My gut feeling is if Schiller is in the US, he'll enlist escaped German prisoners and commit sabotage in the US.*

The sly German saboteur's personality was one of charm, a Lucifer in disguise. In sabotage strikes, Schiller, the enemy of humans, used innocent individuals like Miss Reed with no regard for their ultimate well-being. Was Lucinda Reed helping Hans Shiller? Where would Schiller strike next?

CHAPTER 17

Waging War

*H*ans Schiller fingered a camera button on his single-breasted sports coat. He preferred double-breasted jackets and cuffed trousers, but the war shortage dictated US clothing styles.

Masquerading as small-town businessman Jim Waters, a country gentleman, he kept an eye on the rearview mirror. Happy no cars followed him, he drove south on the highway toward his SS base in the United States, removed the porkpie hat, and finger-combed his blond hair.

"Handsome and irresistible," he said, admiring his reflection until a patrol car appeared beside his gentleman's image in the rearview mirror.

He quickly replaced the hat and checked the speedometer. His speed was okay, but capture was first in his thoughts. He felt the pistol in his pants pocket and fingered a compass and silk map, marked with an escape route to New Orleans.

The patrol car passed, and the officer didn't glance his way. "Routine patrol," Hans surmised. "If he's not looking, he's not searching." Keeping a safe distance between the two vehicles, he followed the patrol car. Relief washed over him when the police officer pulled into a roadside restaurant.

Mr. Waters visualized the patrolman drinking a scalding cup of coffee and enjoying a hot breakfast, and hunger pangs gripped his stomach. Hans reached for a brown bag on the passenger side of the coupe and took out cold sausage biscuits. Not as good as a warm German meal, but he had a thermos of lukewarm coffee.

Arnold had issued a less expensive car to him because it attracted less attention. Driving a luxurious Cadillac or Lincoln with Mademoiselle Retroussée, Miss Turned-Up Nose, by his side would be more fun, but not a chance.

What was he thinking? He had to put the girl out of his mind. *Nein.* He was alone, and no one could share his thoughts. He visualized what he pleased and imagined holding the girl close and kissing her.

Unlike Germany's superb Autobahn, the US highway was mediocre, but the drive was therapeutic. South of Brookhaven, a road sign marked the exit for Roxie, a town he visited over a decade ago. A saboteur's life did not come with sentimental entitlements, but he indulged in memories of Roxie.

"Hans, if you learn to speak English fluently, I'll reward you with a trip to America," said his uncle Ernst. True to his word, Uncle Ernst rewarded Hans with an extensive tour of the United States and a stopover in Roxie for a visit with distant relatives.

"Your cousins are descendants of German immigrants who came to America in 1830," his uncle said. Who cared how long they'd lived in America? He had more fun in Roxie than any other place in the United States. His cousins taught him to play football, and he taught them a few soccer rules. He laughed at his cousins' choppy German; they laughed at his British accent.

In German spy school language courses, he'd lost the British accent, but he never lost the ability to mimic his cousins' American southern drawl. Reminiscing about Roxie and his cousins' hospitality stirred up the possibility of a surprise rap on their door. He calculated the distance to the town and shook his head. *Nein.* He couldn't risk contacting his cousins.

Paradoxically, the Deep South accent led to his command of Operation Heil. To overcome the poignant and disturbing feelings for his cousins, he practiced mental disciplines learned in German Intelligence classes.

Staring at himself in the car mirror, he repeated over and over, "I am a German citizen in disguise." Psychologically and emotionally, he slipped back into his role of sleeper saboteur in the United States.

Next, he passed a road sign labeled McComb, Population 9,989. Wary of a speeding ticket, he let up on the gas pedal and drove slowly past the neat brick and framed homes with red and green wreaths on front doors. Angels and stars decorated lampposts on Main Street. "It's almost Christmas," he said and sighed.

On a church lawn, a straw-roofed manager and banner heralded "Unto us a child is born, Our Savior, Christ Our Lord," from the chorus (Messiah) composed by Frederick Handel. The banner roused long-ago memories. In Germany, he walked with carolers singing "Stille Nacht"

("Silent Night"), lyrics by Joseph Mohr and melody by Franz Xaver Gruber. The memory prompted singing the famous carol first in German and then in English.

The beautiful German carol revived the days he attended church with his parents in worship and celebration of Jesus's birth and chipped at his confidence in Germany's Nazi regime. "But not my German heritage," he said and continued singing Christmas carols while he drove south to his base.

The sound of a horn blowing behind his car startled him, and he caught sight of a jeep in the rearview mirror. He flexed his foot on the gas pedal to speed off, but the American officer driving in the light utility vehicle pulled alongside his coupe and motioned him off the highway. Hans felt the cyanide tablet in his coat lapel and stopped the car. He expected the officer to get out of the jeep and come at him, but the officer motioned for Hans to roll down the window, "Sir, we are clearing the road for a convoy. Please remain parked until we signal all clear."

"Yes, sir."

The officer pulled off, and Hans breathed out a sigh of relief and relaxed. Within seconds, several army trucks, followed by flatbeds loaded with tanks, rolled by him. He identified the Sherman 4A1s tanks by the second escape hatch for a gunner. He gritted his teeth and said, "Tanks with hatches that will never reach Germany."

Designers of the American tank stressed mechanical reliability, and American factories churned out ammunition and standard parts for repair to keep the light Sherman tanks in action. The sight of the trustworthy, American, death-spewing tanks elevated Hans's adrenaline level. He stifled an urge to drive out in front of a flatbed and stop the convoy.

Why was the convoy traveling in the direction of the New Orleans port on the Gulf of Mexico rather than toward an Atlantic port? He checked the map on the seat beside him. US 51 South intersected with a major highway that led to several Atlantic seaports. He hit the road map with his fist. He'd have his team of demolition experts following the convoy within the hour. The tanks would never reach any seaport and cross the Atlantic. He boiled with a rage that equaled the wrath he experienced in New Orleans, his first illegal day in the US.

Living undercover rendered him powerless to wage war. He calculated the number of Sherman tanks on the flatbeds and mulled over the best approach to destroy them. American soldiers smiled and waved to him.

He forced himself to smile at his enemy, returned the waves, and mouthed, "I'm a German saboteur."

The driver of a jeep went by and signaled all clear. Hans looked into the car mirror at the American sports coat and tie he wore. "I am not James G. Waters," he said roughly through clenched teeth. "I am a German espionage agent, a saboteur."

Glaring through the windshield at the disappearing convoy, he roared, "I'll destroy your tank convoy before it reaches an American port for shipment to Germany."

CHAPTER 18

Second Rendezvous

On a roundabout route to his secret base, disguised as James G. Waters, Hans Schiller turned off US 51 onto LA 10 at Fluker, Louisiana, and drove west.

At St. Francisville, he turned north on US 61 and detoured on Bains Road. On the unimproved road, he drove along with ease under trees with overlapping leafy limbs that seemingly touched the sky and blotted out the sun rays. In the middle of the dark lane, he spotted a black hound, slammed on the brakes, and sounded the horn.

The snoozing dog didn't budge. Annoyed, Hans climbed out of the car, closed the door with a bang, picked up a roadside pebble, and sailed it toward the motionless creature. The small nugget bounced off the dog's rump. The stubborn canine looked up and growled. Hans threw a larger stone that hit the dog's bony rib cage. The pathetic animal weakly barked, stood, and limped behind an abandoned, rusty car, half-covered in tall grass and weeds on the roadside.

Jim picked up more pebbles and patted his coat pocket. "Ammunition for my return trip," he said to the hound and went on his way until he caught sight of the 1942 Ford coupe that Arnold Keller issued to him in New Orleans.

Parking on the skimpy shoulder of the road, Hans got out of the car he picked up earlier in the fairy-tale forest and tipped his hat to the blond man sitting in the Ford coup acquired in New Orleans.

"A dog delayed me." He grinned.

The German agent smiled and handed Jim a cold sausage biscuit. "A treat for the dog on your return trip."

Hans handed him a few pebbles. "Weapons for the canine on your return," he said and laughed.

"We have a radio message for you. The agents you sent to Middleton College reported classes are out for the holidays. The girl is on a train on the way to New Orleans. Our agents on the train reported the girl is sitting by a priest and surrounded by men in uniform."

Hans frowned. "Radio the agents on the train to follow orders. Eliminate the girl."

"Yes, sir," said the agent and drove off to return the older Ford coupe to Keller's SS garage in New Orleans.

Keen on getting to his home base, Hans started up the newer Ford coupe and drove toward US 61. Standing in the middle of the road, the thin, starving hound flagged him down with his wagging tail.

"Smart dog. My agent bribed you."

He stopped the car, rolled down the window, and threw a sausage biscuit into the tall grass. The dog ran, retrieved it, gulped it down, and wagged his tail for another treat. Jim smiled and threw the second biscuit into the roadside grass. The dog wagged his gratitude and begged for more food. Hans tossed him more treats.

The canine's winning personality suggested great companionship. Hans wanted to scoop up the mangy dog, clean him up, and keep him.

"Impossible." He shook his head at the dog and said, "Sorry, no more tidbits."

Arnold Keller had equipped the forties' Ford coupe with hidden devices for espionage work. Hans opened the car door, pulled out the cigarette lighter, and found three German Intelligence dispatches. He expected the first dispatch: *Send the college surveillance report today.*

He smirked at the second message: *Locate the 99th Infantry Division.* "Locate the 99th?" He pursed his lips. The 99th Division had transferred from Camp Van Dorn to Camp Maxey in November 1943. How could German agents assigned to Camp Maxey lose the 99th Division?

Hans looked at the message again and slapped his head with the palm of his hand. He had enough to do without chasing after the 99th Division.

He unrolled the third strip of onionskin paper and blinked at the communiqué: *Vorbereitung für den frühen Morgengrauen sechzehn hier. Stehen zu.* (Prepare for Early Dawn Sixteenth. Stand by). Calculating US central standard time, a seven-hour difference, the message meant "Begin US sabotage at midnight December 15, tonight." The long-awaited words from Berlin exhilarated him and he said, "Finally!"

The hound cocked his head at his elated friend and barked in response.

"Sorry, Fritz. You can't go home with me today." The dog's tail fell between his hind legs, and he looked at Hans with soulful eyes.

Hans focused on his orders. Germany's major offensive stratagem concentrated on taking over the Port of Antwerp, a massive assault that bought time for the launch of Germany's new secret weapon. But why synchronize the major German offensive in Europe with sabotage in the States? For months, the Operation Heil team geared up for the destruction of American factories and obliteration of the elite 63rd Infantry Division.

His team members asked, "Why does German Intelligence specify 'wipe out the 63rd Infantry Division'?" He brought his team up to date on the SS-targeted division.

"During the January 1943 Casablanca Conference, with President Roosevelt, Prime Minister Churchill, and Allied military advisors, German Intelligence wrangled security clearance for me. I served meals to conference leaders seated at a table with hidden microphones. We overheard critical intelligence about Allied military resources and strategy, and Churchill's renowned promise—*the enemy shall bleed and burn in expiation of their crimes against humanity.*

"In keeping with Churchill's formidable promise, the US organized the 63rd Infantry Division, a division of trained infantrymen skilled at wiping out German infantry soldiers in combat. The division commander designed the 63rd shoulder patch with an up-thrusted golden sword. The insignia boldly proclaimed Churchill's provocative statement, to *bleed and burn the enemy.*

"Incensed by Churchill's proclamation and the organization of the US 63rd Division and their bleed and burn insignia, the SS established our sabotage base in Myrtle for the purpose of wiping out the elite 63rd Division on American soil.

"Now do you understand why we have to destroy the 63rd?" he'd asked. Astonished, his men grasped the significance of the 63rd Infantry.

The latest Operation Heil orders overwhelmed Hans. He raked fingers through his hair and rubbed his hand across the back of his neck. How could he destroy the 63rd Division, locate 99th, sing in the choir, and initiate massive sabotage at different locations?

The 99th Division order puzzled him the most. The 99th left Camp Van Dorn more than a year ago. Why did the SS saddle him with finding the 99th now? Was the division shipping out and traveling on US 51 or

61, on the way to a port of embarkation for Germany? Who could he ask without raising suspicion?

He wrinkled his nose. Workers at fruit and vegetable stands scattered along US 61 would know about convoys. He pulled into the first produce stand on the highway.

"Merry Christmas," he said to the tired-looking woman and her husband. He extended a hand to the farm man and received a handshake from a calloused palm. "Your produce looks good."

The wife smiled and wiped her hands on her apron. "We don't have much produce to offer—a few fresh eggs, a couple of jars of honey, homemade cakes, and a little candy. We used our sugar ration stamps to make the sweets."

"I'll take the honey, that cake, and this candy. You're almost sold out. Have you had a lot of traffic driving by your stand?"

"A large convoy, headed north, stalled here yesterday," said her husband. "That's why we don't have much left for local folks."

"Large? Guess that means about twenty-five trucks." Hans browsed the jars of honey, avoiding eye contact with the farmer.

"Twenty-five?" The farmer laughed. "I figured nearer to a hundred."

"Is that so?" Hans nearly dropped the jar of honey he'd picked up.

"Yep, flatbeds loaded with tanks and artillery. We're gonna whup those Germans good and those Jap-pa-neeze too. Our boy here draws pictures of convoys and soldiers. Yesterday, soldier boys bought his drawings to send home," said the proud father.

"Is that right? Any left, son?"

The boy held up several drawings. Hans was amazed. The kid's sketches included rank and insignia on soldiers' uniforms. The emblem was not the 99th checkerboard patch but still excellent intelligence information. The boy was a genius.

"These are good. Would you sell a few to me?"

"Yes, sir."

The detailed images were worth a thousand black-and-white photos. While Hans negotiated a fair price for all the sketches with the boy's mother, the young artist went back to his drawing. Hans glanced at the boy's sketchpad and cringed at the sight of his own image.

"Hey, that's good. I'll buy it and give it to my mother for Christmas."

Unnerved by the portrait of himself, he paid the mother and looked at his watch. "I am late for an appointment. My mother will like your son's drawing of me. Thank you for your hospitality."

The boy's accurate portrayal rattled him to the core. His mother would love the picture of him. For the first time in years, the holiness of the Christmas season crept through him. He ached over his dishonest, evil, sneaky occupation, a life of trickery and sham, and his assumed names in many disguises depressed him. He was irked German leaders concocted postponing sabotage in America until the major German offensive began. Hans doubted sabotage would cause the chaos in the States that German Intelligence anticipated.

* * *

Hans drove away from the fruit stand on his last lap to Operation Heil's base. After being up all night at Middleton, the boy's drawing at the fruit stand and the encounter with the fräulein at the parade field stressed him out. "Silly girl, she could have been shot for trespassing. I could have been shot!"

He fingered the knife in his side pocket. While the tilt of a feminine chin, a turned-up nose, and cupid-bow lips had captured him, the girl, an enemy, had escaped. Thoughts about the girl had to stop. Jolted by the gnawing in his stomach and feeling anxiety over multifold assignments from the SS, his mind played tricks on him. He rubbed his temples to clear his head and stifled an urge to drive faster toward his home base.

It was December 15, 1944. He was on MS 24 at the intersection of MS 33. The No Trespassing highway sign at Camp Van Dorn, home of the 63rd Division, irritated him. He could have wiped out the "bleed and burn" division a month ago, but he held off, waiting for orders from SS Intelligence.

At the entrance to the camp, he saluted the weathervane antenna atop the white provost marshal headquarters building. "In a few hours, black smoke will curl from the three vent towers on your roof."

The mighty and powerful 63rd Division trained at Camp Van Dorn, eight miles from The Café, his home base. Soldiers wearing the striking red and gold sword emblems on their shoulders frequented his restaurant daily, and he walked amid their tables while he waited for orders to annihilate them. The tables turned tonight. Within a few hours, the 63rd Division would hemorrhage and be ablaze.

CHAPTER 19

Home Base

*E*very mile closer to home base, Hans struggled with the multiple requests from Berlin headquarters: radio the Middleton report, sing in the Christmas program, carry out Operation Heil's sabotage mission, destroy factories and ships, and destroy the 63rd and the 99th divisions.

Searching for a clue to the 99th's whereabouts, Hans slipped his hand into a hidden pocket on the left car door and pulled out *The United States Guidebook for Army Posts and Towns.* The booklet, patterned after Germany's Baedeker travel guides, listed pertinent information on US military bases. Scanning the copyright page, he read "First Edition 1942, Cancelled; Second Edition 1942, Censored."

"Zilch!" He threw the censored booklet on the floorboard, stomped it, and bellowed, "Useless." A careless Berlin Intelligence agent provided Arnold Keller with censored copies of the military publication. Unknowingly, Arnold stashed the worthless booklet in SS cars parked in the New Orleans garage. Nothing Berlin Intelligence agents concocted made his secret life easier in America.

Saboteurs existed in perilous environments wherever they operated. Intelligence agents behind desks in Berlin made colossal mistakes. An ignorant SS Intelligence agent billeted him in Myrtle, a small town, putting him at higher risk.

He learned the town's 1940 county census documented only four naturalized citizens, and all four were German Americans with the surname of Weide, a German surname that originated with those who lived among the *weides* or willow trees. The Weide family changed their name to Willow. When the Willows bought a large Victorian home, they converted it into a small hotel named The Willow. He lived with the Willows in their hotel filled with German furniture and china.

Hans complained to his agents. "Every move SS Intelligence makes endangers my life. The Weide family left their birthplace and changed their surname to Willow, but they did not leave behind their German heritage. Organized and structured individuals, the Willows monitor guests closely. I live in a fishbowl under the eyes of the Willow family. Don't ever contact me at the hotel."

A natural gift for foreign languages and the southern accent learned from his south Mississippi cousins helped him converse easily with the Willows and others. He often spoke about his *muhthuh, sistuh, and bruthuh* (mother, sister, and brother), the pronunciations common with villagers in the town.

Townspeople accepted the newcomer and never questioned his acquired accent and 4-F disability classification, but the pressure of covering up his clandestine activities in the small town stressed him out.

Today, other events splintered the saboteur's confidence in the ultimate success of Operation Heil. First, he bumped into Mademoiselle Retroussé, Miss Turned-Up Nose. Her composure and unflappable behavior stunned him, and the sketch by the boy at the roadside stand alarmed him. He snatched his image on paper out of his pocket and tore it to shreds. Alone in the car, he said, "Muhthuh, you'll never see this picture of your handsome son."

Disguised as Jim Waters, he exited SR 24, drove downhill, passed the Gilead Baptist Church, turned into a Main Street alley, and parked the coupe in the back of The Café, home base for Operation Heil. When Hans walked through the back door, he gave the chef a thumbs-down.

"What's up?'

"You tell me, Bernie. I bumped into a female student who can identify me."

"What happened?"

Hans filled him in on the Middleton girl and said, "The fräulein slipped by our agents when she left the train at the Carrolton, a suburban stop in New Orleans. The agents spotted the girl getting into a sedan. They hopped into a taxi and followed the vehicle but lost sight of the car in traffic."

"Is a young girl a major threat, Hans?" said Bernie Koch.

"Any threat is major, Bernie. You know that. She's a student at

Middleton. Unless we come up with her address in New Orleans, we'll never find her in the crescent city. After the holidays, we'll take her out at the college."

Bernie winced. "Stress is making you edgy, Hans."

"The girl has to go, Bernie. I have to get some sleep. Wake me up in a couple of hours."

"Okay, boss. I'm just the chef." Hans punched Bernie on the shoulder and slipped through the concealed door.

Hans and Bernard Koch were classmates in Berlin and Hamburg spy schools and worked together during Hitler's takeovers and invasions of European countries. Their association was one of respect and trust, and they enjoyed a true friendship. Under orders and funding from the highest authority in Germany, Hans, disguised as Jim Waters, was the proprietor of The Café, a legitimate business in Myrtle, Amelia County, Mississippi, a hangout for Camp Van Dorn soldiers, civilian camp workers, and Amelia County's residents.

Microphones mounted under restaurant tables relayed patrons' conversations to receivers in the secret back room. On The Café roof, camouflaged cameras focused on the railroad station for surveillance of troop trains to and from Camp Van Dorn, critical information for German leaders evaluating the military strength of the US 63rd Division.

During daylight hours, only Jim Waters, Chef Koch, and an assistant cook had access to the kitchen, but at night, other German agents slipped through the restaurant's back door and entered the concealed room.

In the hidden room, Hans checked for radio messages behind another false wall before he hung his Jim Waters coat and trousers in a shallow closet.

Exhausted from the all-night surveillance at Middleton, Hans shaved and showered. In less time than usual, he dressed in clean clothes, loosely knotted a tie around his neck, and draped another Jim Waters sports coat over a chairback before he buzzed for Bernie, his master chef and chief demolition expert.

Bernie popped into the secret room and said, "What now?"

Hans sat on the edge of the cot, pulled on socks, slipped his feet into polished shoes, and stretched out on his back. "Wake me in a couple of hours, Bernie."

Bernie left, and Hans closed his eyes. He fell asleep in a stupor and dreamed he walked on the magnolia-lined streets of Myrtle, filled with people who warmly greeted him. In the dream, he entered The Café's front door and saw three large portrait frames on the back wall. One frame held a portrait of him as Monsieur Jacques Herbert, and the middle frame enclosed his likeness in a US Navy officer uniform. The third frame was blank. Wearing Jim Waters's clothes, he climbed into the empty frame, pulled up his pant legs, and revealed withered limbs to diners.

"Sit down with us and rest your legs," he heard.

"It helps to get off my feet," he said. He climbed out of the frame and sat at a table with his mother, sister, and brother. The Middleton girl, with her long auburn hair trailing behind her, floated over the table.

"Wake up, Hans," Bernie said, interrupting the dream. The girl floated away, his mother, sister, and brother, a Luftwaffe pilot killed in flight over the English Channel, vanished.

"Wake up," said Bernie, shoving his shoulder. "Get up, Jim Waters. Time to go to work."

Part II

*H*old fast to the Bible. To the influence of this Book we are indebted for all the progress made in true civilization and to this we must look as our guide in the future.
—General Ulysses S. Grant, United
States Civil War, 1861–1865

* * *

CHAPTER 20

The Coffee Club

December 15, 1944

 eticulously dressed and refreshed from his nap, Jim Waters greeted patrons in The Café dining room and stopped at the table of three well-known townsmen who were drinking their afternoon coffee.

"Good to see you gentlemen today. May I join you?" he said with his hand on the only empty chair.

"Sit down, sit down," the men chorused.

"I'm ready for my afternoon coffee and pie. How about pecan pie with me?" Most of The Café's patrons knew that Jim Waters talked the Willows' cook out of her pecan pie recipe.

"No pie for me."

"It's on the house, Mr. C."

"Well, you talked me into a slice, Jim," said Tom Cunningham with a grin.

"Mr. Tom, how is the cornmeal business?"

"We stay busy."

"Not surprised," Jim Waters said and turned to the other men at the table. "We only use Mr. Tom's meal at The Café. The freshly ground meal makes the best cornbread."

"We all enjoy Tom's fresh cornmeal," said the banker at the table. After he retired, Tom set up the grist mill in his garage, and the mill became a gathering spot for customers waiting for Tom's custom ground cornmeal.

"We are happy if our patrons are happy. We collect a small portion of the coarse, medium, or finely meal from farmers and sell our measure to other customers."

Jim cleared his throat. "The chef tells me with extra Christmas meals, we'll need more meal for cornbread dressing."

"We'll have some ready for you."

"Most folks eat Christmas dinner at home. Guess you gentlemen will eat Christmas dinner with your families," said Jim. The men nodded in agreement.

"The Café business may be slow over Christmas. If my gas ration stamps hold out, I plan to spend Christmas Day with my muhthuh, sistuh, and my bruthuh, if he has leave from the army air force. Before I go home for Christmas, I need to stock the pantry for the cooks. But estimating supplies for a holiday is difficult. Soldiers may or may not come in for our home-cooked meals. Do you all expect your soldier boys home for Christmas?"

"We all have relatives in the military, but none of us expect anyone in the service home for Christmas," said Tom Cunningham.

"You have my sympathy. I'm not surprised. The war is heating up. Soldiers are shipping out. I hope my bruthuh doesn't ship out before I see him at Christmas. Are there many folks in town with loved ones in the 99th?"

"Several town girls married 99th soldiers," said one of the men at the table.

"Is that so? We could have 99th boys and 63rd boys in the restaurant during Christmas week."

"Could be," remarked Tom. He pushed back his chair and stood. "Thanks for the coffee and pie."

"I'll stop by for extra cornmeal."

"Yes, do that. In the meantime, see you in church, Jim."

"You bet," said Jim. A tiny red light blinked over the kitchen door, signaling a radio dispatch. Jim stood and nodded at each man who remained. "I need to get ready for the church program tonight. Thank you all for dropping by The Café."

"Thank you for the coffee and pie."

"Anytime."

* * *

Pleased he'd found out that a few 99th soldiers' wives lived in town, Jim knew church women would talk about guests and any 99th soldiers expected in town for Christmas. Jim walked away from the coffee club, hurried into the secret room, and switched on the radio for the latest dispatch.

"German Intelligence infiltrates report an advanced unit of the 63rd Division entered Port of Marseilles December 8, 1944."

Jim smiled. From conversations he heard on The Café's mikes, he'd alerted German Intelligence about the advance 63rd ship out, and SS followed up on the report, a feather in his cap. The major 63rd Division deployment for Europe would be any day. But the division would never reach France to fight in Germany. Explosives he and his team placed on tracks and under bridges would destroy the bleed and burn 63rd Division in Amelia County, Mississippi.

He left The Café and walked to The Willow hotel. After his devious conversation with the coffee club men, he felt dirty inside. A hot shower always helped wash away internal muck.

CHAPTER 21

Top Secret

*T*om Cunningham left The Café and spoke to people on Main Street. The friendly gestures to passersby did not reflect his concern about Jim Waters's restaurant.

Strangely, The Café never seemed to run out of the finest cuts of beef. The Café cooks prepared large portions of tuna salad and thick tuna sandwiches. The US rationed canned fish and meat. For meals served in The Café, the cooks had to have a plentiful supply of lard, shortening, oils, cheese, and butter, all rationed. At home, women substituted margarine, colored with red, for butter.

He suspected Jim Waters dealt with black marketers. While The Café owner sipped on-the-house coffee with customers, he brought up a shortage of holiday supplies. A few 99th infantrymen on leave for Christmas would not create a problematic situation for the restaurant. Why did holiday supplies concern the owner of The Café?

Jim's questions about the 99th weren't the only problem. Tom was curious about other things he'd observed about the well-liked café owner. Today, Jim finished his pie and put his fork with tines down on his plate, a European custom. When the other men at the table placed their forks tines up on their plates, Jim quickly flipped his fork tines up.

Years ago, the curly-white-haired man attended Middleton College. Male students ate at long tables hosted by faculty members. He'd noticed then a European student who finished eating and placed his fork tines down on his plate. Jim claimed he grew up in Alabama, USA, a fork-tines-up location. Jim putting his fork tines down by his uneaten pecan pie triggered suspicion about The Café owner, and Tom was determined to keep an eye on Mr. Waters.

No one in town, not even Tom Cunningham's family, knew he was an OSS agent and one of a few railroad men used by the US military for transporting more than a million men a day on trains headed for ports of embarkation to Europe and the Pacific.

Tom traveled with the 99th Division to their port of embarkation, and he considered 99th soldiers his boys. The 99th insignia, a checkerboard with white squares superimposed on a five-sided black shield, suited the 99th Division well. The symbol represented Pittsburg and the Pennsylvania iron district. True to the icon, Checkerboard soldiers, conditioned by the hard work of building Camp Van Dorn, were men of iron.

At Camp Van Dorn, sprawled across acres of red mud, newly enlisted 99th soldiers slept in the icy-cold barracks built overnight. The soldiers, not yet men, had never before experienced elements comparable to southwest Mississippi's frigid, wet winter of 1943, the most miserable winter in decades.

During the day, the young recruits, freezing in full uniform and heavy backpacks, marched over ruts and holes through thick, thick, Mississippi ice-covered mud while sergeants yelled, "Crack the ice. Forget the mud. March! Push 'em down. Pull 'em up and push 'em down! Up, down, march!"

The hot, humid summer brought on another grueling challenge for 99th soldiers. Mosquitoes were a' biting and chiggers were a' chomping. The draftees learned the first rudiments of marching, soldiering, and bivouacking fundamentals in Mississippi's brutal, unforgiving frigid winter and hot summer weather.

Come fall of 1943, the fast, aggressive, hard-hitting 99th Division left Camp Van Dorn for Camp Maxey, Texas. The night the 99th entered Camp Maxey, they marched so quietly most of the other troops on base didn't know the 99th Division was there. Camp Maxey and Louisiana maneuvers had fine-tuned the skills of young warriors. The 99th gained the reputation of the finest disciplined troops ever seen. "I know. I was there," whispered Tom.

In OSS service, Tom worked with the railroad dispatchers who engineered complex, secret routing for the highly classified deployment of the 99th Division. Sworn to secrecy, conductors never revealed the looped and twisted southwest-northwest-northeast path of trains carrying the 99th from Camp Maxey to Camp Miles Standish near Boston and deployment.

At Miles Standish, telephone companies provided long-distance calls, gratis, for all of the soldiers. The origin of the calls remained a secret with telephone employees and Checkerboards. In OSS service, Tom had monitored the tight security for the efficient 99th Division until the soldiers boarded ships on the eastern seaboard, a first trip across the Atlantic for most Checkerboards.

Tom promised himself that one day he would write about the 99th Division and tell the world about the Checkerboards, the railroad men devoted to the military deployment of the 99th Division and other divisions headed for Europe and the Pacific. He'd include the patriotic, tight-lipped telephone operators who put through calls, the last calls ever made to the families of many young 99th soldiers.

"Until the war is over, the classified information will remain written on the tablets of my heart, a heart aching for young soldiers I witnessed become men," whispered Tom to himself. "If I were younger, I'd follow my Checkerboard boys on to the battlefields in Europe.

"Wherever the 99th lands in Europe, there'll be no chaos and no confusion. The unproven, formidable 99th infantrymen, silent sentries poised to strike defeating blows, will advance and stand fast on the battlefield." The 99th knew how to be quiet.

"Shh, we're moving out. Hold fast. The Boards are coming. No one is telling, but we're coming, we're coming, we're coming—shh, quiet. Fire!

"While my boys stand steadfast in battle, Jim Waters flipped his fork from tines down, a European custom, to tines up, the American way, and confirmed my suspicions. Jim Waters is not an Alabama native.

"Tonight, on my daily OSS report, I'll report my suspicions of snooping Jim Waters," Tom Cunningham said aloud to no one.

CHAPTER 22

Welcome Home

December 15, 1944

*T*om walked into the Myrtle depot and spoke to the stationmaster. "Is the train from New Orleans on time?"

"Nothing is running on time these days, Tom."

"I'm meeting Lucinda and will wait." He slipped a folded paper out of his coat pocket. The Amelia County Historical Society asked him to speak at the next meeting. If he had to be out of town the night the Society met, he'd asked another member to read his speech. With pen in hand, he read over his talk.

Amelia County 1940

In 1940, the railroad provided work for a few Myrtle people, but the lumber industry employed most Amelia County's workers.

People planted vegetable gardens and struggled to buy groceries. Ten pounds of sugar sold for about forty-eight cents. Round steak was twenty cents a pound. Twenty-five cents bought a hamburger and a drink; restaurants charged thirty-five cents for lunch, fifty-five cents for dinner. Two dollars bought a pair of men's dress shoes.

But life flourished in Amelia County, a county with an abundant water supply, rainfall, and fertile soil. Despite a lack of material things and not much money in their pockets, with homegrown vegetables, a cow or two, and a bit of honey, most people had plenty to eat.

Schools were excellent, pews filled at churches on Sunday mornings and nights, and God-fearing people in Amelia County enjoyed stable lives.

That stability changed with the 1940 Selective Service and Training Act, draft registration of male citizens, ages twenty-one to thirty-five, subject to call for military service. After the US entered the war, conscription for military service extended to men between eighteen and forty-five years of age, and all men ages eighteen to sixty-five had to register with the draft board.

With his pen, Tom circled the numbers.

Women left the county to work in factories churning out war equipment. A sprawling army camp sprung up in 1941 at Amelia County's back door. Fantastic human strength and the unique energy of Amelia County citizens went to war, an extraordinary and phenomenal effort seen in all patriotic Americans.

Tom penciled, "We will win this war."

At the rumbling sound of the train, Tom slipped the speech into his pocket and walked out of the depot. Two army officers stood on the station platform. Tom recognized the taller officer but did not acknowledge him.

"Myrtle, Myrtle, Myrtle. All off for Myrtle!" said the conductor who stepped off the train. Lucinda rushed by the soldiers standing in the train doorway.

"Lucy!"

"Oh, Granddaddy. It's so good to see you!"

"How was the wedding?"

"Wonderful," Lucinda said and fell limply into his outstretched arms.

Lucinda's lack of vibrancy surprised her grandfather, but he said, "Lucy, is all this luggage, yours?"

Two soldiers on the platform stepped toward him and said, "Sir, we can help you with the suitcases, the box, and the laundry bag."

"Well, thank you," said Tom and rolled his eyes at Lucinda's belongings at his feet. "Sure will save a few trips to my car." Lucinda held onto Tom's arm while the soldiers gathered and carried her belongings to her grandfather's black sedan. Lucy opened the door and slid into the front seat.

Tom opened the trunk and said, "We may have to put some of her things in the back seat."

"We've got it, sir," the soldiers said and wedged the box and laundry bag into the trunk. "We are in no hurry. Our car is parked here. We can help you unload the luggage at your house."

"We're on our way to church. We'll unload the car later. Thank you very much for your help."

"Our pleasure," they said in unison. One of the soldiers stepped close to Tom and said,

"Colonel Matthews wants to arrange a meeting with you."

"Follow me to the church. I'll see him in the parking lot."

* * *

Once settled in the front seat of his car, Tom turned to his granddaughter. "Lucy, your mother went early to practice for tonight's Christmas program and asked me to drive you to the church. Your train was late, but we'll be on time. The service begins at seven o'clock. Sorry we couldn't drive to New Orleans for the wedding and drive you home. We didn't have gas stamps to make the trip."

"Ration stamps." Lucinda groaned. "My food stamps, shoe stamps— everything issued by the government had to be turned in when we enrolled at Middleton. I wonder if I'll ever get them back."

Tom turned the key and pulled out of the parking lot. "Why would you need to get the ration booklets back?"

Lucinda brushed off the question with a shrug of her shoulders. "Mama wrote Cousin Emma would sit with us."

Tom deadpanned his surprise at his granddaughter's abrupt change of subject. "Yes, Emma will be at the church. Look at you, girl. We sent you off to the girls' school, and you wound up in the US Navy."

Lucinda rested her hand on his shoulder. "Granddaddy, you know Middleton combined with the girls' college because of the war, and I am not in the navy. Making a good grade at Middleton is hard. V-12 sailors are top academic students and set grade curves in my classes."

Tom's eyes narrowed. He tilted his chin and turned his head toward his granddaughter, who looked wilted. Perhaps low grades explained why she collapsed in his arms at the depot. He'd confront her later about her classes and grades. "With the army camp close to town, soldiers are everywhere around here. Guess you are about as well off with the Navy V-12 as you would be here with the 63rd Division."

Lucinda wiggled her shoulders, sat up straight, and looked out the window. "Miss Mamie's dress shop sign is gone. Is that a new café in her building, Granddaddy?"

"Yep, fellow opened that a few months or so ago. He is 4-F. While you are home, stay out of that café, Lucy. Civilian camp workers and soldiers hang out there." He had served in WWI and remembered girls lingering in cafés in Paris."

"Granddaddy, you surprise me. Most soldiers and sailors are my age."

"Before your father left for England, he asked me to take care of your mother and you children. The Café is not a place for you."

Tom didn't expect a response from his precocious granddaughter. She knew when to keep quiet, but he knew Lucinda well enough to know she would broach the issue again. He broke the silence and hummed George Cohen's WWI melody, "Over There," a song he sang to his granddaughter when she was a baby.

Lucy joined him, singing, "Send the word over there, the Yanks are coming, the Yanks are coming, and we won't be back—" She stopped singing and said, "Granddaddy, do you know about the WACS, WAVES, SPARS, and WAFS for girls?"

"You are not old enough to join the WACS, WAVES, SPARS, or WAFS. You have to be at least twenty-one," said Tom.

"Oh no," Lucinda said and grinned. "I can join the WAVES when I turn eighteen." She slipped her arm in his and looked up pleadingly at him.

"You are not joining the WAVES. Your father is away. I'm the boss. I forbid it."

Lucinda let go of his arm when he turned into the church parking lot, leaned back against the seat, and said, "There is our beautiful church."

Tom cut his eyes at Lucinda. Tears rolled down her cheeks, and she said, "Coming home and seeing the church makes me cry."

Tom patted her on the knee. "If you need to talk, I'm always here for you."

"I'll be okay, Granddaddy," she whispered.

Tom raised his eyebrows and said, "We'll talk later."

CHAPTER 23

Christmas Program

*T*om eased the car to a stop at the historic church and opened the passenger door for Lucinda. Lucinda clutched her grandfather's arm,

"The church glows in the blue, violet, and coral sky," said Lucinda with a catch in her voice.

"Your grandmother said 'the stained glass windows bathed in the last light of day and the steeple silhouetted in the sunset appear as though heaven comes down and engulfs our place of worship.'"

"I miss Grandmother and know you do too, Granddaddy."

"I do. Memories of our beautiful years together keep me happy," Tom said as they walked arm in arm up the steep church steps. In the familiar foyer, Lucinda's knees buckled, and she tightened her grip on her grandfather.

"Jason will usher you into the sanctuary."

"Jason is too young to be ushering," she whispered.

"With the war on, we recruit ushers out of the Cradle Roll," said her grandfather as he placed Lucinda's hand on her brother's arm.

"Jason, please walk Lucy to our pew. I need to check out the car."

"Sure, Granddaddy." As Tom hurried down the steps, her lanky, thirteen-year-old brother winked at Lucinda, offered her his arm, and escorted his sister down the left church aisle.

In the vaulted sanctuary, blackout curtains covered the triple Gothic-style stained glass window that faced Main Street and the tall, narrow Gothic windows in columned galleries on each side of the church, but candles inside sparkling hurricane shades cast a rosy radiance, an aura of holiness.

Lucinda sighed. Except for faded red grosgrain bows on the ends of the antique walnut pews, the consecrated interior of the church appeared more beautiful than ever. The military needed new grosgrain ribbon for campaign bars and medals fastened on servicemen's jackets.

At the family pew, Lucinda patted her brother's arm and sat on the velvet bench cushion.

"Surprise," said Priscilla.

"Pris! I thought you were in New York City. I expected to see Emma, not you." Lucinda hugged her sister. "Where is my brother-in-law?"

"He shipped out a week ago. That's why I'm home."

"Oh, Pris, I am so sorry to hear that. How did you get here?"

"Rode for hours on jampacked trains. Where is your coat? We sent that coat to you from New York City. Why aren't you wearing it?"

"It's in the car," said Lucinda, visualizing the wet coat jammed in the laundry bag.

Her strikingly beautiful and fastidious big sister would never understand cramming the wet coat in a laundry bag, but neither had her sister committed a military offense.

"Where is Emma?" said Lucinda, avoiding more talk about the coat.

"Emma left an hour ago for San Antonio to see John before he ships out."

"My boyfriend shipped out. David is a Baptist, and can you believe he asked me about my religion?" Lucinda whispered. David's voice echoed in Lucinda's mind—what he said and the way he said it with his indigo eyes boring into hers.

"I don't know if he was serious or not. David said being a Baptist doesn't mean you are a Christian. I asked, 'What if I were Methodist, Catholic, Presbyterian, or Episcopalian? What would you say?' He said 'The Old Testament heralds Christ's birth. I respect Jewish people, God's chosen people. To say you believe in nothing. How could I respect nothing?'"

Priscilla grinned. "David was thinking marriage, Lucinda. He wanted to know what you believe," said Priscilla in a low voice. "We're in church. Be quiet."

Lucinda murmured in Priscilla's ear, "I believe in what the church believes. I don't know what David meant, and I want to know."

Priscilla raised her eyebrows. "Shh. We'll talk later, Lucinda. The choir members are taking their places."

Lucinda looked up at her beautiful mother, regal in the gold choir robe draped with a red, satin stole. Her mother smiled, and Lucinda fought tears. *How can I keep what I've done from you, Mother?*

* * *

James G. Waters took his place in the choir and scanned the crowded sanctuary. His eyes rested on a side pew near the front of the church, and he froze. The Middleton college girl sat in Tom Cunningham's usual seat.

A spontaneous expression on the girl's face told him the girl thought, *The man in the choir resembles the Middleton navy officer.* For an instant, their eyes locked into each other's, and he gazed into the windows of her soul. He liked what he saw and instinctively thrust his chest toward her. Magnetized, he couldn't divert his eyes from the girl. In response, the girl lifted her eyebrows, and Jim Waters stared into her eyes until her eyebrows twitched. She blushed and lowered her eyelids. The twice-in-one-day physical attraction to the American girl sparked a desire to dash to her side. Impossible! He was a German agent trapped in a choir loft.

* * *

The new choir man's penetrating gaze disturbed Lucinda. Avoiding eye contact with the man in the choir, she looked down at her shoes and fidgeted with her fingers.

Priscilla reached over, patted Lucinda's knee, and said, "Stop fiddling with your fingers, Lucinda."

Lucinda sighed and said, "I'll try."

Reverend Kelly stood at the pulpit and addressed the congregation. "Welcome to our annual Christmas program. We thank any visitors for celebrating the holy season with us. Those of you from other churches, please save seats for us at your Christmas program. We'll be there." The congregation laughed in appreciation of Reverend Kelly's promotion for their church's Christmas programs.

"Please stand for prayer," said the pastor.

Lucinda stood but searched her soul in silence, humbly confessed her sins, and asked the Lord for mercy and grace. She shivered when the minister closed the prayer with, "Thy will be done, in Jesus's name. Amen.

"Remain standing, turn to page thirty-five in the hymnal, and sing with the choir, 'How Firm a Foundation,' the traditional American hymn attributed only to K."

Physically and emotionally exhausted, Lucinda held onto the pew in front of her while the congregation sang. At the close of the familiar hymn, the choir director motioned for the worshipers to be seated. Lucinda settled back on the maroon, velvet-padded cushion, pressed against the gentle scroll of the wooden church bench, and felt His comforting arms about her.

The chairman of deacons stood to make announcements. Lucinda shuddered when the church leader spoke of young men killed, missing, and wounded in action. She knew everyone on the causality list. She pondered over male friends who faced injury and death yet fought for America.

"Lord, help me to pray unselfishly about David, and when I pray for my beloved, to be in Thy will," she mouthed.

The choir director stood and said, "We dedicate our Christmas music to the wounded and those we've lost in the war. Please join the choir as we sing timeless carols that speak and bring hope to us in these hard days.

"Our first carol is a poem of despair, faith, and hope written by Longfellow after the tragic death of one son and a second son wounded during the Civil War." In 1872, John Calkin composed the music to "I Heard the Bells on Christmas Day." The carol brought tears to the eyes of many in the congregation. Priscilla held a wet handkerchief, and Lucinda patted her sister's arm. War was wretched, so wretched. She wished she could cry and wash away her troubles with tears, but the cold reality of war enveloped and angered her. *David knew he was leaving. The fact he did not tell me prompted my sneaking out of the dorm to find out.*

Sitting amid others, she prayed under her breath. "Lord, my stealing out of the dorm was wrong. But a premonition, the sixth sense you gave me before birth, told me David was leaving. So my intuition about David wasn't exactly my fault. Why did David ask me about my religion? You heard him, Lord, and You know we'd never discussed faith until David said, 'Tell me about your faith.'

"What was David thinking, Lord? Was David saying, 'I love you'? If David was interested in marrying me, I need to know. God, You know everything. Tell me, heavenly Father. And about marriage, Lord, You wrote 'equally yoked.' Remember? Second Corinthians 6:14? 'Be ye not unequally yoked together with unbelievers.' And you mentioned 'like-minded.' 'Fulfill ye my joy, that ye be likeminded, having the same love, being of one accord, of one mind.' Philippians 2:2. I'm not into theology and not sure what 'one mind' means.

"David and I do not have the same kind of minds, but we are believers and would be 'equally yoked' believers. You know everything about me. You know I love David, and I'm serious. David tried to talk to me about my faith, and I joked about it. Shame on me. Forgive me, Lord. I'm not a very patient person, but I'll endure waiting for Your RSVP."

"Remain standing for A. J. Skilton's 'No Room in the Inn,' page 273 in your hymnal." Lucinda blinked away her thoughts and sang with the congregation.

"Please be seated for solos of rejoicing and praise," said the choir director.

CHAPTER 24

Christmas Solos

December 15, 1944—7:00 p.m.

ucinda glanced at the choir members, resplendent in antique gold robes that were fluted with free-flowing pleats and wide crimson stoles cascading down the front. She knew all the singers except the newest member, James G. Waters.

Opening the Christmas program, she read the following:

"There's a Song in the Air" Soloist, Louisa Reed
Poem by Josiah Holland, 1872.
Earlier in life, Holland lived
in Natchez, Mississippi.
"Christmas Song"
by Karl Harrington, 1904

* * *

"Good Christian Men, Rejoice!" Soloist James G. Waters
Latin Christmas carol translated
by John Mason Neale mid-1800s

"Gesù Bambino"
Italian Christmas carol
by Pietro Yon, 1917

Lucinda scrutinized the male soloist's face. Where had she seen him before tonight? She frowned, pressed her lips together, and closed her eyes. Was she losing her mind? James G. Waters resembled the naval officer she encountered at Middleton, but he couldn't be the same man. *After hours of no sleep and no food, my brain cells tricked me,* she thought and peeked at the newest and youngest man seated in the choir loft.

The handsome chorister locked his eyes with hers. She tucked her chin to avoid his stare and looked at her feet until she heard her mother's sweet voice. Lucinda looked at her precious mother, tears filled her eyes, and she whispered under her breath, "Oh, Mama, you'll hear about my behavior this morning. I am so sorry."

Where was her grandfather? He could have waited to go to his car until Mama sang. After her mother's second solo, Lucinda glimpsed through her eyelashes at James Waters and watched him step up to the altar. The soloist gave her a hard look with icy-blue eyes that matched the officer's eyes.

The thick-blond-haired soloist sang in a rich baritone voice. After the first solo and an interlude of soft music by the organist, James Waters sang "Gesù Bambino" with his eyes fixed on her. Lucinda looked about at her mother and the other choir members.

The pastor asked the congregation to stand for the closing hymn. Jason slipped into the pew, elbowed her in the ribs, and slid a small folded note under her hand. Lucinda saw her grandfather's handwriting. *Do not let anyone see this memo.* She shielded the message in her hands and read. *While the congregation sings the last hymn, (1) excuse yourself to Priscilla; (2) do not speak to anyone else; (3) do not question Jason. Follow him out of the church to me.* Baffled, Lucinda stood, leaned over, and said, "Excuse me," to a surprised Priscilla. She walked with Jason toward the foyer.

* * *

James G. Waters watched the girl's every move. He saw Jason walk down the side aisle and stand beside Lucinda. The two slipped out of the pew, tiptoed up the side aisle, and entered the foyer. During the benediction, he stood rigidly in place and waited his turn to leave the choir loft.

Closing the service, Reverend Kelly prayed, "For all our boys, men, and women who serve, especially those at sea, in the air, and on foreign soil, we ask for Your special blessings. In this season of celebration of our Lord and Savior's birth, we commit the husbands, sons, brothers, and other family members who serve our country during these dark days. In Thy will, in Jesus's name. Amen."

Jim Waters scowled at the pastor's prayer for the US soldiers, his enemy.

* * *

Jason and Lucinda walked out of the church and crossed the parking lot to Tom Cunningham's car. "What is going on, Granddaddy? Is this a joke?" said his granddaughter.

Tom took Lucinda by the elbow and opened the rear door. "Get in the back seat, Lucy. Colonel Edward Matthews needs to ask you some questions. Jason, come with me."

Tom walked Jason to the car parked next to his sedan. "Son, something critical has come up. We need your help. Go back for Priscilla. She'll be looking for you and Lucinda. If Priscilla questions you, say quietly, 'Granddaddy has urgent business. We have to leave with him.' Do you understand?"

"Yes, sir."

Lieutenant Wiley lowered the window and said, "Hello, Jason. I am Lieutenant Wiley, and this is Lieutenant Snyder. Do as your grandfather said. Get Priscilla, walk her to this car, and the two of you get in the back seat."

"I'll do as you say, sir."

* * *

After the closing prayer, Reverend Kelly walked to the back of the choir loft. As Louisa Reed passed by him, he put his finger to his lips and took her arm. Perplexed, Louisa walked out of the choir loft with her pastor. The minister moved her quickly down the hallway, opened his office door, and nudged her into his office, motioning toward the uniformed men before them.

"Louisa, during your solo, the officers before you contacted me. They need to speak with you," he said and left his office. Showing their credentials, the uniformed OSS agents said, "Mrs. Reed, Lucinda may be in danger. We want you to come with us."

"What can you possibly mean? Lucinda sat in the pew only moments ago. How could my beautiful daughter be in danger? Why?"

"We'll get to that later. Do you have a coat?"

"It's in the other choir room."

"You'll have to come as you are. We have a blanket in the car. We have to move fast." Almost lifting her off her feet, they ushered her to the back office door.

"I saw Lucinda and Jason leave the sanctuary before the service closed, but I cannot imagine Lucinda in danger," Louisa said. Then she clutched her throat, struggled for breath, and her knees buckled. The officers grabbed her arms and eased her into the back seat of their car.

"Hand me the first aid kit. She's having difficulty breathing and passed out." The officer patted Louisa's face and said, "Mrs. Reed, can you hear me?"

Louisa opened her eyes, moved her index finger, and closed her eyes again. "Stay awake, Mrs. Reed. We know this is a shock. We are doing all we can to protect your daughter." Louisa's head fell against the officer's shoulder, and he shook the woman in his arms. "Mrs. Reed has a pulse, but she's unconscious. Hit it! We've got to get her to the base hospital."

CHAPTER 25

Seeking the Truth

ieutenant Colonel Matthews sat beside Lucinda Reed on the back seat of Tom Cunningham's car. Lieutenant Harris sat behind the wheel, and Mr. C. was in the front passenger seat.

The young woman chewed on her hair and tapped her foot. Was she uncomfortable with his aide and her grandfather in the car or frightened? Despite the circumstances, he had to question Miss Reed now.

Ed tapped Harris on the shoulder and said, "Lieutenant, ease out of the church parking lot and drive Mr. Cunningham's sedan to OSS headquarters in the army camp. He turned to Lucinda and said, "Miss Reed, we'll appreciate your answering a few questions. We'll record my questions and your answers. Do you understand?"

"Yes, sir."

"Lieutenant, please turn on the recorder."

Ed spoke into a small microphone. "December 15, 1944, 7:50 p.m., location, Gilead Baptist Church parking area, Main Street, Myrtle, Mississippi, interrogator Lieutenant Colonel Edward Matthews; witnesses Tom Cunningham and Lieutenant Harris.

"Miss Reed, please give your full name, date of birth, and present place of residence."

Tongue-tied, Lucinda stared at the recorder.

"Your full name, birth date, and residence?" repeated the colonel.

"Yes, sir." Lucinda gave her name, birth date, and hesitated.

"Residence? Where do you live at present?" said the colonel in a stern tone.

Lucinda answered, "Myrtle."

"But at present, you are a student at Middleton College and live in Adalia Hall."

"Not exactly. Adalia Hall is temporary. I live in Myrtle."

"You're in Myrtle for Christmas, but you reside at Adalia Hall. Right?"

"Yes, sir."

"I want to know what happened where you lived this morning. Were you behind a hedge in the off-limit military area at Middleton?"

Lucinda glanced at her grandfather and lowered her eyes.

"Yes, sir."

"An American naval officer was with you in the restricted area. How long have you known the naval officer?"

Lucinda's eyes popped wide open. She shook her head and said, "Know him? Until this morning, I'd never seen him—ever."

Ed Matthews hoped she spoke the truth. "How did you get in the restricted military area?"

"I climbed the fence."

"Why?"

"Because I wanted to find out about something."

"What and why?"

"The Navy V-12. Because ..."

Her grandfather turned, glared at her, and said, "Answer Lieutenant Colonel Matthews, Lucinda."

"Well, because I wanted to know if someone was shipping out."

"Who?"

"My boyfriend, sir."

"His name?"

Lucinda hesitated, glimpsed at grandfather's angry stare, and murmured, "David."

Ed narrowed his eyes, leaned forward, and said, "David who?"

"Atherton."

At the disclosure of the seaman's full name, the lieutenant's mouth sprung open, his body jerked, and he gripped the steering wheel. Ed Matthews clenched his jaw, but his face did not register surprise with Lucinda's response. Calmly, he said, "Did the seaman know you were behind the hedge?"

"Oh, no, sir. I didn't know myself until five minutes before I left the dorm. David hadn't called in two days, and I decided to find out if the navy ordered a blackout and was shipping him out."

Tom Cunningham looked at his granddaughter and raised his eyebrows.

"How long were you behind the hedge?"

"I'm not sure. In equestrian class, when we saddled up our horses in the morning, we hear reveille. This morning, halfway up the back lane on my way to the main campus, reveille sounded earlier than usual. I ran on up the lane. The off-limit area was the only place to find out what I wanted to know, and I climbed over the fence surrounding the parade grounds. About the time I reached the hedge, I heard David give a command. He's the leader of the platoons."

"What happened next?"

"David gave another command. I sensed I wasn't alone at the hedge and spun around."

Ed rubbed his chin. Footprints at the scene confirmed a spin at the hedge. "The navy officer stood behind you?"

"Yes, he did."

"How long did you stand there with him?"

"As I said, I wasn't with him."

"How long, Miss Reed? Give me a time. Five minutes, three minutes, a minute?"

Lucinda's mouth scrunched from side to side. "At least three minutes."

"How close were you to the officer?" Lucinda held up her right hand and stretched the space between her thumb and index finger. "He was this close to me."

"Interviewee displays a distance of about six or seven inches between her and the unknown officer. Lieutenant Harris, you don't perchance have a tape measure?"

"Colonel, there's a tape measure in the car dashboard pocket," said Tom.

"Will you measure the circumference and length of your granddaughter's right hand and the stretched-out distance between her thumb and forefinger?"

"On the right hand, the circumference measures eight inches; length from wrist to the tip of the middle finger, seven inches. Stretch distance between thumb and index finger, six inches."

"Did the officer speak to you?"

"He said, 'Young lady, report to the dean of women.'"

"You said you'd never seen him. How did he know you were a student?"

"I have no idea." At Lucinda's cheeky reply, Tom glowered at his granddaughter. Ed raised his hand and mouthed "Forget it" to the white-haired grandfather.

"After the officer told you to report to the dean, what happened?"

"He walked toward College Drive and disappeared in the misty dark."

"Did you report to the dean of women, Miss Reed?"

"No, sir. I signed out with her for the Christmas holidays."

"Do you think the officer could identify you?"

"He flashed a light in my face and looked me square in the eyes."

"Did he have a camera?"

"I didn't see a camera. The officer had a flashlight."

"The corner light pole provided some light. Could you identify him?"

"He stared at me with cold steel-blue eyes and a straight nose for what seemed like forever."

"Do you think the officer was a blond or brunette?"

"A navy officer's hat covered his hair, but I'd say a blond."

"Height? Tall? Short?"

"Not short but not as tall as David, who is six three."

"Did you notice anything else?"

"Yes, sir. The officer had a row of ribbons on his uniform and two stripes on his coat sleeve."

Ed listened without comment at the young girl's portrayal of the officer. Except for the flashlight, Lucinda Reed's depiction of the unknown man agreed with David Atherton's description of the intruder.

"After your encounter with the officer, what did you do?"

"I moved away from the parade ground, crossed the main drive, walked into and out of the chancellery building, and hurried toward the lane. The dim headlights of a vehicle leaving the campus flashed on. The lights weren't that close, and I ran across the highway. Would you believe the driver switched on the bright headlights, and the car stopped? The hedge officer jumped out of the car and chased me almost to the dorm door."

Ed listened impassively to the young lady's account of the aggressive officer and said, "Miss Reed, you stated you could identify the officer."

"Yes. If you asked me who the arrogant officer resembled the most of any person I've ever seen in my whole life, I'd say"—she squinted her eyes—"the new man in mama's choir."

Ed's pulse raced. Had Lucinda Reed unmasked the master of disguise, Hans Schiller? He reached inside his coat, flipped on the radio strapped to his body, and said, "Lieutenant Harris, pull the car off the road.

"Urgent, all OSS agents, stand by for orders. Lieutenant Wiley, drive to my location on the road and park."

"Message received."

The colonel looked at Tom and said, "Mr. Cunningham, please step outside with me.

They walked a few feet from the car before Ed said, "Do you know—"

"Jim Waters, the man in the choir?" said Tom. "Yes, and I planned to file a Suspicious Person Report with OSS tonight."

"And we interrupted your plans."

Tom nodded. "That's it exactly, Colonel."

"Tell me what you know."

"James G. Waters opened The Café sometime in late July and joined the Gilead Baptist Church by letter and the choir. Waters claimed a 4-F deferment for a vague disability that kept him out of service. The restaurant became a hangout for soldiers, civilian workers from Camp Van Dorn, and local folks. Diners flocked to The Café for the finest cuts of beef and an abundance of rationed food and beverages printed on The Café menu.

"Afternoons, some of us menfolk meet for coffee at The Café. Today, Jim sat at our table and ordered coffee and pie for us, on the house. I noticed when he finished eating his pecan pie, he placed the fork tines down on his plate, European style. We coffee clubbers placed our forks tines up on the plates. Jim blinked and quickly flipped his fork with tines up. While we talked, Waters asked if we knew of any 99th Division soldiers coming to town for Christmas. His intense interest in the 99th confirmed my distrust of him."

"Where does he live? What kind of car does he drive?"

"He lives across the street from me at The Willow hotel. In retrospect, his vehicle sparked my first doubts about him. Jim Waters drives a 1942 Super Deluxe V-8 Ford sedan coupe with a copper radiator and leather upholstery. Buying that '42 Ford model is impossible. I know. I tried. The Ford company stopped production of the model and all models for most civilians in 1942, but Jim Waters arrived in town with a new and 'unavailable' 1942 Super Deluxe V-8 Ford coupe."

"Your mistrust of this songbird is enough for me, Mr. C. You are one of us and know the ropes. My team is unaware of your OSS connection. We have a severe situation going on here. We'll keep your OSS work between the two of us. Your family does not need to know about Lucinda's dangerous involvement with a person we believe to be a Nazi spy. OSS took over the guesthouse at the army camp. It's best for you and your family to be our guests for a few days.

"Until we capture the unknown officer, we'll hold your Lucinda for her safety at a separate location. An OSS agent will be with your granddaughter at all times. No visitation allowed."

"You are right. I'll take care of the circumstances with my family, Colonel."

"I'm glad you were here for us, Mr. C. Keep your radio on. I may need you in town. Do you mind if the lieutenant drives your sedan? Under the lieutenant's pass, camp entrance guards will admit everyone in the car."

"Yes, of course."

Lieutenant Wiley stopped the OSS car, and Ed said, "Lieutenant Synder, drive Mr. Cunningham's family to the guesthouse."

Tom, Priscilla, and Jason joined Lucinda in his sedan. "Lieutenant, check in with me when you arrive at the camp."

"Yes, sir."

Ed signaled "come here" to Lieutenants Harris and Wiley and said, "We are going back to town. Check your firearms and ammo."

CHAPTER 26

Another Search

hoir members patted Jim Waters on the back and praised his Christmas solos. He thanked them, hung up the choir robe, and grabbed his jacket. He didn't see Louisa Reed in the choir room, but she'd know the girl who sat by Priscilla and left with Jason. He had one thought in mind. Find the girl.

"Where's Louisa?" he asked a nearby choir member.

"She left the choir loft with the pastor."

"Did they go to the sanctuary?"

"Maybe. Louisa hasn't left the church. Her choir robe hanger is empty," she said and pointed to the choir closet.

"Thank you. I'll look for Louisa in the sanctuary."

The people lingering in the candle-lit sacred room applauded and congratulated The Café proprietor on his performance. Deacon Stuart grabbed his arm and said, "Jim Waters, we heard Metropolitan singing from you tonight."

While eyeing the girl, he'd never sung better. In sham modesty, he said, "Thank you, sir. Have you seen Louisa?"

"Only Louisa's daughter Priscilla, walking toward the vestibule," said Mr. Stuart.

"Who was the girl sitting with Priscilla?"

Mr. Stuart grinned at Jim Waters's apparent interest and said, "Lucinda, her sister."

"Louisa's daughter?"

"Yes, and Tom Reed's granddaughter. Tom calls Lucinda 'Lucy' after his beloved wife, who died several years ago. In high school, Lucinda played on the basketball and tennis teams. She's home for Christmas from Middleton College."

"Is that so?" said Jim and smiled.

Eager to share a word about one of Myrtle's favorite daughters, Mr. Stuart said, "Lucinda is an all-around American girl, spirited."

Mr. Stuart's description of Lucinda Reed fit Hans Schiller's assumptions about the Middleton girl, a spunky personality and steel backbone; Lucinda Reed defied him. At the sight of the attractive, gutsy girl sitting near the front of the church, he forgot he was a German agent and sang his heart out to her.

The deacon solved Hans's problem. He'd locate the girl and liquidate her. He brushed off a desire for the girl. Patting Mr. Stuart's shoulder, he said, "Come by The Café for coffee on me anytime, Deacon."

"Thanks, Jim. I'll do that soon."

Jim walked up the middle church aisle and into the foyer and questioned several people as he left the church.

"I am looking for Louisa and the Reeds. Have you seen them?"

"Before the program, I saw Tom in the foyer. I haven't seen Louisa or Lucinda, but Priscilla and Jason walked out a few moments ago."

"Thanks. I live across the street from Tom. I'll catch up with them later," he said and walked down the steps. On the sidewalk, he scanned the people coming out of the church and other people standing under the triple-arch windows. In daylight, the glorious stained glass image of the Good Shepherd surrounded by children reminded him of his childhood church and plunged a spear deep in his soul, a soul trapped in sabotage, hades.

Kiss or kill? His mood was mercurial. What chance in a thousand did he have with Lucinda Reed or any other American girl? He'd kill Miss Turned-Up Nose before she squealed on him.

Jim Waters squared his shoulders in a military brace and, snake that he was, slithered up Main Street. A block before he reached The Café, he slipped into an alley and broke into a run for his room at The Willow hotel, a perfect location to take out Miss Reed with his Luger P-08.

On entering his dark hotel room, he closed the blackout curtain and switched on a lamp. Sliding back a false wall behind his bed, he pulled out the Luger and muzzled the gun with a silencer. Snapping off the light, he pulled the curtain to the side and waited for the Reed family's return.

After waiting ten minutes, he swiped his hand across his mouth and looked at his watch. The Reeds should be home. Where were they? Orders from the SS could come through at any moment. He had to get to The Café's hidden radio room for the US sabotage command, synchronized with Germany's major offensive, an assault that bought time for Hitler's secret weapon, rumored to be a far-reaching missile.

Under his command, Bernie had planted explosives under Mississippi River docks in New Orleans and Baton Rouge, tributary river bridges, and railroad tracks used for troop trains.

The SS assured his sabotage men that after the Axis victory, they'd return to Germany for a heroes' welcome. Bernie guffawed at the SS orders to destroy New Orleans and Baton Rouge ports and stow away on neutral ships docked there. How could his men board vessels destroyed by German sabotage?

"My brave men will never ride in open vehicles along a parade route and wave to happy Germans in Berlin," he said and sighed.

His own SS orders read that after the destruction of ports, he was to return to Myrtle. Hiding in plain sight in the small town, he'd keep The Café open and fare better than the men he led.

Thinking of Arnold brought on nausea. What if the OSS arrested Arnold and he talked?

The Jim Waters cover-up would be over, and until the ports reopened, he'd be in the same circumstances as his team, unable to stow away on neutral ships to South America and work his way back to Germany. Hans groaned. He sat on a keg of dynamite, waiting for sabotage orders from the SS.

Seated by the window in his room, Jim Waters waited, with the pistol in hand, to kill the guiltless American girl. He was a man of experience with women. If he had more time and a fair playing field, he'd win the girl over. His passion spelled fatal attraction for her and for him. A romantic pursuit of the young woman was not to be. She had to die.

Restless and with one finger on the Luger trigger, he sneaked a quick look out of the window. Where were the Reeds? He was popular in the community. If someone threw a party after the program, they'd invite Jim Waters.

At the restaurant, Mr. Tom said, "See you in church." He didn't say, "See you in church tonight." Mr. Tom never appeared in the sanctuary, but his tall, white-haired neighbor often traveled. Jim twisted his mouth from side to side. If the retired railroad man left town, killing his granddaughter would be easier.

He couldn't wait any longer; he had to get back to The Café and the radio. Lucinda was in Myrtle for the holidays; there'd be other opportunities to get rid of her. Closing the blackout curtains, he placed the Luger into its secretive space, caressed it, and said, "We'll get Miss Reed later." He left his hotel room for The Café.

CHAPTER 27

Astonishment

*J*im Waters hurried from his room at the hotel to The Café. After events, the Myrtle community gathered about on Main Street and dropped by his restaurant for late snacks. He saw few people on the street, but he anticipated a crowd in his restaurant.

Surprisingly, he found only one couple in The Café, but the scarcity of customers provided the best scenario for checking the SS radio for sabotage orders. He turned the door sign from open to closed and approached the man and woman seated at a side table with two additional half-filled goblets on the table.

"Good evening. Are others with you?" Jim said and motioned to the extra goblets and plates.

"Yes and no. Our friends finished eating and left." Jim called the waiter to remove the used water goblets and plates.

"Was there a problem with their food?"

"Oh no. Our friends have a long drive ahead of them and were eager to get back on the road," said the young man.

"May I get anything else for you?"

"Thank you but no. We enjoyed steaks you could cut with a fork, perfect, and the best cornbread I've ever eaten."

"We do our best. All local ingredients." Jim looked at the young lady and said, "How about you? Is there anything I can bring you?"

"Nothing," said the young woman. "After eating the scrumptious pecan pie, I could not eat another bite."

"Thank you. There are plenty of pecan orchards around here, and the pecan pie is our specialty."

"Sir, I believe this is the cleanest restaurant I have ever been in," said the woman.

"We try to keep it spic and span," said Jim. "Lots of scrubbing goes on here. We sterilize everything, and our cooks take pride in a spotless kitchen."

"And the immaculate waiters' uniforms trimmed with an unusual shade of dark green," she said.

"Fabrics capture bacteria and harbor microorganisms. Waiters change uniforms frequently," Jim said. The Café monogram and trim on the waiters' uniforms matched the gray-green field color of German uniforms, a daring tribute to the homeland.

Jim didn't want to talk. He had to get the couple out of the restaurant and turn on the hidden radio for Unternehemen Wacht am Rhein (Operation Watch on the Rhine) orders.

"I would like an extra slice of pie," the man said and rubbed his stomach. "Honey, sure you don't want another slice of pecan pie and a cup of coffee?"

"The pie was delicious but no, and no coffee. And you do not need more pie and coffee, my dear," the woman said sternly.

Jim glanced at the wedding rings on their fingers and smiled at the wife. "Bring him back for the pie."

"Indeed, I will," said the woman.

"The meal was excellent. We'll be back," said the man.

"We're happy you enjoyed our food," Jim said and motioned to a waiter. "Check for this table, please."

While the man took care of the check, Jim pulled the shade over the front door.

"Good night. Thank you for the wonderful food," said the talkative couple, lingering at the front door.

"Good night," their host said. Opening the front door, Jim inserted a key into the deadbolt and inched the door closed. "Have a good evening. Come back soon," he said with a deceitful smile.

"We will," the couple said and left the restaurant. Jim exhaled held breath, turned a key in the deadbolt, and fastened a safety chain lock high on the door.

Turning to the waiters, Jim said, "We'll close early this evening. Finish up quickly, toss your uniforms in the dirty-clothes hamper, and enjoy an early night out of here."

Placing his hand on the cash register, he said to the cashier, "Balance out in the morning." He moved toward the back of the restaurant, but a thump on the door stopped him. Raising the front door shade a bit, he peered through the glass. Several people rubbed their stomachs and pantomimed eating. He yelled through the window, "Sorry, closed." After snapping off every light in the dining room, he rushed into the kitchen.

Karl Lutz stopped scrubbing the sink, and Bernie said, "No soldiers showed up for food tonight."

"I know. The 63rd Division could ship out, and Wacht am Rhein orders come through tonight. I have to get on the radio. Bernie, leave the kitchen as is, and both of you head out for the demolition sites. Be careful, and you too, Karl. Keep your radios tuned in and wait for my orders. If the SS radio confirms Wacht am Rhein, I'll signal. Tonight, we'll crush the enemy on their turf."

Bernie took off the chef's toque, his pride and joy, and placed the tall hat on the shelf in the closet. The white stovepipe hat with a hundred pleats represented one hundred different ways he could cook an egg. He threw his double-breasted jacket and pants into a hamper and held up the lid for Karl to toss in his assistant cook floppy hat, jacket, and pants. There were no shoes in the closet. Agents wore steel-toe boots suitable for both gastronomic and espionage activities. Bernie and Karl scurried into street clothes and dashed out the back door.

Jim Waters bolted the door after them and in the dark dining room eased open a blackout curtain and looked up and down Main Street. Only a few civilians strolled the street, and he saw no soldiers. The 63rd must be shipping out. He needed final orders to hit troop trains on bridges north and south of the camp and town. Walking out of the dark dining room, he turned out the kitchen lights and entered the pantry. Pulling back the false wall of the pantry, he stepped into the darkness of the secret room.

As he walked toward the concealed radio, he paused, cupped his ear, and recognized a barely perceivable whistle "= = o =": an engine signaling the train approached a public crossing. After the initial sound, he closed his eyes and, listening intently, heard an intermittent "= o," the long and short sounds warning people, animals, or vehicles near a railroad track. In the German Supreme Command school on an estate at Quenz Lake near Berlin, he'd learned to distinguish the train horn sounds and calculate a train's speed. The repeated "= o" told him it was a fast-moving train at 45 mph, the rate and speed for a troop train pulled by two locomotive engines.

The continuous rumbling train noise and loud long and short whistles resonated in his ears. The train deploying the 63rd Division moved fast and closer to Myrtle's Main Street crossing. His agents had time to trigger explosives under railroad bridges north of Myrtle, destroy the troop train, and obliterate the 63rd Division. A flashing red light signaled an SS message. Whether the Wacht am Rhein sabotage orders came through or not, he'd destroy the 63rd tonight.

Jim yanked back the wall concealing his powerful radio unit. Reaching for the radio switch for the saboteur agents standing by railroad tracks north of Myrtle, he felt strong hands grab his neck and muscular arms pin back his shoulders. He struggled with his assailants and kicked at his attackers' shins. Hans yanked his left arm free and stretched his hand out for the cyanide underneath his shirt collar. A hard chop hit his forearm.

"Oh, no, you don't."

"Handcuffs snapped over both wrists, a blindfold covered his eyes, someone locked shackles around his ankles, and he heard, "Lights and insert earplugs." Someone inserted plugs in his ears and pulled a hood over his head. Hans saw pairs of feet around him but no faces.

The café proprietor scrunched his eyes and recalled the scarcity of people on Main Street. His radar missed a café stakeout. Two diners and their missing friends captured him. He gritted his teeth at his stupidity.

CHAPTER 28

Groundwork

*E*d Matthews dialed Mike Ward's direct line in Washington.
"What's up, Ed?" said Mike.
"You know we raided The Café and hold a Jim Waters. We caught another suspect at The Café's back door, but one got away. In the restaurant, we found a secret room, and a false wall concealed a high-frequency shortwave radio and radio transmission interceptor unit."

"Are you telling me there is a continent-to-continent radio setup with access to US intelligence radio communiqués?" said Mike.

"Exactly," said Ed. "Berlin, Germany, to Myrtle, Mississippi, frequency and the capability for listening to OSS radio messages. Also, we found components for explosives. To me, The Café spells headquarters for sabotage commanded by Waters, a python out of his natural habitat, hungry for a strike. When, where, and what—we don't know."

"Jim Waters is a saboteur, and under a Geneva Convention article, he falls into a prisoner of war category. You're an attorney and know the American judicial system assures, no matter how guilty or heinous Waters's crime, he cannot be condemned without due process of law. Document, document, document every fact."

"You're right. The slightest data can become competent evidence. Our radioman picked up a coded message in German and forwarded it to Washington for cryptanalysis and interpretation."

"I know. We're working on it, and demolition experts are on their way down there. You have a top secret investigation underway in Myrtle."

"We do, and we staffed the shortwave setup twenty-four seven. We'll snag Nazi commands until German Intelligence gets wise."

"What else will help in Myrtle?"

"Keep The Café open and catch stray saboteurs."

"I agree. Our OSS agents come from all walks of life, including food-service workers. A chef and restaurateur will arrive by morning."

"Great. It'll be tricky, but with professional restaurant know-how, we'll pull it off. In a few moments, we interrogate Jim Waters. Our captive may be Hans Schiller."

"Before you begin questioning Waters, switch your silver oak leaf for the American eagle emblem."

"What's that? Change the silver oak leaf insignia for the American eagle one? What are you talking about?"

"Great work and a well-deserved promotion, Ed."

"I'm speechless. Rank is the last thing on my mind."

"Pin on the eagle, Colonel Matthews," said Mike.

"Unexpected, Chief. Thank you."

"Your aide has the eagle pins. Wring a confession out of Jim Waters."

Lieutenant Wiley opened the door. "Excuse me, sir. Chief Ward sent this package, and Mr. Cunningham is here."

"Thank you. Send Mr. Cunningham in." Ed slipped the small package in the desk drawer, murmured, "The eagle," and greeted his distinguished visitor. "Bring me up to the minute, Mr. C."

Tom placed a folder on the colonel's desk. "The assistant cook, Karl Lutz, caught at The Café's back door, admitted Waters commanded a team of saboteurs and expected orders from Berlin soon. Lutz planted bombs under railroad bridges across the Amite River and the streams north of Myrtle."

"To wipe out the Camp Van Dorn trains," snapped Ed. "Vicious madness."

"Yes. You'll find the bridges marked for timed explosives on this map," said Tom and pointed to the sites.

"Fast work, Mr. C."

"Just doing my job, sir. Lutz said Waters expected orders for an onslaught of the terror at any time."

"You know the area. We'll need your help locating the marked bridges. OSS demo experts are on the way and will be here shortly. Wait in my aides' office until they arrive."

"Yes, sir."

"A minute before you go, Mr. C. The army doctor called."

"The doctor called me, sir. Louisa had a laryngeal spasm, a rare and terrifying breathing difficulty, but she began breathing normally in a few seconds. Scary for her, but it seems not life-threatening."

"The army doctors want to keep her under observation tonight. You may see her, but no other visitors are permitted tonight."

"That's good news, Colonel. Thank you."

"During our investigation, the OSS will provide security for your family. Your granddaughter's problems at the college and with the navy take a back burner to our investigation. OSS can hold Miss Reed indefinitely."

"Under the circumstances, I understand. I'll keep you informed on the bridges, Colonel." Tom left, and Lieutenant Wiley entered the office.

"Sir, this came in from Washington." He handed the colonel a file stamped top secret.

Ed opened the file and read, "All OSS Agents: December 15: German troop movements reported on Belgium border." Ed rubbed his ear. He'd accompanied the 99th to the Ardennes Forest on the Belgian border and remembered an OSS brief stated local witnesses reported questionable German military movements near the forest.

Ed closed his eyes, squeezed his chin, and slumped in the chair. Although well trained in defensive arts, the Checkerboards had never been in battle. Thinly positioned in the woods on the Belgian border, the 99th soldiers would be battle babies.

"God, help them," he prayed.

Wiley returned and said, "Sir, another top secret message just in from Washington."

Ed opened the envelope and scanned the memo: "Coded message intercepted at The Café, Myrtle, Mississippi, December 15, 1944, time 8:00 p.m. Sonnenaufgang 16. Dezember 1944 0800 translates U 15 December 1945, 23:5; 11:59 CST."

The colonel placed the two top secret messages side by side. Did Nazi troop movements along the Belgium border connect with the onset of sabotage in the United States? Did the "U" signify Jim Waters and "15" mean today? He looked at the clocks on the wall of his office. With the time difference between Germany and US Central Standard time, sabotage on American soil could begin in several hours. A gnawing permeated his being. He clenched his teeth and said, "The only German saboteur capable of carrying out the lunacy of massive destruction in the US was Hans Schiller, Mr. James G. Waters." He slammed his fist on the messages and shouted, "Lieutenants Wiley and Harris, on the double!"

The lieutenants burst through the door, and the colonel said, "Wiley, call the pastor of Gilead Baptist Church and request a recording of the Christmas program. Pick up the recording immediately. Harris, double the guards on the prisoner and transport him for interrogation."

CHAPTER 29

The Truth

USA; Germany
December 15, 1944; December 16, 1944

*J*im Waters studied the two silent guards who shackled his
ankles, plugged his ears, and handcuffed him. A third guard
blindfolded him, and another pulled a hood over his head.
Assisted by the guards, he shuffled out of his cell into a corridor and
crossed a doorsill.

With his head covered and his breath stifled, he welcomed the crisp
morning breeze across his body, and the guards loaded him into a vehicle.
Inside the conveyance, he sat on a bench. With his hands cuffed behind
him, he felt a hard surface and assumed he rode in a truck. The chains
about his ankles grated into his skin. Where were they taking him?

Events of the day raced through his mind. Who talked? Bernie Koch
and Karl Lutz were out of The Café before he opened the hidden pantry
door. Did they escape? If caught, Bernie would never talk. He wiggled his
nose. Lutz might talk. Someone squealed on him. Lutz or the girl. *The
fatal attraction? Nein. Impossible.* The girl had never been inside The Café.

Who spilled the truth? Had OSS arrested Arnold or an agent in New
Orleans? Baton Rouge? How much did his captors know? Did someone
crack the code on his radio?

In Berlin, he and Bernie questioned the sanity of espionage in America
and considered bailing out of Operation Heil. After he and Bernie arrived
in the US, they could have turned coat, but German victory fueled their
passions for massive destruction in the US.

The vehicle slowed to a stop, and Jim heard the doors open. Strong hands grabbed his upper arms and pulled him forward, lifting him to the ground. He dragged his shoes on concrete until a shod foot hit wooden stairs. His guards helped him up five steps onto a flat surface. He brushed against the side of a doorway and stumbled into and out of an elevator. The ankle bracelets clanged about his legs until he stopped walking and guards relaxed their grip on his arms. Who had captured him? The OSS or US Army Intelligence?

* * *

Colonel Matthews looked at the manacled man who stood before him. Newly intercepted German radio messages verified that a massive German assault, synchronized with sabotage in the US, would begin within hours. He had mere seconds to break Waters.

"Remove the sensory items and unshackle the prisoner."

Guards uncovered Waters's face and unfettered his ankles and hands. Dressed in prison clothes, Waters leaned over, massaged his ankles, and rubbed his wrists before he stood ramrod straight.

Chipping at the prisoner's obvious military stance, the colonel said, "This is not a military court." Ed Matthews observed Waters's shoulders loosen up slightly. "You are held as a prisoner of war by the Office of Strategic Services for preliminary questioning."

The bailiff motioned for guards who escorted the prisoner to the witness stand. Ed stood in front of Waters, focused on the captured man's facial expression, and said, "What is your name?"

"James G. Waters," said Jim with his head held high.

"Give the date and place of birth."

"I was born October 7, 1920, in Short Creek, Alabama," he said, looking confidently and directly into the Matthews's eyes, a liar's tactic for the seasoned interrogator.

"You were dressed in civilian clothes when apprehended. What is your US service rank?"

"4-F," said Waters with a guiltless gaze.

"Have you ever committed treason against the United States of America?"

"No, sir," Waters said truthfully and raised his eyebrows in innocence, but his blue eyes widened at the word treason, and his tensed posture presented the reaction Ed Matthews desired before he threw out a shocker question.

"You are then a foreign agent in the United States. Answer yes or no." Jim Waters answered, "No."

Ed caught an almost imperceivable ripple in Waters's jaw muscle, and the prisoner thrust out his chin, displaying determination. This did not escape Ed Matthews. *Hans Schiller would face a firing squad rather than talk.* Was it possible an ounce of remorse existed in the emotionless man in the witness box?

Colonel Edward Matthews looked directly into the expressionless eyes of the prisoner and spoke as softly as a father to a child. "Hans."

Visibly shocked at the sound of his given name, Jim Waters blinked, and his eyes confessed, "I am Hans Schiller." The interrogator became the parent; the prisoner became the son. Ed Matthews tapped into the weakness he'd sought in Schiller.

The colonel stroked his nose, signaling Lieutenant Wiley to play the Christmas carols that Jim Waters sang in the Christmas program. Jim's jaw dropped, and his shoulders slumped, erasing all tautness of military posture.

Ed motioned with his hand to Lieutenant Wiley, and the music stopped.

Ed moved closer to Jim Waters and said, "You are a German espionage agent." Jim stiffened his military posture. "You are a German espionage agent," repeated Ed.

Hans did not cave into the repeated question, a mark of his strength and fighting capability.

Ed Matthews took a quick stride toward the prisoner and said, "We do not need a firing squad. I'll put a bullet in your head."

Under bright lights, the full colonel silver eagle insignias glistened on Ed Matthews's shoulders. "You have five minutes. Confess and face trial by a military court or dig your own grave tonight. Guard, get a shovel."

Ed Matthews walked out of the room and crossed the hall to the restroom. Bending over the washbasin, he splashed cold water over his face.

The colonel's fury was not feigned; the anger reached the depths of his soul. He wanted to strangle Hans Schiller. "For as he thinketh in his heart, so is he" (Proverbs 23:7).

"Lord, I've lost it. I want to murder Hans Schiller. Germany has lost the war, and the massive assault in Belgium will not win the war. In a few hours, German troops will mow down American battle babies on the front line in Ardennes Forest, and German agents might obliterate countless citizens in the US. Senseless killing. Lord, I don't have to tell You the prisoner has explosives rigged to blow on American soil. I am powerless to stop the carnage. Quell my murderous intentions. Killing Schiller is not the answer. Make him talk. I put my trust in Thee. In Jesus's name, help me," he whispered.

* * *

Hans sat motionless in the interrogation room, but his mind was whirling. Colonel Matthews's sudden rage and the look in the officer's cold, hard eyes shocked him. The colonel's voice compounded his extreme anger. *He'll execute me.* Interrogations were nothing new to the colonel. *Why the colonel's abrupt wrath? The full colonel knows something unknown to me. Something other than confronting a suspect ticked him off. Has a faulty timer set off explosives? Has Hitler's major assault begun in Europe?*

Has the OSS captured Arnold? Other than him, only Arnold and Bernie knew the locations of all the explosives set and ready to blow. He and his men deserved a military trial and a firing squad, an honorable death. But until the OSS captured all of his men, the intelligence agency wouldn't turn him or his men over to the military for trial, and then with a sure death sentence. *My death will happen on Hans Schiller's time, not on an enraged colonel's. I won't dig my grave and fall dead into it because of your anger, Colonel.*

* * *

Ed reentered the interrogation room, took his seat at the table, and prayed silently, *Take over, Lord.*

"Hans Schiller, five minutes are up. The shovel is ready. It's your call. You can cooperate with us or walk out that door to your death."

The prisoner looked fiercely at the colonel. "I am due a trial."

"That is my call. Confess now, or execution takes place within seconds."

Hans squared his shoulders and, with boldness, said, "Trial."

"You are Hans Schiller?"

"Yes."

"Hans Schiller, you are under my command. The conditions for a confession are the whole truth immediately. Give the names of espionage agents under your command and the exact location of every explosive planted by your team. The slightest deviation from the truth, you pick up the shovel and dig your grave. Do you fully understand and agree to the conditions for a reprieve of execution at this moment?"

"I do," said Hans.

"Where have you placed explosives? I remind you, I said confess all."

"New Orleans and Baton Rouge factories, docks and bridges, railroad tracks and bridges near Myrtle."

"And you expected orders for the onset of destruction and bloodshed tonight?"

"Yes." Ed glanced at the open phone line. Mike Ward heard Schiller and would act instantly.

"Under the supervision of our demolition experts, you and your team will defuse every explosive you have planted. Agree or walk out the back door of this room."

"Agreed," said Hans.

Ed Matthews silently thanked God and spoke to Lieutenant Wiley privately. "Accompany the prisoner and guards to the chart room. Set up a phone open to Washington. Ask Schiller for his agents' names and locations. Mark on a map the location of every explosive they've planted. I'll join you in the chart room in a few moments."

Matthews thanked the officers seated at the table and said, "You heard the testimony of Hans Schiller, famed German spy and saboteur. A major German offense is underway in Europe. With or without Schiller's orders, his espionage team will detonate all of the explosives set up for destruction in the US. If Schiller continues talking, we'll arrest his espionage agents and bomb experts. We'll need your help. Stand by for further orders.

"Colonel Wilson, cancel all passes and leaves for soldiers at this camp. MPs, soldiers, and trucks for the operation are under your command. Close all roads leading to factories, docks, and bridges in New Orleans, Baton Rouge, and bridges north of Baton Rouge."

Matthews dialed the red phone in front of him. "Mike, you heard the interrogation proceedings on the open line. Waters is Hans Schiller and plans sabotage in the US synchronized with the massive assault in Europe. I have to enlist the help of Schiller and his agents in locating and defusing explosives."

"I heard your orders. I'm not sure I agree. You're running huge risks with our men working with German saboteurs."

"The situation is perilous. I have a gut feeling. Captured German saboteurs working with American demo experts is the quickest way to defuse the explosives. Schiller's men don't want to die any more than he does. Pray that enough of our American way of life rubbed off on Schiller and his team for the SS hates, intravenously needled into their veins, to be drained out, and under the eyes of American demolition experts, the saboteurs will disable every bombsite they set up."

"I pray you are right. You have a hazardous night ahead of you, and time was never more crucial. Ed, your brilliance broke Schiller."

"No laurels for me, Mike. I was helpless. Schiller cracked under a greater power."

CHAPTER 30

A Long Night

Mississippi
December 16, 1944

olonel Edward Matthews arrived at his temporary OSS office. After working all night defusing bombs with American agents and captured German saboteurs, Ed propped his tired legs and feet on the desk.

Lieutenant Harris opened the door. "Good morning, sir. Ready for breakfast?"

"Good morning, Lieutenant. Thanks. Smells great. I'll eat at my desk. Has the team eaten?"

"Yes, sir. The agents ate and continue monitoring the docks, plants, and bridges at the sabotage sites."

"News of the massive German assault on the Belgian border limped through intelligence channels. Few know the German breakthrough in Belgium's Ardennes Forest synchronized with the massive destruction plans in the US."

"Under your command, Colonel, the army and OSS agents saved thousands of American lives."

Ed Matthews leaned back in his chair and gestured with his hand toward his aide. "Harris, you and your fellow OSS agents' heroic work stopped the monstrous sabotage planned by Schiller."

"Thank you, sir, but your leadership prevented devastation in the US by the enemy."

"We worked together, Lieutenant. In the grueling hours ahead, we will document last night's events and prepare transfer papers for the captured saboteurs for army trials."

"Colonel, you worked all night tirelessly. Take time to eat." The colonel forked into ham, eggs, grits, and southern buttermilk biscuits but pushed the tray aside when an aide handed him a packet stamped top secret. Ed opened the envelope and grimaced over the message:

"During heavy fighting in Belgium's Ardennes Forest, the 99th suffered many casualties yet tenaciously held their defensive position."

Ed buried his head in his hands. The Checkerboards endured the initial thrust of Hitler's massive assault in the Ardennes. The hundreds of 99th soldiers captured, wounded, and dead brought overwhelming sorrow to his heart. Tightening his hands on the edge of his desk, the tired colonel sat upright in the chair and checked over a list of Schiller's men.

Bernard Koch, The Café's chef, escaped. Capturing Koch was a priority. But how many more German saboteurs lurked close and waited to kill Americans on the home front? Mike had OSS agents working on every angle and all clues for other saboteurs hiding out in the US.

Ed looked at his schedule. Dean Wright's name topped the list because of Schiller's confrontation with Lucinda Reed and the girl's indisputable testimony. He needed the Middleton dean's expertise with the college student under guard at the camp.

Ed buzzed his aide and said, "Call Washington and requisition travel expenses and counsel sessions for Helen Wright, Middleton College, dean of women."

"Yes, sir," said Lieutenant Harris.

Ed Matthews pulled Dean Wright's card from his pocket but dialed the number from memory.

Dean Wright answered his call, and he drew a line through her name on his schedule.

"Hello, Dean Wright. Colonel Matthews. Checking back with you regarding Miss Reed."

"Good morning, Colonel Matthews. I am glad you called. I am concerned about Lucinda. Have you spoken to her?"

"Yes, she's fine. I cannot go into details. She's at an army camp for her safety."

"An army camp?"

"Yes. Miss Reed is worried about her situation at school."

"I can understand why. Lucinda was well aware of the rules and consequences. The board scheduled an emergency meeting this afternoon.

After the board's decision about Lucinda's school status, I need to speak with her."

"My early call has an urgent purpose. We need your assistance. You'll have to come down here, about 125 miles from your location."

"I cannot drive that distance on my gas ration stamps."

"OSS will provide gas ration stamps, but we requested approval for train travel and professional counseling sessions with Miss Reed, and we need to debrief you."

"Debrief me?"

"Excuse me, a law-related term. There will be a military court and testimony by Miss Reed. We need an official statement or deposition from you."

"I understand, Colonel Matthews. You do not have to pay me to counsel with Lucinda, talk with you, or for my travel expense."

"I am following OSS protocol for reimbursement of professional services."

"Please. Under no circumstances will I accept payment for counseling sessions with Lucinda or discussing my student with you, and I will pay for my travel expenses."

"We're dealing with the military here, Dean Wright. OSS will arrange for travel by train and reserve a room for you at The Willow hotel, the only hotel in town." Ed frowned at her silence. *She's a stubborn one.* "Is this a problem?"

"I will make my hotel reservations," the dean said primly.

Ed smiled. *Nothing inappropriate about reserving a hotel room for you. You'll be well chaperoned. My children won't let you out of sight.* He cleared his throat and said, "My family will be at The Willow. I'll make the reservation for you."

"No, no," she said.

"We have urgent military business down here, Dean Wright. The OSS handles all expenses in any situation like this."

"The college president will have to be informed about a trip down there."

"I'll take care of that." He heard a sigh on the phone and silence. He grinned and waited for her reply.

"Is that necessary?" she asked.

Ed smothered a chuckle at the dean's curt response and said, "Yes, and under my orders, OSS will make arrangements for you to come down here tonight and schedule a deposition for next week. Is that acceptable?"

"Yes," she said meekly.

"Are you on Christmas break?"

"Yes and no. I have responsibilities here before the students return."

"I'll ask the college president for a week, if needed, for counseling services."

"A week?"

"Yes. Our investigation here may take a week." OSS held Schiller, a POW. Preparation for trials took time, especially a military trial with an expected death sentence. "I'll call in an hour or so, confirming all arrangements. Is that satisfactory?"

"Yes, that will be fine."

* * *

Intrigued by Colonel Ed Matthews's warm voice, Helen Wright scowled and placed the receiver on the hook. The colonel was married.

CHAPTER 31

A Welcomed Interlude

December 17, 1944

*U*ntil he heard the train's engine throttle and saw steam bleed from the pistons, Ed Matthews waited with his children inside the depot. Outside, while the locomotive wheels came to a grinding, screeching halt, Ed's six-year-old son stood straight as a soldier, but his four-year-old daughter covered her ears and held onto her father.

The conductor stepped from a passenger coach and placed a stool for exiting passengers on the platform. Expecting the Middleton dean dressed in tweeds, Ed was unprepared for the beautiful young woman who stood in the train exit wearing a stunning black suit. Ed's heart pounded, and he extended his hand to help Dean Helen Wright step onto the platform stool. Thad offered his chubby little hand to the dean, but Penny dashed between her father and brother and threw her arms around the dean's knees.

Helen swayed, rocked on her stiletto heels, and tumbled into Ed Matthews's arms. Breathing in her perfume, Ed held Helen close for a long moment before he stood her up and said, "Are you all right?"

Helen pulled away from him, smoothed her skirt, and said, "I'm fine."

Ed gently brushed the dean's back and silently thanked his little girl for tossing the dean into his arms but turned to his daughter and said, "Penny, what were you thinking? You grabbed our visitor by the knees and made her fall."

"But, Dad-dee, you caught her," said the curly-red-haired moppet. Moving over by Helen, Penny rolled her eyes and said, "What is her name?"

"I told you her name earlier, Dean Wright.

"Grandmother told us to call her Miss Helen," said his solemn young son.

Ed ignored the comment and said, "My children, Thad and Penny. Penny, please apologize for knocking Dean Wright off her feet."

"Hello, Miss Helen. I'm sorry."

Helen put her hand on Penny's shoulder. "Thank you, Penny."

Chagrined by Penny's *Miss Helen* salutation, Ed glared at Penny and said, "Welcome to Myrtle."

Miss Helen reeked of his mother's passion for southern tradition. Even though she had been informed of the dean's title, his mother had coached Thad and Penny to say, "Miss Helen," a greeting of familiarity reserved for close family, friends, and household servants. He wanted to nurture and guide his children. Provoked by his mother, he frowned.

Helen smiled, and the annoyance with his mother vanished. What would he do without his children's full-time keeper?

"Is everything okay?" she asked.

"Yes, of course," he said and handed Thad his car keys. "Son, open the car trunk, and we'll load up the luggage." Penny ran ahead with her brother, and Ed walked with the dean toward the car, saying, "When Audrey died, Mother moved in with us and accepted full responsibility of the children."

Helen paused a second and said, "I am sorry for their loss and yours."

"Thank you."

Ed placed the large suitcase in the trunk and handed Thad the smaller one. The manly little boy heaved the handbag into the trunk and helped to close the trunk. Ed opened the back door for the children and ushered Helen to the front door, saying, "Mother is waiting for us at The Willow."

Easing into the car, Helen said, "Penny and Thad, I can't wait to meet your grandmother."

"But I'm hungry," said Penny.

Ed grinned, slipped behind the steering wheel, and said, "Penny, we plan to eat at the hotel." He winked at Dean Wright and said, "Did you know The Willow hotel, formerly a residence, has a huge yard with a playhouse?"

Helen's eyes twinkled. "It's been a long time since I was in a dollhouse. It'll be fun to check it out."

* * *

Mrs. Willow met them at the door of the charming Victorian hotel. "Welcome. We do everything we can to keep our guests happy. Let me know if you need anything." She summoned the porter and housemaid. "Please show Dean Wright to her room."

"Dean Wright, the Willow has a great menu. We'll meet you at six thirty in the dining room."

"Thank you, Colonel Matthews. I look forward to meeting your mother."

He motioned to the children. "Come with me. I want you to thank Miss Mettie for the food she sent to the room."

Earlier, he heard Mettie complaining. "Mr. Jim left town for Christmas to visit his family in Alabama. He leaves town all the time, and The Café never closes. His cook runs The Café. Someone said there's a closed-for-repairs sign on the door. I'm thinking Mr. Jim *and* the cook left town for Christmas. I have more to do with breakfast and dinner today than taking care of The Café's clientele, domino-playing men who drink coffee all afternoon in The Willow dining room. Mr. Jim's always asking for recipes for his chef. I sometimes wonder if his chef knows how to cook." Mettie was sharp, and she'd had issues with James G. Waters before The Café closed.

"Good afternoon, Miss Mettie. Thank you for the refreshments you sent to our rooms this afternoon."

"I figured the children needed a snack." Mettie wiped her hands with a clean dish towel and hugged the children.

"Thank you, Miss Mettie," Thad and Penny chorused.

"If you get hungry or thirsty, just let Miss Mettie know."

"Does that go for me too, Miss Mettie?"

Mettie laughed. "Colonel, that goes for you too. I am always happy to serve polite people. You all are respectful folk."

"The coffee and meals at The Willow are excellent, the best I have ever eaten. You are a gourmet cook. The aroma of your coffee hit me the moment I walked into the dining room. Do you roast and blend the coffee beans?"

"No, sir. I don't do that. We buy Community Coffee from New Orleans, the finest coffee in the world," she said with a hearty laugh.

"Community Coffee? Well, your coffee is perfectly blended and roasted, unsurpassed."

"Thank you. Thank you, Colonel."

"We'll see you at dinner, Miss Mettie."

Leaving the dining room, Ed overheard Mettie at the domino table. "Welcome to The Willow. How is the game going? May I serve you a cup of coffee?"

Ed breathed a sigh of relief over Miss Mettie's change of heart. The less talk about The Café, the better. OSS still had to keep Waters's capture top secret, clear out the electronic equipment, and reopen The Café under new management. He walked the children to his mother's room and called her aside. "I don't want to get you up in the morning, but I have to be on base early."

"Don't try to get the children up, son. Call me, and I'll crawl in your bed with Thad. Sometimes he sleeps with me."

"I know. Thanks, Mother."

CHAPTER 32

Surprises

 olonel Matthews's announcement of his wife's death surprised Helen. She dismissed misgivings over the colonel's insistence on the trip to Myrtle and anticipated having dinner with him.

"I'll be ready shortly," she said to Ed with a lighthearted smile, then followed the porter and housemaid to her hotel room.

Blue velvet love seats flanking a white marble fireplace with a crackling fire stirred memories of home. The corner Christmas tree with familiar handblown ornaments brought tears to her eyes. Her mother bought the same ornaments in Germany. Was Mrs. Willow German?

She wondered if her parental home and furnishings survived the ongoing German bombings and thought about all the people displaced, injured, and killed by the war. While the porter placed her suitcase on a rack in the bedroom, Helen looked about the spacious accommodations with guilt.

"Anything we can do for you, ma'am?" asked the porter.

"No, indeed. The Willow hotel room is the loveliest I've ever seen."

"Mrs. Willow is German, and she decorates the rooms with furniture she brought with her from Germany," said the maid.

The porter scowled at the young maid and said, "The Willows are loyal American citizens and have lived in the United States for years."

"I know, but they are Germans," said the perky maid.

"We have many Germans who left their homeland living in our country," said Helen.

"We sure do," said the porter, frowning at the maid. "If you need anything, call us, ma'am."

"Thank you. Everything looks perfect to me," said Helen, tipping each generously. She closed the door, walked back to the bedroom, and admired the four-poster bed covered in a blue and cream toile de Jouy fabric counterpane with matching drapes on floor-to-ceiling windows.

In the bathroom, beautiful pastoral scene wallpaper coordinated with the bedroom color scheme. After sniffing her black suit that reeked with train smoke, she opened the bathroom window, took the suit off, and hung it on a hanger on the door. Grateful she had time for a bath, she slipped out of her underclothes, cleansed her face with cold cream, and filled the bathtub with water. The clawfoot tub had a shower attached. After lathering her hair with Camay soap, she drained the tub and switched on the shower spray. Leaning over in the tub, she rinsed her locks and watched black soot-filled water run into the tub drain until the clear water poured off her head.

In her robe and slippers, Helen set her hair with bobby pins and then sat in the parlor by the fireplace. The fire's curling flames quickly dried her hair. Rid of smelly train smoke and refreshed from her bath and pleasant surroundings, she relaxed with cheerful thoughts about the colonel, but she couldn't overcome a sharp sense of sadness about Lucinda. Didn't the young girl realize the gravity of sneaking off campus onto the military grounds? She had to believe her highly perceptive ex-student had a positive future.

Psalm 118:24 came to mind: "This is the day which the Lord hath made; we will rejoice and be glad in it."

"It's time to dress for dinner with Colonel Matthews," she whispered.

In the bedroom, Helen opened the suitcase and pulled out a garter belt, silk underwear, and the silk stockings she bought in Switzerland. She kept the stockings wrapped in tissue paper for special occasions. Most days, she wore ugly, sagging rayon and cotton stockings. Japan was the primary producer of silk. After Pearl Harbor, the US government seized all raw silk in the US for war needs. She carefully unfolded the silk stockings and eased the sheers over her toes and legs, then fastened the tops on tabs attached to long straps on her garter belt. Turning her back to the long dressing mirror, she made sure the stocking seams were straight.

Helen had debated when packing for the trip to Myrtle and decided to include something she'd never worn, a blue silk dress and slip purchased for her trousseau. She put on the silk slip and dress and slid her feet into black patent high heels. She draped a bed jacket over her shoulders, unpinned her curls, and brushed her shimmering sable hair until it suited her. After she powdered her face and applied two coats of a warm red lipstick, she tossed the bed jacket over a chair.

Opening a green velvet jewelry box, she fingered the shell-shaped clasp with an M on the pearl necklace, a gift John gave to her in Gstaad. She held the necklace and remembered John fastening the luminous strand of Mikimoto pearls about her neck, handing her a small velvet box with matching earrings and gently kissing her. The blue dress and pearls embodied John's love and her love for him, but she'd met a man who opened her heart again. Helen pinched herself to make sure she wasn't dreaming, then dabbed Chanel No. 5 on her wrists and beneath her ears.

Pleased with her reflection in the mirror, she left her room for dinner with the colonel and his family.

* * *

Ed waited for the dean outside the dining room at The Willow and caught his breath at the appearance of the radiant woman walking toward him. His desire for Helen Wright overwhelmed him. He was on a roller-coaster ride and thrilled. He shipped out after Christmas. What was he thinking? He said cordially, "Shall we join the family?"

"Indeed. I am looking forward to being with your mother and the children."

Diners turned and gazed at the tall, handsome couple who joined the attractive older woman and two children seated at a round table.

Natalie's face glowed with approval of the lovely young woman who stood by her son's side. "We are delighted you could join us, Helen."

"It's a pleasure to be with you, Mrs. Matthews."

"Natalie, let's call each other by our first names. Sit down, my dear," she said, patting the chair beside her. Ed pulled out the chair for Helen, eased it closer to the table, and sat on the other side of the beauty who joined them for dinner.

Edward Matthews eyed his mother. He could read Natalie Matthews's mind. *She thinks Helen Wright looks great for the mother of my children.* His attraction to Helen had nothing to do with his children, and he didn't want the dazzling young woman beside him to get that idea.

"Natalie. Call me Natalie," his mother said. "You look lovely, Helen,"

"Please do call me Helen. Even though this is a business trip, it is nice hearing my given name."

"During off hours, first names are acceptable," Ed said, smiling. The look in the dean's eyes quietly expressed her thanks to him.

Mrs. Willow handed them menus. "With the war on, we don't have everything listed.

Local and Gulf fishermen keep us supplied with fresh fish. Mettie's fish en papillote is popular. Colonel, we have one or two porterhouse or T-bone steaks from Amelia County farmers."

"An Amelia County T-bone for me, Mrs. Willow." He kept an eye on the children while Natalie and Helen exchanged pleasantries and agreed on the fish en papillote.

A waiter placed water and appetizers on the table. Natalie cut her eyes toward her son and nodded toward Thad. Colonel Matthews acknowledged the cue.

"Let's say grace. Son, you say your blessing first."

Thad glanced at his father and said, "I've already said mine silently."

Helen and Natalie looked up with amusement, and Ed asked, "What did you say?"

"I don't know. I didn't hear it."

The hilarity of Thad's answer generated warm companionship, and Ed prayed, "Father, we thank Thee for this day, our friends, this food, and all the blessings You provide. In Jesus's name."

They all whispered, "Amen."

The children sampled Mettie's Santa salad, a red-tinted pear with raisin eyes and a whipped cream beard, and ate fried chicken. A waiter placed green salads and the entrees ordered before the adults. Mrs. Willow served hot, homemade rolls from a covered basket, and Mettie held out a tray of desserts.

"Think I'll skip dessert," said Natalie. "It has been a long day. Edward, it's the children's bedtime." Natalie pushed her chair back and said, "Helen, please join the children and me for breakfast."

"I'd love to join you, Natalie. What time?"

"Not too early."

"Mother, my driver's scheduled to pick up Dean Wright at nine o'clock tomorrow morning."

"Edward, that's too early. Tell him to be here around ten."

Ed chuckled and helped Natalie from her chair. "Mother, I need to go over tomorrow's schedule with Dean Wright. Put the children to bed in my room and leave the connecting door open to your room. I'll close it when I come up."

"That's fine. I'll be reading."

"Don't read too late tonight. Remember, when I leave for the base, you get an early wake-up call."

Natalie groaned and said, "Good night, Helen. I'll see you later in the morning."

Ed smiled at his mother and said, "Thad and Penny, finish eating Miss Mettie's caramel cake, and it's off to bed for you two."

"Is Miss Helen going to bed too?" said Penny with a bounce of her red curls.

Ed placed his hands on the table and looked into Penny's beautiful green eyes. "Yes, when it's her bedtime, not your bedtime."

"I want Miss Helen to put my pajamas on me. And I want to sleep with her too."

"You are not going to sleep with Dean Wright. While we are at The Willow, you and Thad sleep in my room."

"I don't wanna sleep with you and Thad or grandmother. I wanna sleep with her," said his daughter, wrinkling her face and pointing to Helen.

"We do not point. Mrs. Willow put a nice little bed for you by mine. You are going to sleep in your bed."

"I want Miss Helen to put on my pajamas." Mrs. Willow and Mettie stifled giggles at the colonel's persistent little daughter.

Exasperated, Ed lifted his hands off the table. "Dean Wright, do you have a solution? Any ideas would be appreciated."

Looking at Penny in her most professional manner, Helen said, "Obey your father, and I will help you dress for bed."

The colonel silently mouthed "thank you" to Helen. "Finish your cake, Penny."

Penny jumped up and kissed her father. "I've finished," she said, grabbing and pulling Helen's hand.

CHAPTER 33

Moments to Cherish

*I*n his hotel room, Ed handed Penny frilly pink pajamas, and Helen motioned for Penny to come to her.

"I can put on my pajamas," said Thad and closed the bathroom door.

"Daddy, you go with Thad and put on your pajamas while Miss Helen puts mine on me."

"Penny, you have two seconds to get into your pajamas," said her father, and he turned his back to Penny and Helen.

Thad came back into the bedroom, kneeled beside the massive bed, bowed his head, blessed each in his family, and prayed the familiar child's prayer. Penny repeated her "Now, I lay me down to sleep" prayer.

Ed lifted his little girl, kissed her, tucked her into bed, and said, "Good night, sweetheart."

"I want Miss Helen to kiss me," whispered Penny. Ed stepped back, and Helen kissed Penny good night.

Ed looked down on his daughter. "She's asleep. Penny is a flip-flopper and a kicker. She sleeps better alone, and so do we." He hugged and kissed his little son. Thad clung to his father, pulled his head down, and put his mouth on his father's ear. Ed smiled and said, "I will." *You don't know and won't know until you are older how much I want to do what you asked.*

"Promise?" Tears filled Thad's eyes.

Ed often wondered how much his young son remembered about his mother. Tonight he knew. Thad remembered that both his father *and his mother* kissed him every night.

Ed kissed his son again and whispered, "I'll see Miss Helen to her room and be back soon." He opened his mother's door and said, "The children are in bed."

Helen slipped out the door, and Ed caught up with her. "We can sit in the parlor, but the fire may be out."

"I'll get a sweater and join you."

Ed waited in the parlor for Helen, an unexpected pleasure in his life. Their professional relationship quickly melted into a very personal one. Did she feel the same? His children couldn't have been sweeter tonight. He smiled about Thad's request. Was it too soon to kiss Helen Wright good night? He nodded. *Yeah, too soon.* He moved two parlor chairs close together before she returned.

When Helen walked into the parlor, he said, "Sorry, the fire is about out. I want to thank you for coming down here for Lucinda and your help with the children. I have been with Thad and Penny very little since the war began. I try to make it up to them when we're together."

"Your children are darling, and it was a joy to help Penny. For years, I've worked with children, but I'd never had the privilege of tucking them in and hearing their prayers."

"You came down here for another purpose, but I am grateful for your help with Penny and will never forget it. This evening with the children became more personal than I'd expected," he said with a friendly smile. "May I call you Helen?"

"You may. I live in an institutional environment, and the college title gets a bit old. It is nice being with your family. My parents died in an accident several years ago. I was their only child."

Although he'd read the OSS file on Helen Wright, he did not blink when she mentioned her parents. He hoped she talked about the deceased fiancé to get the tragedy out of the way. He shared, "Audrey died when Penny was born. The day we brought Penny home from the hospital, Thad was two years old. It hasn't been easy, especially for Thad. He cried for weeks."

"Death is never painless and more difficult for a child. Before the war and while working at a boarding school in Switzerland, I met an RAF pilot. We fell in love, and John asked me to marry him. That summer, I resigned from my job and went home to plan a Christmas wedding.

"We were completing plans for our wedding when my parents died in a car accident. I had no family in London or the UK. John insisted we move our wedding date up to late September of that year, 1939. On September 3, England declared war on Germany, and all servicemen reported immediately to their bases. Within weeks, John's plane took a hit, but he flew the crippled aircraft home. Three days later, he died from injuries sustained in the fatal flight."

"A crushing blow—your parents and fiancé, lost within a few weeks."

"Yes, it was hard. No one escapes the emotional upheavals of death."

"You are right. The shock of death creates waves of grief."

"And war stresses everyone out."

"What did the board decide about Miss Reed?"

"They expelled her. Lucinda was an excellent student, and Lucinda's professors vouched for her outstanding academic achievement and urged the board to let her take the semester's exams. I agreed with the board. Lucinda made a poor choice. I'm not sure why she left the dorm in the middle of the night, but I suspect a boyfriend had something to do with it."

"OSS has to hold her for now, and Miss Reed spending empty hours in a dark army barracks is another problem. You'll have to administer the exams here. What do I need to do for her?"

"Keeping Lucinda mentally active, studying for the exams, doing correspondence courses and physical activity is the answer. She plays tennis. Girls her age surround themselves with color. Decorate her space with colorful curtains, a bedspread, pillows ..."

"Scheduling tennis for her is no problem. You're the professional. The exams and correspondence courses are your responsibility, and I'm adding decorations for her room."

"I'd love to help brighten up her surroundings, administer the exams, and arrange for courses by mail from another college. Lucinda is resilient. She'll work through her problem."

"She will, but your help will make the situation easier for Miss Reed and me.

The army keeps me busy. Our professional get-together and first night at The Willow became a pleasurable one for me. How about you?"

"Yes, a happy day. I enjoyed being with Natalie and the children."

"I kind of like them." He folded his hands across his lap. "And now it is back to business. I go in early, but my driver will pick you up in the morning at ten o'clock, thanks to Mother." He laughed.

"And I'll enjoy a leisurely breakfast with your mother and the children." Helen stood and moved toward the parlor door.

Ed walked with her down the hallway. At her room, he took her key, opened the room door, and said, "There is something else. Do you mind if I come in for a moment?"

"No. I thought we'd finished our meeting. It's warm in here. Do come in."

"Thanks. Thad made me promise to take care of something for him. He'll ask, and I don't want to lie to him. You see, Thad has a problem."

Helen sat on one of the love seats and said, "How may I help?"

Ed stood before the fire and said, "I'd say you have to ... uh, cooperate."

"Certainly. What can I do?"

"You'll be surprised at how." Ed leaned over and kissed her on the cheek.

Helen batted her eyes and laughed uneasily. "How sweet of your little son. After I kissed Penny, I wanted to kiss Thad but thought he'd be embarrassed. Tell your dear little boy thank you for me."

"I promise." He resisted kissing her again. *Don't rush it, Ed.* "Good night, Helen."

"Goodnight, Colonel," she whispered and edged the door closed.

Ed pushed the door back and said, "Thought we agreed on first names."

"Only my first name. Shall it be Edward?"

"Ed." He chuckled and closed the door.

CHAPTER 34

Mirror on the Wall

Sunrise
December 18, 1944

*H*ans stared at the first hint of sunlight creeping through the small window in his cell and heard keys rattling in his cell door. Four silent guards entered, shackled and blindfolded him, pulled a hood over his head, and inserted plugs in his ears. A guard handed the prisoner thick gloves to wear and walked him out of the cell.

Outside, Hans heard a small plane coming in for a landing, while unseen guards loaded him into a vehicle and sat him on a bench. His handcuffs clanged against a metal panel of in a truck or van. Where were they taking him?

* * *

At the camp landing strip, Colonel Matthews watched David Atherton jump from the plane and walk across the tarmac to meet him.

"Good to see you, seaman. Our first stop will be for breakfast."

"Thank you, Colonel Matthews. The pilot had food on the plane. We ate on the way."

"We'll go straight to work then. You know why you are down here?"

"The unknown officer?"

"Yes. We captured the unknown, a German agent subject to military trial. You reported the unknown officer, but can you identify him?"

"I don't know, but I can try," said David.

"That's all we ask. You could ship out before we complete our investigation. The option, a lineup identification before you ship out. You may or may not recognize the unknown officer in the lineup today, but that's okay," said the colonel.

* * *

After a short ride, guards helped Hans out the vehicle. His ankle shackles clanked against some steps. He counted four rises and entered a building that was new to him. Inside, guards removed the hood, blindfold, and earplugs and pulled off the gloves. Hans squinted in a brightly lit room, looked about him, and spotted a mirror on the wall. In spy school, he'd learned the fingernail test for mirrors. Touch a one-way mirror with your fingernail, and a gap appears. On a two-way mirror, there's no gap in the image. He couldn't touch the mirror for proof, but he knew he stood before a two-way mirror.

Who was on the other side of the mirror? The girl? *Nein, nein.* She wouldn't report herself to the dean of women.

"Unshackle the prisoner and have him remove the outer garment." With no privacy, Hans peeled off orange coveralls stamped "Prisoner," front and back, and stood in his underwear before the mirror. The colonel would never exhibit him in his underwear before a female. Whoever stood on the other side of the mirror was a male.

A guard handed him a navy officer uniform. Hans pulled on the uniform pants over his raw ankles, smarting from the iron shackles. He examined the stinging abrasions on each ankle before he pulled on socks and put on black navy regulation shoes. Pushing his hands through the white shirtsleeve cuffs and wool sleeves of the officer jacket, he winched from chafed wrists. He stared at the two stripes on the coat sleeve and knew who stood behind the mirror. *The sailor who spotted me at the hedge and reported me to superiors watched me change from the orange prison uniform.*

Five navy lieutenants entered the room and stood beside Hans. This stunned him. How had the colonel found five lookalikes for a lineup in less than two days? In Germany, doppelgangers, doubles, were omens of bad luck. The officers who looked like him gave him the creeps and heralded a military trial and death sentence. He and his men had POW rights. When he confessed, he thought it would be months before the OSS captured all his men and turned him and his men over to the army for trial.

Standing second from left in the lineup, Hans squared his shoulders but deferred snapping his heels, a characteristic of German military officers.

* * *

David Atherton scrutinized the six navy lieutenants. "Sir, the man second from the left is the officer I sighted at Middleton."

Surprised by David's quick assessment of the lineup, Ed Matthews asked David, "Are you sure?"

"Yes, sir."

The colonel thanked the young seaman. "My driver is waiting to take you to the airfield. You will be in the air in a few minutes." Atherton saluted the colonel and rushed out the door.

Ed beckoned his aide. "Return the prisoner to his cell and have the medics treat the prisoner's chafed ankles and wrists."

Pleased with the lineup results, Ed Matthews eased back into his office chair and dialed his boss's number.

"Mike, we'll wrap up Schiller's case in a few days. Defense lawyers may rip the lineup ID to pieces, but Atherton's identification of Schiller won't help a defense plea. I hope the lineup ID goes as well with Miss Reed."

"So do I. Defense lawyers will argue faulty memory to spring Schiller. If we have two IDs on Schiller, we'll have better support for the prosecutors seeking a conviction and death sentence."

"Mike, Hans Schiller is looking after his own neck. He's slick and bold and has the eyes of a fox. The camp prison barracks lack maximum security. The slightest slipup, Schiller will break out of the camp guardhouse and vanish."

"I know. We're working on housing Schiller in a windowless cell hidden from public scrutiny in the basement of OSS headquarters. The cell should be ready by the end of the week. Schedule transporting Schiller on Christmas Eve to DC."

"In the meantime, we'll double up guard on Schiller. Until we capture Bernard Koch, Schiller's right-hand man may be lurking about to spring our prisoner."

"You're right. Keep Schiller under heavy guard. Your leave won't begin until after Schiller is off your hands. After your leave, you return to Europe for counterintelligence duty."

"Our boys are taking a beating in Belgium. I'm anxious to get back over there."

"Enjoy your leave, Ed. You'll be behind enemy lines until Germany surrenders."

* * *

The colonel turned to Lieutenant Harris. "At a trivial blunder, Schiller could break out of prison. Station extra guards with the prisoner and remind them of standing orders. Absolute silence. No talking with the prisoner or talking among themselves."

"Yes, sir."

Ed looked at his watch. "Dean Wright should have arrived at the WACs' barracks at about ten o'clock. Send my driver to the barracks for her. The dean has to sign the payroll papers, and I want to speak with her before the next lineup. That's all for now."

* * *

Lieutenant Susan Sanders met Helen at the provost marshal's building at the camp entrance.

"Welcome to Camp Van Dorn, Dean Wright. A jeep is parked outside, and the driver will take us to Miss Reed's quarters."

The jeep driver maneuvered through a sea of tarpaper buildings before he stopped the vehicle at an army barracks labeled WAC Headquarters. Susan and Helen looked at a small aircraft climbing over the barracks.

"The airfield is in back of the WAC barracks, and we hear the planes landing and taking off," said Susan as they entered the barracks. "Lucinda's room is to the right."

They walked down the cheerless corridor to Lucinda's room, and Susan tapped on the door. "Lucinda, you have a visitor."

Lucinda opened the door and shrieked, "Dean Wright, I am so happy to see you! Colonel Matthews told me you were coming, but I didn't expect you so soon."

"I came last night so that I could visit with you this morning." Helen stared at the plain room and compared it to Lucinda's bright, eye-catching room at Middleton.

"Miss Reed, Colonel Matthews okayed sprucing up your room. Dean Wright is here to help you. Please call if I can assist you. I'll be in my office."

"Thank you," said Lucinda with a quiver in her voice. She closed the door behind Susan and burst into tears. "Dean Wright, I apologize to you. I knew better. I don't know what got into me, and I'm devastated. There is a verse in the Bible that says, 'Jesus wept.' I know He wept over me. My parents never will trust me again or get over the hurt," said Lucinda.

Helen handed her several tissues. "Dry your eyes, Lucinda."

She dabbed at her eyes and blew her nose. Helen waited a moment and said, "Lucinda, the board expelled you from Middleton."

"I knew they would, Dean Wright," said Lucinda, wiping her nose with another tissue.

Helen pursed her lips and said, "I'm here to help you, and we'll begin by perking up this room."

"I feel the way the room looks—miserable," said Lucinda.

"A pretty bedspread with a matching curtain for the window would help. What colors do you like?"

Lucinda's eyes brightened. "I like pink and green."

Looking about the room, Helen said, "I'll see what I can find." Then she turned and gazed at her former student. "Lucinda, we need to talk about your future. You know you can enroll in correspondence courses from other colleges."

"My dictionary, thesaurus, and everything I'd need is in my grandfather's car."

"That's not a problem for Colonel Matthews, and I'll ask him for a desk, chair, and bookcase. Finish the courses, and when the military releases you, I will do all that is possible for your enrollment in a university."

Lucinda cried again and said, "After letting you down, you'll help me finish college?"

"Certainly," said Helen. She handed her the box of tissues. "Lucinda, I am your friend and advisor. Colonel Matthews brought me down here to help you."

At the sound of the colonel's name, Lucinda twitched her nose and said, "Dean Wright, do you want to know what I believe happened?"

Puzzled, Helen's brow crinkled. "Well, uh, yes, I do," said Helen.

"I saw a spy at Middleton."

"Really?" said Helen with a raised eyebrow, but she turned her head at a knock on the door.

Susan entered and said, "Dean Wright, Colonel Matthews's aide called about your signature on official papers. A driver is on the way for you."

"Thank you, Lieutenant. I'll be back soon, Lucinda," said Helen.

CHAPTER 35

More for the Record

December 18, 1944

Lieutenant Harris buzzed the colonel. "Sir, Dean Wright signed the payroll papers."

"I'll be right there," said Ed. He jumped up and opened the door for Helen.

"Hello," he said and offered her a chair. "How'd the meeting with Miss Reed go?"

"Very well. Lucinda wasn't surprised by the board's decision, but her eyes spoke of the depths of shame, self-disappointment, and the misery for her parents."

"We've arranged for Miss Reed to see her mother this afternoon, and you and Lieutenant Sanders will go along for the visit.

"I'm glad you have the responsibility, not me, of informing Mrs. Reed that Middleton expelled Miss Reed. We cannot allow Miss Reed alone with anyone, not even her mother. Miss Reed is not permitted to talk about what happened at Middleton."

"Colonel, you need to know—"

"I thought we agreed on first names."

"But this morning, I speak on official business, Colonel. Lucinda theorized about the Middleton officer and told me he was a spy."

"Lucinda Reed doesn't know who she saw. For her safety, Miss Reed is confined to the barracks unless escorted by her guard, and Miss Reed's contacts are restricted to me, my aides, Lieutenant Sanders, and you, my official advisor and Miss Reed's mentor."

Ed sat back. "Helen, I know Miss Reed trusts you, and I trust you. The integrity of a case is always a priority. We don't jump to conclusions. We probe for facts. While we investigate, we isolate potential witnesses for their protection. Only you and Lieutenant Sanders are on the shortlist of those with whom Miss Reed can be left alone. Except for Sanders, Miss Reed must eat alone in her room. If you would like to eat lunch with her, we can arrange it."

"Yes, I would enjoy having lunch with her in her room. I eat alone most of the time. It's no fun. Before all of this happened, Lucinda ate at a table of twelve. I know Lucinda misses the lively dormitory life, and I understand the confinement for her safety."

Ed looked at Helen and said, "Miss Reed may very well disclose something with you she'd never divulge to me, but I have to weigh in. No talking with her about the Middleton officer. I have complete confidence in you, and I am indebted to your counseling."

"You have my word."

"I know, and I appreciate your being here. Miss Reed and Lieutenant Sanders will arrive momentarily for a meeting with me, and we scheduled the first hospital visit for you and Miss Reed with her mother. After the hospital visit, you're free to go to the hotel in my car."

"The ideas of decorating the room and studying for college credit lifted Lucinda's spirits. If it is okay with you, I'll shop for the decorating goodies on the way to the hotel."

"Of course. Direct the driver where you need to go. Keep receipts for reimbursement."

"Lucinda needs a desk and chair, a lamp, and a bookcase."

"We'll take care of the furniture for her room. I'll see you at dinner tonight, Helen," he said with a boyish grin.

Helen gave him a friendly smile. "Of course, Ed."

The colonel buzzed for his aide. "Dean Wright will wait in the officers' lounge until time for the hospital visit."

* * *

Hans waited with his guards in a room without a mirror. *If this weren't a windowless room, I'd overpower the guards and break out of here. Am I in a holding area? Did the colonel's lineup ID fail?* A second monkey performance before the mirror on the wall galled Hans, and he pantomimed an ape scratching his sides. Guards observed the prisoner's weird actions but stood by without facial expressions.

* * *

Colonel Matthews welcomed Lucinda Reed and Lieutenant Sanders into his office, served refreshments, and poured himself a cup of coffee. After sitting behind his desk, he said, "Miss Reed, I understand the US Army Air Force stationed Colonel Reed in the UK."

"Yes, sir. Daddy's in England."

"I regret your father is not here to explain the seriousness of your situation. No one can take his place in your life. In his absence, I must counsel you. First, you are not to discuss the officer and what happened at Middleton, the church, or the camp with anyone."

"I already have."

Ed cocked his head at her. "With whom?"

"Dean Wright."

"Keeping Dean Wright informed is my job, not yours." He shuffled the papers on his desk out of his way and folded his arms across his chest. "This afternoon, Dean Wright and Lieutenant Sanders will accompany you for a visit with your mother. Do not discuss what happened at Middleton with your mother."

"But the board expelled me."

Ed leaned forward, looked directly into Lucinda's eyes, and said, "Mrs. Reed feared you were in danger and collapsed. We don't want that to happen again, do we?"

"Oh, no. I don't want to hurt Mother."

"I'm sure of that. Do not discuss anything that's happened with your mother, Dean Wright, Lieutenant Sanders, or the WACs in your barracks.

"Your situation is complicated. Your mother deserves a professional account and answers about your problem. Let Dean Wright explain the board's decision. You may express the sorrow you feel about being expelled, but that is all.

"Navy Intelligence and Judiciary may question you, but for now, OSS overrides all other authority. Anytime you feel the need to talk, I'm here for you. Do you understand?"

"Yes, sir." Lucinda raised her hand.

"You want to talk to me now?"

"Yes, sir. I finished the semester, and school was out on Friday, but the college schedules the first semester's exams after the Christmas holidays. My parents paid for the semester. I want to take the exams the first week in January for the semester credit."

"I don't have any authority with the college. Dean Wright may be able to help you."

"Take the exams at Middleton?"

"No. If Middleton allows the examinations, you'll take the exams here. Talk to Dean Wright about the examinations."

"I will, but there is something else. Colonel, I need to write a letter to someone."

"Who?"

"Well, my ... well, David Atherton." At the name, Lieutenant Wiley's eyes popped wide open, and he dropped a pencil. Lieutenant Sanders reached out with her foot and rolled the pencil back to him.

"We censor mail at the camp, Miss Reed."

"Censor? You're kidding, sir?"

Astonished by Lucinda's cheeky reply, Susan put her hand on Lucinda's arm and said, "Lucinda, Colonel Matthews is—"

The colonel lifted a palm toward Susan and said, "Yes. We're at war. Personal mail coming and going out of the camp is censored."

"Sir, I'd rather not have what I write censored. If you'll let me write the letter, censoring it would be okay." Lieutenant Wiley rolled his eyes at Miss Reed's reply.

"We'll take care of the letter for you, and I have something for you to write. We need a written description of the officer you saw, what he said to you, and what you said to him. Will you type that up, sign it, and give it to Lieutenant Sanders?"

Lucinda sighed. *How many more times do I have to tell the colonel about the officer?* "I need a pen and paper for the letter and a typewriter," she murmured.

Ed swept his arm toward Susan. "Round up pens, onionskin paper, and an envelope for the letter, and a typewriter and typing paper for her report for me."

Susan nodded in acknowledgment.

"Miss Reed, the other purpose for our meeting deals with a lineup."

"I'm in prison?"

Unfazed by her question, Colonel Matthews said, "You are not in prison. You violated military orders, seldom justified, especially during war. We are holding you for your protection. We want you to view a lineup. We'll sit behind a two-way mirror and view suspects. If you recognize anyone, you tell me. Do you have any questions?"

"No, sir."

In the viewing room, the colonel said, "Lieutenant Harris, have each officer step forward, turn around, and step back in line. Miss Reed, look over the men and tell me if you see a man you recognize."

Lucinda gasped and took a deep breath at the sight of the officers on the other side of the glass.

"Take your time, Miss Reed."

Lucinda studied the officers. "All of the officers have blue eyes, sir," she said, but her eyes rested on one man. She moved closer to the colonel and lifted her finger toward the lineup. "The officer, second from the right, has the same steel-blue eyes and arrogance of the officer I saw at the hedge."

"Lieutenant Harris, prepare for the second lineup."

The guards took Schiller to the holding room and dressed him out in a Gilead choir robe, then returned him to the mirror room. Hans stood with his lookalikes before the mirror. Ed Matthews stood by Lucinda and watched the color drain from her face. "Miss Reed, can you identify anyone you see?"

"Yes, sir," she said with her face white as a ghost. "The man third from left is the man in mama's choir."

Ed glanced at his aide. "Recorded, Lieutenant Wiley?"

"Yes, sir."

"Lieutenant Harris, escort Miss Reed to my car for the hospital visit. After the visit, have the driver take the lieutenant and young lady to their barracks, and the dean wherever she wants to go. I'll wait for you in my office."

* * *

Hans squeezed his fists tight and held his head high, but shame flooded his soul. He took off the choir robe, and the muscles in his jaw twitched. *Who viewed me in the robe? The choirmaster? The Gilead pastor? Louisa Reed? Myrtle friends?*

* * *

Harris returned to the colonel's office, and the colonel said, "Be sure they're keeping the prisoner under double guard. Schiller confessed, but he is shrewd, and I have no doubts he has escape on his mind. We haven't captured his accomplice, Bernard Koch, and for all we know, Koch might try to help Schiller."

"Yes, sir. We'll double the guard detail."

"If you need me, I'll be at The Willow," said Ed.

CHAPTER 36

An Eventful Evening

Tuesday
December 19, 1944

E d and Helen walked into the hotel dining room together, and Penny ran to them. Ed picked his daughter up and walked over to Natalie and Thad.

"Thanks for waiting for us. We had a busy day."

"I let the children order," said Natalie.

"And here's their food," said Mettie. They're hungry, Colonel."

"Thad, say the blessing for us, and you and Penny may eat."

"I wanna eat, but I want Miss Helen to put me to bed."

"I'm hungry, Penny," said her father. "If you talk Dean Wright into helping you, you have to wait for us to eat."

"Miss Helen, will you put my pajamas on me?"

"Yes, Penny."

* * *

Helen walked with Ed to his room, helped Penny into her pajamas, tucked her into bed, and said good night to Thad. Ed kissed his son, and Thad whispered in his ear again, "I promise." Tucking the covers around Thad's shoulders, his father winked and said, "Go to sleep, son, and I'll walk Miss Helen to her room."

Thad closed his eyes, and Ed opened the door to Natalie's room. "They're asleep, Mother."

Ed took Helen's elbow and walked her into the hallway. "It's later tonight—no fire and chilly for the parlor. I'm trying to figure out where we can sit and talk."

"You know there's a fireplace with flames in the suite reserved for me."

Ed grinned. "Is that right? May I join you?"

"Please do." She held out the key and eyed him. "You saw the suite before I came."

"I did. The rooms appeared fitting for a dean of women."

"And far grander than I expected."

They entered the foyer of Helen's suite, and Ed took the light jacket from Helen's slender shoulders and hung it on a coat-tree. Helen motioned to the love seats and sat across from him.

He smiled at her choice. "Helen, you did say I could address you by your given name?"

"Yes, of course."

"How did the meeting with Mrs. Reed go?"

"Mrs. Reed and Lucinda were overjoyed at being together. My explanation about the expulsion seemed to satisfy Mrs. Reed. She understood Lucinda had not fallen into an endless black hole. Lucinda followed your orders and said very little."

"Good. We cannot allow mother and daughter alone, and it'll be tough keeping them apart. Miss Reed asked about taking examinations today. I told her to talk to you."

"Before I talk to Lucinda about exams, I'll have to clarify it with the college about my giving the exams here. I don't believe it will be a problem, but you never know. I may need your help convincing the board, Colonel."

"I thought we agreed on first names," he said, then sat beside her, leaned over, and kissed her cheek. "That's for Thad. This one is for me." He took Helen in his arms, gently kissed her cheek, and pressed his lips against hers.

Helen went limp in his arms. "Oh, not so fast."

I expected you to say that." Ed held her tighter and kissed her again.

She popped him lightly on the arm, and they laughed together. "We've only known each other a matter of hours," said Helen.

"We've known each other since we met on December 8, plus a couple of days here, sweetheart. I've wanted to kiss you since you fell for me at the depot."

"Fell for you?" asked Helen.

"I didn't want to get caught kissing the dean of women in public and put off kissing you until tonight. Two or three days can be a lifetime. We are singles, loners. We've both lost loved ones dearest to us. Tonight, we're caught up in war and a fragile time frame. Let's make the most of this week, Helen."

She tipped her head to the side, and her hair touched his cheek, tickling his heart.

"An interesting analysis. May I say one thing?"

"Yes."

"You're right. Let's make the most of the week."

He kissed her again and said, "I want to court you properly with candy, flowers, dinner dates, and fun togetherness. My time is not my own."

"I've felt courted since I fell into your arms," she said with crinkled eyes and a magical smile.

"Now, have you really? I didn't know that." The light in her eyes told him their feelings were mutual. She wanted to be in his arms. They'd both found love again. "We have three more evenings together before we part ways."

"Three days before I have to wash train smoke out of my hair and clothes again."

He nestled his face into the crook of her neck. "I smell perfume. What is it?"

"You're in intelligence. You tell me."

"That I am." Her coquettish smile fascinated him, and he said, "Don't make me sniff at perfume counters until I find my favorite scent. Tell you what. Your next bottle is on me." He released her and dug into his pocket. "The army issued me a car and driver. I don't need my car." He handed the car keys to her. "You buy the perfume and wrap it up pretty. After I come in from work tomorrow, I'll have a gift for you." He chuckled, stroking her hair. "And I'll take a whiff."

Laughing with him, Helen said, "You're impossible, Mr. Deep Pockets," and threw her arms about him. They kissed and whispered their joy of being together.

Someone rapped on the door and said, "Colonel, a call for you."

Ed jumped up and opened the door. The porter said. "Lieutenant Harris is on hall phone."

Ed ran to the phone. "Colonel, Schiller grabbed a guard's gun and got out of the guardhouse."

"I'll be right there." Ed ran by the porter, grabbed his car keys from Helen, and said, "An emergency."

CHAPTER 37

Lockdown

*E*d jumped into his car, raced to Camp Van Dorn, and flashed his ID to the armed sentry at the main entrance. The colonel's driver pulled up in a jeep and said, "Lieutenant Harris sent me for you, sir."

Colonel Matthews threw his car keys to the sentry, said, "Park it," and hopped into the army vehicle. "Where's Lieutenant Harris?"

"Harris went into the woods after the prisoner, sir. That's where we're headed." The driver hit the accelerator, drove onto the camp road bordered by a dense forest, and stopped before a battery of army trucks and soldiers. Lieutenant Wiley appeared and ran to their vehicle.

"What happened?" said the colonel.

"An unarmed medic with two guards went into Schiller's cell. When the medic leaned to examine the prisoner's wrists, Schiller threw the medic on the floor and grabbed a guard's gun. A second guard rammed his gun into the unarmed guard's back, and Schiller snatched up the medic. Schiller and the fake guard walked out of the cell with their captives. Schiller then shouted to his prison guards, "Throw your guns down. I shoot to kill." The pretend guard picked up the guns."

"Koch," said Ed.

"Outside, Schiller and his accomplice shoved the medic and unarmed guard into a jeep and sped off. Harris arrived and took off after them in his army vehicle. Harris was unarmed."

"We found both the jeep and the army vehicle here. Moments ago, we heard two shots in the forest. The camp is in lockdown."

The colonel picked up a machine gun and said to Wiley and a group of soldiers, "Quietly, follow me."

170

Walking among trees and listening, Ed and Wiley heard a twig snap. They eased toward the sound and found Harris facedown on the ground. He motioned for them to get down, pointed to a thicket, and mouthed, "He's alone in there."

Ed put a finger over his lips and motioned for soldiers to surround the area before he said, "Schiller, we have machine guns. Come out with your hands up."

"The medic and the guard are with me. Shoot," said Hans.

Ed turned his back on the thicket and shot, and bullets ricocheted off trees. "One more second, and you'll be history, Schiller."

"Ich komme als Kriegsgefangener heraus," shouted Schiller. ("I come out as a prisoner of war.")

"You're an escaped prisoner of war," said the colonel, "and in no position to negotiate. Time has run—"

Schiller thrashed out of the thick tree undergrowth and held his hands high. Harris searched Schiller, and Wiley plunged into the thick brush and combed for stolen pistols. Searching for the faked guard who was armed, soldiers found the medic and guard tied up and gagged. Matthews questioned them about the two shots heard earlier.

"The prisoner shot at a rattlesnake."

Ed shook his head and said, "Fearless Schiller?" He stomped back into the woods, searching for Bernard Koch. He radioed his agents. "The fake guard is out of the woods by now. Close all roads leading to the camp and beef up the search for Bernard Koch."

CHAPTER 38

Bracing for Battlefields

Wednesday
December 20, 1944

t daylight, Ed called Mike Ward. "We're searching for Bernard Koch, no doubt the armed guard who helped Schiller escape. Dogs picked up a scent that led south out of the camp, but the trail stopped at a creek.

"When Koch walked into the provost marshal's office, he had forged papers assigning him to Schiller's guardhouse. He got away, Mike. At least we have Schiller in chains."

"Koch's not exactly gone; he landed at the top of our most-wanted list. The provost marshal photographer snapped a picture for the guard badge, and for the first time, we have a description and a photo of Bernard Koch posted in every post office, sheriff's office, and military base in the US. Excellent work, Ed. I wasn't surprised you put your neck out to recapture Schiller, and your unarmed lieutenant deserves a captain's rank for going after them," said Mike.

"Frank Harris is a good man, Mike. He'll appreciate promotion."

"Transfer Schiller to Washington on Christmas Eve. We'll arrange for the move, but security for the flight is your call.

"Ed, your leave begins at midnight, December 24, and ends midnight, December 31.

We'll cut overseas orders for the men you select and meet with you and your team in DC on January 1, 1945, the day you fly out for Europe."

"We'll be battlefield ready, Mike,' said Ed. He cradled the phone receiver and summoned Lieutenant Harris.

"Congratulations, Captain. Orders were cut for a well-deserved promotion."

Surprised, Harris cocked his head. "Captain? For me?"

"Mike Ward initiated, and I endorsed the higher rank for you 1,000 percent. Unarmed, you followed Schiller and his guard friend, both armed, into the woods, the heroic action that led to Schiller's recapture."

"Sir, sometimes in this business you act before you think. I'm no hero."

"Your bravery imprisoned Schiller again," said Ed. He pinned the double bars, captain rank insignia, on Harris's shoulders.

"Thank you, Colonel Matthews."

"Captain Harris, let's check out the guardhouse security for our nimble prisoner."

* * *

Schiller heard a key rattle at his door, and Colonel Matthews and Frank Harris entered his cell. When the captain motioned Schiller to the far corner of his cell, he spotted the double bars on the officer's shoulders. Irked his escape promoted the lieutenant to captain, Schiller jutted his jaw out but lowered his chin and looked at his chains. The guard moved the steel bedstead beside the toilet, secured an end of a chain on the bed frame, and locked the opposite end of the chain around Schiller's ankle. The captain checked the chain for enough slack for toilet use, and without a word, he and the colonel left the cell.

Schiller lay on the bed with his feet near the porcelain, stretched out on the thin mattress. He said, "I'm officially a POW. You can't keep me in chains forever, Colonel."

* * *

Outside the prison barracks, Ed said grimly, "In chains, we knew Schiller wasn't going anywhere, but now, chained to the bedstead, he knows it.

CHAPTER 39

Critical Conferences

December 20, 1944

*S*atisfied with Schiller's maximum security at the camp but dismayed and fed up over Hans's escape and outwitting him again, Colonel Matthews shoved the breakfast tray aside. Hunching over his desk, he flipped open the daily intelligence report from Belgium.

Thunderstruck at the 99th Division casualty list, Ed murmured, "How many more men will lose their lives in this war?"

His overseas orders for counterintelligence work behind enemy lines meant a minimal chance of survival—for his children and Helen—and increased his despair. Giving the food tray another shove, he squelched thoughts of marriage. He and Helen had no future together.

A knock on his door interrupted his thoughts. "Dean Wright, sir."

"Thank you. Have the dean come in." Hiding his depression, Ed greeted Helen with a smile. "More forms for your signature." Handing Helen his pen, his hand brushed over hers. He gritted his teeth at the touch.

Helen signed the forms and gave several receipts to him. "Lucinda and I had a great morning decorating her room. Thank you for making it possible."

"Glad it helped. We scheduled the deposition for Thursday."

"The word scares me."

"Nothing frightening." He walked her to the door. "See you tonight," he said with a grin that covered his emotional upheaval and a weighted heart.

He'd looked forward to their after-dinner time together, but the last thing he wanted was to lead her on. After last night's coziness, how could he cut off a relationship with her? He thumbed through the slim phone book on his desk until his finger rested on the county courthouse number for a marriage license.

What if he married her and never returned? Shimmering with anger, he slammed the phone book shut. He had to break off what he'd started with Helen, no matter how much he loved her and wanted to marry her.

Brewing with disappointment, he muttered, "I've got to get out of here." He walked to the officer's club for coffee and found Lieutenant Wiley sitting alone at a table. "May I join you, Lieutenant?"

Wiley laughed. "You can. I'm waiting for someone."

Ed saw Susan Sanders enter the dining room, smiled, and said, "Is your guest walking in the door?"

Wiley's eyes lit up. "Yes, sir. You may join us, Colonel."

"No, no. All I want is a cup of coffee," Ed said, then turned to Susan. "Thank you for picking up lunch for Miss Reed every day."

"The club food is more inviting than the mess hall trays."

"I agree. See you all later."

Ed sat alone and watched the two young lieutenants talking and laughing. He'd never noticed them together, but obviously, they were in love. Since he'd lost Audrey, Natalie and her friends schemed to find young women for him to date, but no one interested him until Helen. His heart ached for the love and companionship with his newly found sweetheart, but he dreaded being with her tonight and telling her there was no future in their relationship. He arched his back and braced for overseas duty.

Ed picked up his car at the provost marshal's office and arrived at the hotel in time for a shave and shower before for dinner. Glancing out the window, he saw Helen and his mother walking with the children toward the hotel.

Penny and Thad dashed into the room and hugged him, bubbling over about their afternoon with their grandmother and Miss Helen. The warmth of their bodies boosted his spirits. Ed held onto each word, keepsakes in his heart for the rough days to come. Holding his dear ones close to him, he said, "It is about dinnertime. Wash your hands. Son, change your shirt. Penny, choose a dress for dinner."

With her father's help, Penny struggled into a shamrock-green dress and pinafore. Ed brushed through her red curls and hugged his daughter.

"Don't wrinkle my pinafore, Daddy." Fighting tears, her father swallowed and took a deep breath.

Natalie and Helen joined them in the dining room. Helen would never look more beautiful than tonight, and he prayed for strength to walk away from her. After a delicious dinner, his scheming mother winked at him and said to her grandchildren, "I have a surprise for you in my room. Are you ready for it?" Penny and Thad jumped up from the table.

"Wait a second. Sit down and—"

"May we be excused, Daddy?" they chorused.

"You may," he said.

Heartbroken he had to break up with Helen, Ed walked with the woman he loved to her room. "May I come in?"

"Please do. The porter has a nice fire going in the sitting room."

He sat on the love seat facing her and began his retreat. "Fate brought us together, and we are both mature adults. Do you agree?"

"If you are asking me if I agree we are mature, I don't. I don't feel old, only forever young."

Her sparkling eyes spun his heart, and he detested the words churning within him. "My point is we are old enough to know what we're doing. You came here on a professional assignment, and with the children, your role became personal. I don't want to lead you on."

She stared at him. "I don't understand."

"I don't want to lead you on and leave you, maybe never to come—"

She put a hand up. "Don't say it."

"I am going to say it. We both have lived with the pains of death—my wife and your fiancé. I cannot talk to you about my work. The risks are high. My professional association with you developed into an unexpected closeness. My leave will be up after Christmas, if not before. I want to be with you but not leave you hanging." Taking a deep breath, he said, "It's better to fade out of your life."

"That is selfish."

Edward looked at his thicket-scratched hands and broken fingernails. "You think so?" He didn't dare look her in the eye.

"I do. You made your decision without asking how I felt."

He pulled a hangnail loose and with downcast eyes said, "We're not on the same page. In one day, you became the center of my universe. Thad whispered, 'Kiss her for me.' I didn't need the prompting." Looking at the bewildered expression on her face and in her eyes, he said, "Helen, I want to shower you with throbbing kisses forever."

"You're showering me with gloom."

"I am going off to war. Initiating a romantic relationship was never fair to you."

Helen stood and put her hands on her hips. "I decide what is fair for me."

Shaking his head and raising his hand, Ed said, "Stop. Don't say anything you'll regret." Could he stop himself? "You charmed me beyond reason; the joy of being with you has been thrilling. I'm in love with you, Helen."

"Apparently, you're not."

"I don't have the right to court you, marry you. Orders for overseas duty have dashed my hope for a life together."

With fire in her eyes, Helen stepped toward him. "War doesn't dictate love."

"And marriage doesn't stop baby carriages. Racing off to war would not be fair to you."

"All is fair in love and war."

"That, my dear, is an option I plan to avoid. I can't marry you or ask you to wait for me until after the war."

"That's your thinking, not mine." She clasped her hands together in determination. "I wouldn't wait for you until after the war."

"I am glad you agree with me."

"But I don't agree with you. Love doesn't vanish," she said, fluttering her hand in the air. Love lives in your heart," she said with her hand over her heart. "War doesn't have anything to do with love and holy matrimony created by God."

Either she didn't hear him or didn't want to listen to what he was saying. "But war has to do with tragedy, death."

"Not always. A man and a woman in love always know one dies before the other. Only God knows when either of us will die."

"I don't want to put you through any heartbreak."

"You have already. My heart is in splinters, and so am I. Colonel, you'll leave here with me ripped to pieces and not pick up a single throbbing bit of me."

Ed's heart twisted. He had to face reality, but he came out with, "Wisdom tells me to stop now, but my heart ..."

"Yield to your heart, Ed, and I'll follow mine."

"You mean that, don't you?"

"Yes, I do."

"Stop crying. I want to ask you something." Ed caressed her arm and dropped to his knees. "Helen, will you marry me before I ship out?"

"Yes, yes," she said with tears streaming down her face. "I love you with all of my heart."

Ed grinned and looked at the floor. "I thought your heart was in pieces."

"Not anymore." Helen laughed. "You put me together again."

Ed cradled her in his arms. "I never dreamed you'd fall apart over me. Helen, you never know about orders. The army could ship me out tomorrow, but I'll run our marriage by the military, and I doubt that'll be a problem. I'm on duty through Christmas Eve, and my leave begins on December 25. How about a Christmas Day wedding?'

"Perfect."

"All we need is a license and a minister." He kissed her and said, "There is no waiting period in Mississippi."

"You checked that out!"

"I did. I couldn't bear the thought of losing you."

"Really? That's hard to believe after what you put me through, you rascal."

"Meet me on the steps of the county courthouse tomorrow afternoon at one o'clock. They issue marriage licenses in Room 301."

"We need a place for the wedding."

"Well, where is home?"

"The Middleton campus, but the chapel is closed, and the chaplain out for the holidays."

"How about my house in Jackson?"

"Your house is fine with me, but don't you think that is a little sudden for Natalie?"

"Are you kidding?" He rubbed her fingers with his. "Mother loved you the moment she saw you. If it is okay with you, I'll ask the pastor of our church to marry us."

"I love the idea of your pastor marrying us."

"Great. One more problem. Until my orders came through, I'd planned on driving mother and the children back to Jackson. Would you mind driving them home, Helen?"

"Of course not."

He handed her the car keys and his book of civilian gas stamps. "Use the car while you're here, but save enough gas stamps for the Jackson trip."

"Don't worry," she said.

"Except for the deposition, you're off professional expenses and payroll. I settled with Mrs. Willow for a couple of extra days for your suite."

"A car, gas stamps, perfume, and the suite just for me?"

"And everything else for the rest of your life, my love."

"Wait until you get the bills for our wedding at your house, dearest one."

"All we need at the house is a minister."

"Oh, no, more. We'll have a unique and special—"

Helen stopped talking and listened. "Someone's knocking, Ed."

"Not again," he said, walking to the door.

"Call on the hall phone, sir."

Apprehensive, Ed picked up the dangling receiver on The Willow wall phone and heard, "Colonel Matthews."

"Mike?"

"Yes, Ed. German troops and tanks surround the 101st Division battalions at Bastogne. US soldiers captured two German officers on the perimeter of the siege. Before anyone could interrogate the enemy officers, MPs loaded them on a plane with other German prisoners bound for US POW camps. Tonight the two German officers arrived at Camp Clinton, and your interrogation expertise is sorely needed. An army vehicle will arrive in minutes for you. How long will it take to drive from your location to the camp?"

"Two and a half hours."

"Tell the driver to step on it. The two officers' brains are filled with the latest German directives, and tank and troop numbers are crucial intelligence for the survival of US soldiers caught up in the Ardennes Offensive."

"Casualty lists coming out of Belgium hit me in the gut, Mike. I'm eager to wring every detail from two Germans fresh off the battlefield."

"Go for it, Colonel."

Ed sprinted to his room and grabbed an overnight bag (he kept packed) and his briefcase. Tiptoeing out of the room, he cast a forlorn look at his sleeping children. He knocked softly and opened the door to Helen's suite. Helen hurried to him.

"Another emergency," he said. Helen held out his car keys. "Keep the keys. An army vehicle is on the way for me. All you need to tell my mother is I'm at work. Hopefully, see you tomorrow."

Giving Helen a quick kiss, he ran out of the Willow front door and saw an army vehicle pull into the hotel drive. "Don't cut the motor. Drive north on Highway 24 toward Jackson. I'll let you know where to turn."

Ed opened the briefcase, took out a flashlight, and checked over all the daily intelligence reports received since the Ardennes Offensive launched on December 16. On December 17, at Malmedy, Germans captured and executed eighty-four US soldiers, and the nineteenth, six thousand Allied troops surrendered to Germans at Schnee Eiffel. Today, a German Panzer Corps encircled US troops at Bastogne. He studied a Belgium map carefully. *I'm ready for two German officer POWs, who'll live as well at Camp Clinton as any US officer lives on any base.*

CHAPTER 40

Happy Plans

Thursday
December 21, 1944

By daylight, Ed Matthews had interrogated the German officer POWs, squeezed crucial information from them, and relayed vital intelligence to US commanders on the north and south defense lines in Belgium.

Midmorning, Ed arrived at the temporary camp office and finalized Schiller's relocation to DC with Frank Harris.

"Your leave and mine begin on Monday, Christmas Day. Mike Ward scheduled the prisoner handover on a turnaround flight. We'll be back here no later than midnight, the twenty-fourth.

"The transfer plane needs to be on the ground here Saturday, long enough to check out seating for the prisoner, those of us on the security detail, and other measures for a safe flight. There'll be no food service or restroom trips for the prisoner during the flight."

"After Tuesday night's escape, I agree," said Harris.

"Confirm on-the-ground time for the plane, and order food service only for the return trip."

"Speaking of food, Colonel, you haven't eaten breakfast, and you've been up all night. Get some sleep. I'll cover for you."

"And I take you up on your offer. After I finish off this breakfast tray, I'll go to my quarters and sleep. I need to run by the commander's office and keep a one o'clock appointment in town, but I'll be in my quarters for the rest of the afternoon. Would you mind giving me a wake-up call around five?"

"No, sir. You need to sleep."

"Thanks, Frank."

* * *

Ed called Helen. "Hi, sweetheart. The commander congratulated me, waived a waiting period, and completed military papers for our marriage. At one o'clock, I'll see you at the courthouse. I'm on duty this afternoon, but while I sleep off the yawns in my quarters, Frank Harris agreed to cover for me."

"I don't want you to yawn while I go over our wedding plans, and the children wouldn't let you get a wink of sleep here. I'll bring sandwiches to the courthouse."

"You know how to keep me happy. See you at one."

* * *

Refreshed after catching up on his sleep, Ed greeted Helen, his mother, and children at the hotel. The children hugged him and said, "You're marrying Miss Helen!"

"That's what I heard," said Ed, and he kissed Helen, much to the children's delight.

Helen beamed and said, "We're leaving in the morning for Jackson to get ready for the wedding."

"That I haven't heard," said Ed. "I'm counting on you staying until Saturday."

"Edward, you and Helen are having a catered wedding with all the frills," said his mother. "We can't stay here until Saturday."

Amazed, Ed looked at Helen. "After dinner, we need to talk alone." Helen laughed and patted him on the back.

After dinner, Ed said, "Mother, do you have any surprises for the children tonight?"

"I do. Come, children. We're filling gauzy bags with birdseed to throw at a bride and groom."

"Daddy and Miss Helen?" chirped Penny.

"That's right," said Ed, and he pecked his daughter on the cheek and hugged Thad.

In Helen's suite, Ed stood by the fireplace and said, "Let's have it.

What's Mother planning? We're having a simple wedding Christmas morning?"

"Yes. We are having a simple wedding, but it's Christmas. Natalie decorated the house and tree after Thanksgiving, and the children are excited about Christmas. We have to have the Christmas tree for the children first."

"They'll be up before daylight. We'll marry and be out of the house by eight o'clock."

"We're not marrying at daylight and leaving for our honeymoon at eight in the morning. We'll have a tree and eat. Natalie couldn't talk Primo's into catering the dinner, but they agreed to prepare a Christmas brunch with turkey."

"You're holding up marrying me for a turkey?"

"Ed, I agreed in a rush to marry you, but we can't rush the ceremony and take Christmas Day away from the children and Natalie. It's the tree, a Christmas brunch with turkey, our wedding at one o'clock, followed by a reception for guests."

"A reception? What guests? It's just us."

"Dora Farr."

"Who's she?"

"Middleton's retired dean of women and my best friend."

"Is she married?"

"No, she's a widow."

"Recently?"

"No." Helen looked away from him. "I'll tell you about Dora another time. Not now. Lucinda Reed brought us together, and I want to invite her to the wedding."

"Miss Reed is more or less under house arrest, Helen."

"I know you can arrange it. Lucinda is not a criminal."

"I'll have to think about Miss Reed. Brunch will hold up the ceremony a couple of hours, but I know a couple of lieutenants who like to eat, and under my orders could help in the kitchen, serve, and speed up the process. I'll agree to a tree, brunch, and the ceremony but no reception."

"Natalie ordered a beautiful wedding cake for a reception."

More disagreement. But Ed didn't mind. Helen had agreed to marry him. He kissed Helen's forehead.

"The children adore you, and you've thought of everything to make Thad and Penny a part of our wedding. I wish I had the time to shop with

Thad for his first pair of long pants, but you and Natalie will have to do that for me."

Ed pulled Helen to him. "All I've thought about is making you my wife, but you are taking on my children. Our marriage is your first, sweetheart. I want you to have a baby and experience the fullness of motherhood. Are you okay with becoming a mother quickly?"

Helen pulled out of his arms, sat back on the couch with a gasp, and said, "Ed."

He held up his hands in defense. "Just wanted you to know. We have two children, and I hope we'll have more." He winked with a grin. "And I reserve the right to say how many." A coy smile turned her lips upward, and Helen blushed. His bride's shyness caught him unaware, and he knew he'd always be her only love.

CHAPTER 41

A Mission Accomplished

Christmas Week, 1944

On the twenty-fourth of December, Hans Schiller lay on his prison cot, and Christmas Eve traditions in his homeland drifted through his mind. He breathed deeply and remembered the scent of Christmas candles, infused with cinnamon, cloves, and pine, and aromas of goose, apple and sausage stuffing, potato dumplings, and Stollen and gingerbread cookies. The Christmas smells tortured him. Who would have thought in those carefree, happy days he'd ever lie in chains by a smelly toilet on Christmas Eve?

Unexpected movements and the rattle of keys outside his cell brought Hans to his feet, and the colonel, captain, and guards paraded through the door. In seconds, the guards blindfolded him, put him in shackles, and hooded him. He'd thought he'd see fewer guards over Christmas and an opportunity to escape.

Chained to the bedframe for five miserable days, he found the cold outside air pleasurable. Voiceless guards helped him in and out of a vehicle and onto a flat lift that carried him up in the air, and he knew! *They're flying me out of here.* Were they turning him over for the military trial?

Inside the plane, someone removed the hood from his head but not the blindfold. Earplugs muffled sounds, but Hans heard the engines roaring and felt the plane taking off. *What kind of American aircraft am I in?* Pushing around in the seat, he guessed he was in the middle of three flight seats on a passenger plane. *A Boeing 307?* More comfortable than he'd been since his capture, Hans slept until the plane jolted on landing. How long had he been in the air?

A hood went over Hans's face, and guards ushered him out of the plane onto a freight lift, easily identified by the downward motion. They then walked him to an automobile. The car stopped and started at intervals, he assumed for traffic lights. Earplugs muffled more sounds, but he heard car horns. Hans calculated a thirty-minute drive from an airport until the vehicle ride ended. Guards helped him out of the car, and frigid air penetrated his clothing.

In an overheated building, sweat ran down Schiller's hooded face and body. Shuffled into an elevator, he sensed movement to a lower level and the presence of people other than his guards. He counted the down beeps until the elevator stopped, and his guards walked him out of the elevator and moved him along a corridor A noise sounded like a cell door clank, and a guard removed all restraints from him. In a small room with bars on one side and three tiled walls, he saw a showerhead but no faucets. A guard said, "Remove your clothes and throw them on the floor."

A second guard handed him a bar of Lifebuoy, and a guard standing outside the shower stall turned water faucets. Warm water ran over his head and body. He'd bathed two or three times a day until captured, and he hadn't had a shower since the breakout. The water pouring over his sweaty, smelly body enlivened him. He lathered and scrubbed until the guard said, "Rinse off and step out of the shower," and handed him a towel, underwear, and an orange jumper suit stamped "Prisoner," front and back. After Hans dressed, a guard shaved him, and two guards led him to a cell with a steel washbasin and toilet attached to a concrete wall. His eyes rested on his bed, and he felt a thicker mattress than the thin pad he'd slept on in the guardhouse. A fresh paint smell told him his quarters were new and clean.

Two men in civilian clothes entered the cell, read off Hans's POW rights, and advised, "As a prisoner of war, you are allowed books and paper and pen for a letter to a family member."

The civilians walked out of the cell, and a guard brought in a food tray and a clipboard with pen and paper. Hans ignored the two guards who stood outside his cell, grabbed the clipboard, and wrote the first letter to his mother since he boarded the U-boat in Norway.

"Heiligabend 1944, Liebe Mutter und Schwester. Ich bin OK.

Lieben. Hans." ("Christmas Eve, 1944, Dear Mother and Sister, I'm okay. Love, Hans.")

* * *

Mike Ward and his aide took an elevator from the basement to an upper floor of OSS headquarters and Mike's office where Ed Matthews and Frank Harris waited. Ward walked into his office, wiped his brow, and said, "Whew. I know you're as relieved as I am that Schiller arrived without incident. Thanks to you two."

"Thanks for transferring Schiller, Mike. A load off our shoulders."

"We worked a week fortifying the cell space in the basement for our versatile prisoner.

The guards got Schiller showered and shaved, and we read him his POW rights. We'll hold Schiller until we complete our search for his accomplices or release him for military trial. The prisoner could be a guest of OSS for months.

"A librarian will keep Schiller supplied with books, copyrighted before the war, and as a prisoner of war, he'll be allowed to write letters to his family. I doubt Schiller will write a single noteworthy detail, but he might try to code a message. We'll censor every line he writes.

"Ed, thank you for capturing Schiller and eliminating SS sabotage and chaos on the home front. Frank, thanks to you, Schiller dwells behind bars again. You've both received merit leaves beginning at midnight. A driver is waiting with Lieutenant Wiley to take you to your plane. Ed, I know what you've planned for the holidays. Congratulations."

Puzzled, Harris frowned.

Ed smiled. "Thanks, Mike. We'll be back here New Year's Day."

CHAPTER 42

Second Time Around

Christmas Eve, 1944

E d leaned back and looked out the plane window. He'd halfway promised Helen that Miss Reed would attend their wedding, but he debated the risk of checking Lucinda Reed out of the WAC barracks for their marriage ceremony.

Schiller's chances of escaping from the fortified OSS cell were one in ten million, but until OSS captured Bernie Koch, Miss Reed was in danger. After grueling minutes of debate with himself, Ed made his decision. Christmas Day, OSS's Lieutenant Sanders and Lieutenant Wiley, her guards, would accompany the young lady to his home for the wedding.

He looked to his left and spoke to Captain Harris. "Christmas Day, Lieutenant Wiley and Sanders will accompany Miss Reed to my home, and you are invited to come too, Harris."

"Thank you, sir. I have plans."

"I know, but I wanted you to know and extend an invitation for our Christmas Day wedding at my home."

"Wedding? That's a surprise. If I didn't have plans to be with my girlfriend in St. Louis, I'd be there."

"You've shared your St. Louis plans for Christmas, and I understand." The colonel nodded at Lieutenant Wiley, who sat several rows ahead of them. "Miss Reed's guards, Lieutenants Sanders and Wiley, are on duty. I've noticed Lieutenant Wiley enjoys eating with Lieutenant Sanders."

"Phil's enamored with Lieutenant Sanders," said Harris with a laugh.

"All Wiley and Sanders need to know … they're coming to my house for dinner, and no one is to tell Miss Reed where she is going or who she will see."

"I understand. Wiley and I rode in my car to the airport. When we get back to camp, I'll let him know he's expected at your house tomorrow, Colonel."

"Good. Order Wiley to leave the camp with Lieutenant Sanders and Miss Reed no later than 0900 hours. Return hour is indefinite."

* * *

Christmas morning, Susan Sanders checked Lucinda out of the barracks and met Lieutenant Wiley at the colonel's office.

"Shall we blindfold Miss Reed, Lieutenant Sanders?" said Lieutenant Wiley mischievously.

"No, that isn't necessary," said Susan. "We don't want you to be disappointed, Miss Reed. You won't be with your family or Santa Claus, but we do have a Christmas surprise for you."

Lieutenant Wiley opened the sedan's back door for them and jumped into the driver's seat of the military sedan. "Merry Christmas. Sit back and enjoy our drive north."

They arrived in Jackson, and Wiley braked the car in front of an attractive, two-story, Georgian colonial style home and said, "This is it."

Lucinda walked down the brick walkway with the lieutenants and said, "What a beautiful home." Wiley and Susan agreed with Susan, and he tapped a brass ring on the home's black-paneled front door. In seconds, the door opened. Lucinda's mouth sprung open with shock, and she shrieked, "Colonel Matthews!"

"Welcome, Miss Reed. Come in and meet my mother, Natalie Matthews, and my children, Thad and Penny."

Wide-eyed and grinning at the unexpected guests, Thad and Penny stepped from behind their father and shook hands with Lucinda, Susan, and Wiley.

"Welcome to our home," Natalie said and took their coats.

"We have a Christmas surprise for you, Miss Reed," said Colonel Matthews and led them into his living room. Lucinda's mouth popped open again when she saw Dean Farr and Dean Wright standing in front of a glowing fireplace.

Helen Wright put her arm around Lucinda. "We invited you for Christmas brunch with us and to our wedding this afternoon."

Lucinda beamed. "Oh my goodness! You are marrying Colonel Matthews? I would never have guessed."

Penny jumped and clapped. "I'm getting a new mommy."

"That's right," the colonel said. The dean glowed as she watched Ed lift his daughter into his arms and spin her around.

Lucinda hugged Helen Wright and said, "Thank you for inviting me."

Helen hugged her young friend. "Without you, we wouldn't be having a wedding."

Phil Wiley stepped forward. "And are we surprised," he said and tapped Susan on the shoulder. "We came expecting Christmas dinner. You sure know how to keep a secret, sir." He shook the colonel's hand and stopped short of saying, "But then you are an OSS agent," and instead said, "Congratulations, sir."

"We wanted those we are with every day to be our wedding guests," said the colonel. At Ed's comment, Helen raised her eyebrows and with sparkling eyes smiled at him. Ed ignored his bride's silent teasing and introduced the lieutenants and Miss Reed to Dr. Richard Wells and his wife, Madeline. "Reverend Wells will marry us at one o'clock this afternoon."

Helen laughed and said, "*Sometime* this afternoon, my dear."

Natalie returned from hanging up their coats, and Susan said, "Mrs. Matthews, the Christmas tree is beautiful. I know you have been busy with Christmas bells tinkling and wedding bells ringing. What can we do to help?"

"Yes. What can we do?" Lucinda said.

"Thank you. We decorated the tree after Thanksgiving, but things became chaotic around here with Edward and Helen's last-minute decision to marry, and then my son disappeared and missed out on all the work." She laughed. "But Edward did show up in time for the midnight Christmas Eve service at our church."

Susan cut her eyes at Phil, who promised to attend Christmas Eve services at camp with her but never showed up. Phil ignored her piercing stare. After transporting Schiller to Washington, he, the colonel, and Captain Harris arrived back in Jackson at 10:30 p.m. He and Harris drove 138 miles to the camp, too late to attend Christmas Eve services with Susan. Phil gave a slight bow in Natalie's direction. "Lieutenant Sanders, Miss Reed, and I volunteer for whatever and wherever you can use us."

Natalie beamed. "I can use your help in the kitchen. Follow me, Lieutenant Wiley."

"Mrs. Matthews, since this is a family affair, we are Phil, Susan, and Lucinda, at your service."

"Thanks, Phil. We're keeping the food warm in the oven. I would appreciate your lifting out the turkey."

Phil lifted the heavy, perfectly baked bird onto a large oval platter, and at Natalie's direction, he placed a beautifully baked ham on a round serving platter.

Thad and Penny had cut out Christmas bells for name cards. Helen printed everyone's names and put them on the table. Susan and Lucinda placed warm casseroles and hot rolls on a beautifully set dining room table and placed a Christmas coconut cake and a multilayered caramel cake on the sideboard. Natalie handed Penny a silver Christmas bell to ring and announced, "Dinner is ready."

With everyone seated, Dr. Wells read the event of Jesus's birth from the book of Luke. Ed followed the scripture reading with a blessing of thanksgiving for family and food. The colonel masterfully carved the turkey, and Phil stood by with plates to pass the delicious turkey slices to everyone. Mindful of his military orders for Europe and combat zones with field entrées of cold meat and beans, Ed filled his plate with second helpings of turkey and sweet potatoes topped with marshmallows and encouraged others to do so.

After dinner, Phil, Susan, and Lucinda shooed everyone out of the kitchen, washed dishes, and prepared the dining room for the wedding reception.

While the bride and groom and his children dressed for the wedding, Madeline Wells played lively Christmas music on Natalie's baby grand and stroked the keyboard with love songs selected by Helen and Ed. When Natalie signaled, Madeline's fingers coached out more mellow music with George Frederic Handel's "Water Music Suite" and Claude Debussy's "Claire de Lune."

Midafternoon, Colonel Edward Matthews, resplendent in an army dress uniform, entered the living room with his young son, who was dressed in a navy blue suit with a bow tie, firsts for him. Thad carried a white satin ring pillow with ribbons holding the bride's platinum wedding band. Father and son, their eyes glued on the staircase, stood in front of the fireplace banked with baskets of red roses. Phil Wiley escorted

Natalie, dressed in a green, silk, tea-length frock, to her favored high-back Chippendale chair by the fireplace. Madeline began playing Wagner's "Bridal Chorus," the classic here-comes-the-bride melody.

At the top of the stairs, Helen appeared in a long, lily-white, silk wedding gown with a small swish of a train and high-heel, white, satin pumps. She wore an emerald and diamond necklace and earrings, Natalie's gifts to her son for his bride, and carried a large white Bible with pages edged in gold and topped with a bouquet of white roses and streaming ribbons.

In a soft white, ankle-length dress with a pleated green moiré sash about her waist, white stockings, and red Mary Jane shoes, Penny stood beside the bride.

Ed watched in awe as Helen descended the staircase. Penny's red curls bounced with each step, and she scattered white, silk rose petals before the bride until they reached the wedding altar.

The minister began the ceremony. "We gather here today, in the presence of God, to unite this man, Edward Matthews, and this woman, Helen Wright, in holy matrimony. Let us pray."

Friends and family bowed their heads. Ed winked at Penny, and she waved back. His heart flooded with the warmth of a wife and a complete family again.

"Almighty and blessed Father, you brought Ed and Helen together by Thy providence. We ask Thee to sanctify them by Thy Holy Spirit and enrich them and their children, Thad and Penny, with Thy grace. In the name of Christ, we pray. Amen."

Ed took Helen's hands in his and repeated his vows after the pastor. The risks involved in his overseas assignment rang in Ed's ears, and he hesitated before he added, "Until death do us part." The perils he faced vanished when Helen looked into his eyes and repeated her vows in a clear, confident voice.

After their vows of love and faithfulness to each other, the minister asked the children for the wedding bands. Thad untied the slim platinum ring from the pillow and handed it to his father. Ed placed the wedding band on Helen's slender finger next to a beautiful diamond engagement ring. Natalie gave her engagement ring to Ed for the bride. Holding her hand in his, Ed said, "Helen, I give you this wedding ring, a symbol of my love and fidelity, in the name of the Father, and of the Son, and the Holy Spirit."

Dora took the Bible bouquet from Helen and placed a wide platinum band in Penny's palm. Penny grasped the ring in her fist and moved close to Helen, who took the ring from the petite hand, repeated the wedding vows, and placed the symbol of her love on Ed's ring finger. Ed tightly gripped Helen's hand as they faced the minister, and he said, "I now pronounce you man and wife."

Ed hugged and gently kissed Helen, and they both kissed Thad and Penny. Ed chuckled when Thad pulled Helen down to his level and kissed her for the first time. Penny beamed with joy and hung onto Helen until Natalie gently separated her granddaughter from the bride. Undaunted, Penny said, "I love you, Miss Helen-mm-mm. What do I call you now?"

Everyone smiled but Helen, who looked at Penny's solemn little face. "Penny, you may call me whatever you wish."

"Mom, mommy?" said Penny.

"I like mom," said Thad.

"I like either or both," said Helen, and she felt Ed's tight grip on her hand again. Thad tugged Helen down to his face and boldly kissed her a second time.

Ed whispered in Helen's ear, "My competition."

"But he doesn't have your grip," Helen said softly to her husband.

Penny grabbed her father around his knees. He swept her off the floor and kissed her. "Now I have two sweethearts." Penny puckered up her little lips in a tight cupid's bow and kissed him on his cheek.

In the dining room, Dora served ginger ale and lime sherbet punch from a silver bowl, and Susan kept trays filled with finger sandwiches. Natalie surprised the newly married couple with a traditional, white, two-tiered wedding cake topped with orchids.

The children giggled as their father put the cake in Helen's mouth.

"Daddy, you're making a mess." Helen laughed, wiped her mouth, and slipped upstairs to change for their honeymoon.

In the upstairs hallway, Helen laid the Bible bouquet on a table. The night before, Ed wrote his children's mother's name, Audrey Matthews, and her birth and death dates on the Death page in the wedding Bible. "Sweetheart, would you like to write John Carlton's name with Audrey's on the Death page?"

"I'm touched by your thoughtfulness. I wrote John's name in my Bible when he died." She caressed the Bible before them. "The Bible is for us, our children, our grandchildren, our great-grandchildren."

Dressed in a Christmas-red going-away suit, Helen stood at the top of stairs, turned, and tossed the flower bouquet over her shoulder. Penny and Lucinda scrambled to catch it, but Susan jumped high and grabbed the bouquet, much to Phil Wiley's delight.

Ed took the Bible from his wife, gripped her hand, and called the children to his side.

"This is our family Bible. We will read it together every night before we go to bed."

"Tonight, before we go to bed?" said Penny.

Phil and Susan stifled their amusement. Ed said, "Well, not tonight. Let's sit on the sofa and read the Bible together now." Natalie motioned for wedding guests to gather around her son, his bride, and the children.

Ed turned to the dedication page, wrote "The Matthews' Family Bible, Christmas Day 1944," and explained the importance of entering family names in the Bible, God's holy Word. Thumbing to the page titled "Births," he said and entered Thad and Penny's names and birth dates. On the page titled Marriages, he wrote "Edward Clayton Matthews and Helen Wright Matthews, December 25, 1944." He did not open the Bible to the page titled Deaths.

"Each day we read the Bible, we will write the date in the margin by the scripture read." He read Mark 10:16 and wrote "12/25/44" by the verse.

Thad put his finger on the date. "Daddy read that again."

Ed read, "'Jesus took the children up in his arms, put his hand on each of them, and blessed them.'" Penny reached over and patted the page.

Ed looked into Helen's moist eyes. He closed the Bible, handed it to his mother, and put his arms around his children. "When I'm not here, your mother or grandmother will read and write the date in our family Bible.

Helen hugged her mother-in-law and touched the diamond engagement ring, the necklace at her throat, and her earrings. She said, "Natalie, you shouldn't have."

Natalie hugged Helen. "Ed's grandmother Matthews gave Ed's father the necklace, earrings, and ring to give to me. It's time to pass them on."

"Thank you, Natalie. I love you dearly, and thank you for our beautiful wedding."

Ed patted his mother's shoulder and said, "We will be back Friday. My leave is over on New Year's Eve, and I leave early Monday, New Year's Day."

Natalie frowned. "That soon?"

"Yes." He slipped Helen's coat over her shoulders, put his arm about his bride's waist, and said, "Well, folks, we are off."

Natalie held out a basket of seed bags and eyed her grandchildren. "Do not throw these until the bride and groom are out the door. Please!"

* * *

Christmas Day, a guard pushed a tray through Hans's cell door. The food looked better than usual but was not up to Hans's taste for German food at Christmas. Cramming the traditional American fare into his mouth, he chewed on the turkey and swallowed it in disgust.

In Germany, on Heiligabend, Holy Evening, he'd attended church services with his family. After the Christmas Eve service, Weihnachtsmann (the American Santa) appeared in their home. The jolly guy always asked if Hans had been good or bad. Regardless of the answer, Weihnachtsmann left gifts for him under the Weihnachtsbaum.

Hans's mouth watered remembering Weihnachtstag dinners—goose, fondues with meats, powdered-sugar-covered bread filled with fruit and nuts, and all the desserts one desired.

In the war, he'd fought for what he thought was the good of Germany, but victory hadn't happened yet. He pushed the food tray away, sighed, sat on the bed, and scratched twenty-five in the cement on his wall calendar. Germany would never win the war, and he'd spent his last Christmas Day on Earth eating a wretched American Christmas dinner.

He rolled his tongue around in his mouth and imagined the rich flavor of goose.

CHAPTER 43

Duty Calls

December 29, 1944

Ed and Helen returned from their honeymoon early Friday and enjoyed lunch with Natalie, Thad, and Penny. After lunch, Ed said to the children, "We'll be in my office for about twenty minutes. Get your coats out and be ready for a ride to Middleton with us."

"We're going to your office before we go to Middleton?" asked Helen.

"Yes."

Taking Helen by the elbow, he ushered her into his home office, opened a cabinet door, and spun the dial on a hidden safe.

Ed removed a stack of papers and placed them on his desk for Helen to read. "I deploy on New Year's Day." He opened his safe and said, "Here is my safe combination." He put his military service records and survivor documents on his desk and handed her his will and a lawyer's card.

Helen picked up the lawyer's card and said, "Can't we do this later?"

"No, sweetheart. I've changed everything here from my mother's name to yours, and I want to go over the papers with you."

"Ed, I don't need to see this."

"I think you do, darling. You have to know what, where, and why about my affairs." Since the day he'd proposed to Helen, he'd never mentioned the risk of his assignments, but the reality of his possible death never left him. He'd be working behind enemy lines, with a 100 hundred percent opportunity for being killed or, worse, maimed for life. The enemy executed OSS agents. Helen had to know where to find papers she'd need in the event of his death.

"Why don't we go over all this stuff when you return, honey? I don't want to look at the papers now."

"Helen, you have to know about these things. We'll put the safe combo in the top drawer of my desk and lock it. Everything else will be in the safe." Helen took the safe combination and dropped it into the desk drawer. Ed locked the drawer and handed the key to his bride.

Helen had no idea what he faced, and her stoic reserve amazed him. He took the woman he loved in his arms.

"Helen ..."

Helen placed a slender finger on his lips. "Ed, this is morbid stuff and talk. Only God knows our fate. I'm ready for our trip to Middleton."

* * *

Ed and Helen sat on the sofa in her apartment, and Ed explained to Thad and Penny, "When my leave is over, you'll live with your grandmother on school days. After school is out on Friday afternoon, Grandmother will drive you to Middleton. You'll spend the weekends with your mother at Adalia Hall, go to Sunday school and church with her, and late Sunday afternoon, she'll drive you back to your grandmother's for the school week."

Thad frowned for the first time since the wedding.

"What's the problem?" Ed kneeled, putting himself on Thad's level.

"I don't like staying here with girls."

Ed chuckled. "You will not be the only boy at Adalia on the weekends. Other boys will be here. Put on your jacket."

Ed turned to Helen. "Thad and I are going up to the Middleton campus. We'll be back shortly."

"I think that's a fabulous idea." Penny stepped in between them. "I want to go too."

"No, this is a guys' trip. You stay here with ..."

"Mommy?"

"That's right. You stay here with Mom," her father said, smiling at Helen.

On the Middleton campus, Ed walked into the navy headquarters. The door sentry saluted. Ed observed Thad's interest in the salute and said, "We'd like to see the commander."

"Yes, sir." The sentry picked up the phone on his desk and said, "Colonel Matthews to see Commander Kemp."

"The commander will see you immediately, Colonel Matthews. I'll walk with you down the hall." At the commander's door, the sentry gave Ed a snappy salute and returned to the front office.

The commander opened the door and said, "Colonel Matthews. I'm happy to meet you. Come in. Who do you have with you?"

"My son. Thad, this is Commander Kemp." Thad saluted the commander, who returned the salute. " It's a pleasure to meet you, Commander," said Ed.

"Colonel Matthews, I heard about your marriage to Dean Wright … uh, Mrs. Matthews. Please sit down." Ed and Thad sat in the two chairs positioned across the desk.

"We surprised ourselves, Commander. I was a widower with two children, and Helen agreed to take us on. I'm on active duty. Helen plans to finish the school year, and Thad and Penny will spend weekends with her at Adalia Hall. Thad does not like the idea of Adalia Hall and girls. I brought him to the main campus to assure him boys live at Middleton College, and he'll see them when he is with Helen on weekends."

The commander grinned. "Son, our sailors flock to the girls' campus on Saturday and Sunday afternoons, and town women throw a big party every weekend at Adalia Hall." He buzzed his aide. "Bring two passes in here for me to sign. Colonel, visit any of the navy buildings you choose. Feel free to speak with any of the sailors. You'll find off duty seamen hanging out in the ROTC recreation rooms."

The aide entered with the passes, and the commander signed them and handed them to Ed.

"Thank you, Commander. Problem solved. We'll visit a bit with your sailors," Ed said. He pushed his chair back to leave the commander's office.

Commander Kemp raised his hand. "Hold on a second, Colonel. This area is new to my wife. It would be good for her to meet Mrs. Matthews. How about dinner sometime this week?"

"We would like that. I'm under overseas orders, and my leave is up New Year's Eve. We'll be at home this evening if you care to drop by the house. I would like very much to meet Mrs. Kemp. While I'm away, it will be nice for Helen to know another military wife."

"Yes, Dolores will love meeting Dean Wright. We don't have plans this evening. I'll give Delores a ring now. We'll come for a short visit and not take family time away from you."

"We'll be looking for you." Ed wrote down his address and phone number for the commander, and he and Thad left for a visit with sailors.

Ed walked Thad into an ROTC recreation room, introduced his young son to several seamen, and voiced Thad's concern about spending weekends at Adalia Hall with the Dean Wright, now Mrs. Matthews.

"Don't worry, bubba. We'll see you at Adalia," the sailors promised Thad.

Thad's face brightened when the sailors "inducted" him into the navy and presented a navy cap to him.

On the drive back to Adalia Hall, Ed's heart twitched over the baby-face seamen he and Thad met. Trained to fight the Japanese at sea and on islands across the vast Pacific, many of the sailors, less than twenty years old, would never return to their homes and loved ones.

He accompanied the 99th to Belgium. While he met, courted, and married Helen and enjoyed Christmas with his family, young 99th soldiers died. His heart broke over the Checkerboards' casualty numbers in the ongoing Battle of the Bulge intelligence reports.

The advanced 63rd task force arrived in Marseilles on December 8, 1944, and now engaged in the enemy in battles. In hours, he shipped out with the last of 63rd Division's young men. Ed glanced at his six-year-old son proudly wearing the navy cap and agonized over the young V-12 sailors shipping out soon to the Pacific.

Helen greeted Ed with a kiss and hugged Thad. She tugged at his hat and said, "Hi, sailor."

"Mom, sailors promised me we could play football."

"I'm glad, son. You'll have fun at Adalia Hall, Thad," said Helen.

Penny bounced into Helen's living room. "Can I play football with them?"

"Girls don't play football, Penny," said her brother.

"Penny will find plenty to do with girls on the weekends, Thad," said Helen.

"Honey, while I'm away, you'll have a military wife for a friend. Commander Kemp and his wife, Dolores, are dropping by the house for a little while tonight," said Ed.

"That's very nice," said Helen, and she hung her husband's coat in the closet. "I see the ROTC commander in staff meetings and will enjoy knowing his wife."

Driving home, Ed listened to his family. Heaviness invaded his soul, but quoting a well-known commercial slogan, he said, "How about some 'We eat it with a smile' Seale-Lily ice cream on the way home?"

The children's faces lit up, and they pulled on their coats and jumped in the car. For the moment, their smiling faces lifted Ed's spirits.

* * *

At midnight, Hans scratched through December 31, 1944, on his wall calendar. New Year's Eve. He was alive, and the year 1944 was never incised on his tombstone.

Almost a week had passed since he arrived at the new location in a city. But what city?

Except for the first day, no one had spoken to the saboteur, and the constant silence and information blackout tortured him. Aimless without German espionage activity, he faced a military trial and death sentence. Physically and mentally let down, the German agent paced his cell and muttered, "I have to die true to myself, and exercise is the answer."

Hans lowered his body until his chest neared the floor. With his hands on the cold concrete, he pushed up and down, up and down, again and again.

Straightening and bending his arms, he repeated the exercise until he collapsed on the floor. The push-ups accomplished two objectives. He maintained the highest possible fitness level, and exercise kept his mind off of an inevitable death sentence.

Exhausted from exercising, Hans snuggled under the blanket covering his cell bed and considered how, in 1940, Germany annexed the city of Colmar in the French Alsace-Lorraine. Colmar was connected by canal to the Rhine. In his mind, he speculated on Allied and Axis battles during the months of heavy snowfall.

In the severe winter months, German quartermasters issued soldiers gray parkas, trousers, mittens, and headcovers with liners made of cotton or satin. German officers wore stunning, long, black, leather coats as well as their greatcoats for protection from bitter cold air. He fell asleep and dreamed of warmly dressed German soldiers, holed up in strategic, fortified positions in the Vosges Mountains, defeating inadequately dressed Allied troops.

Part III

*O*n the back of Satan's neck is a
nail scarred footprint.
—C. S. Lewis

* * *

CHAPTER 44

Tough Days

January 1945

Every day in West River, Texas, was a busy one for Dr. David Atherton, a general surgeon, but especially in January, with patients who put off appointments until after the Christmas and New Year holidays.

After the last patient left on January 10, a Thursday, Margaret Baker, Dr. Atherton's nurse, locked the office door and went to the file room to pull patient files for the next day's work. Loud banging on the front door startled her, and she dropped the stack of records she held in the crook of her arm. The noise on the door turned into a pounding. Margaret ran her fingers through her white hair. Another patient? The tired doctor was never too worn out to see a patient. She stepped over the files scattered on the floor, walked into the reception room, and opened the door.

Joe Upton, the Western Union dispatcher, held a telegram close to his chest. "This is for Doc Dave. Is he in?"

"Yes," she said. "Dr. Atherton is in his office. You may take it into him, Joe."

The dispatcher held the telegram out to her. "I don't want to take it to him, Margaret."

Margaret's knees buckled, and her breath caught in her throat. "David?"

Joe handed the telegram to her. "Lock this door and take the telegram to Doc." With a shaky hand, Margaret held the telegram close to her heart and hesitated before she knocked on Dr. Atherton's office door. When the doctor didn't respond, she eased the door open.

Dr. Atherton was on the phone, motioned to a chair beside his desk, and silently lipped to Margaret, "I'll be a moment," before he said, "Aaron, call for an appointment tomorrow," and then hung up the phone.

"Margaret, you are pale. It's been a long day. Are you all right?"

"Doctor, I'm so sorry. Joe, the Western Union dispatcher, delivered this telegram." With a quivering hand, she held out the yellow envelope.

The doctor stood, threw his shoulders back, and took the telegram from her. She turned to go, and the doctor said, "Don't go, Margaret." He picked up a caduceus-handle letter opener, inserted the blade into the envelope, removed a half sheet of yellow paper, and read.

We regret your son, Ensign David Bennett Atherton, is missing in action. We'll report more information when available. US Navy Chaplain, Kenneth Goodman.

Dr. Atherton slumped in his chair and handed Margaret the message. "Oh, no. Missing in action? Not David. Not David, Dr. Atherton."

The doctor walked around the desk, patted his nurse on the shoulder, and took the telegram from her. "Please call our pastor and have him meet me at the house. I'll go home and tell his mother."

Crying, Margaret said, "Doctor, I will be on call to help you in any way I can."

"I know you will, and thank you. Close the office for now. We'll get through this tonight. I have surgery in the morning. We'll see patients in the office tomorrow afternoon."

Dr. Atherton had practiced general surgery in the town for twenty-two years. As he drove home through familiar streets, the day of David's birth and his son's first words, first bicycle ride, and first day in school replayed in his mind. He found comfort in remembering the day David committed his life to Jesus. "Please, God, in Your will, I pray David is not suffering. Gather him in Your arms and give him strength, in Jesus's name. Amen."

The doctor turned into his driveway, drove to the back of the house, and stopped the car.

Molly opened the kitchen door. "You're home early," she said with a hug and a kiss.

The scent of something sweet baking in the oven struck his nostrils. "Something smells delicious."

"I'm baking cookies for David. I'll package his favorite sweets and mail them when we hear from him."

The doctor took his wife in his arms and kissed her. "Darling, we received a telegram. David is missing at sea."

Molly shook her head. "Oh, no, he couldn't be," she said, biting her lip. "David was home a few days ago. He called us from San Francisco." Molly sobbed and slipped down in her husband's arms. Dave Atherton tightened his arms around his wife, and they clung to each other.

Clenching his jaw, Dave led his wife into their bedroom, and they dropped on their knees by their bed, where he prayed, "Our gracious, heavenly Father, we know You hold our boy in the palm of Your hand. We ask for Your strength to fill his body and soul. In Your will, we pray for David's rescue and healing. We pray for every sailor injured on his ship and for those caring for them. Be with the loved ones of other sailors missing or killed in action. Fill us with Your strength and draw us closer to Thee. Our son put his faith and trust in Thee. If it is in Your will, bring our boy home to us. In Jesus's name. Amen." Her husband wiped tears from Molly's cheeks.

"Sweetheart, the pastor and friends will be coming. We've stood by our friends when they received telegrams. We must be strong and trust in God's will."

A knock sounded at the front door.

CHAPTER 45

Fierce Fighting

Mid-January 1945

arly New Year's Day, Ed Matthews said goodbye to his family, flew to Washington, DC, for orders, and deployed for Europe with the last of the 63rd Division troops.

On January 14, 1945, at a dock in Marseille, France, an OSS Special Services agent greeted Ed. "Colonel Matthews, you are reassigned to the 63rd's 254th Regiment, embedded with the US Third Division.

"German pilots dropped pamphlets, addressed to the 'Blood and Fire' 254th Regiment, printed with a list of captured 254th men. The message read, 'Have you ever asked yourselves why you are risking lives?'

"The propaganda tactic enraged the 254th Regiment. Despite the bitter mountain weather, the 254th patrols pushed behind enemy lines, but the patrols need a battle-tested counterintelligence agent. Tonight, you will parachute behind enemy lines and help the 254th patrols wipe out the enemy stronghold."

"The sooner, the better."

"We'll drive to the airport. In my jeep is a bag filled with heavy clothing for you to change into on the plane."

"You guys in Special Services think of everything," said Ed.

"We do our best."

* * *

Ed's parachute billowed out above him, and harsh north winds penetrated the combat pants and sweaters layered under his field jacket. He landed, buried the parachute, pulled on a snow cape, and plodded through snow. Uncomfortable shoepacs with felt innersoles and ski socks kept his feet from freezing.

Ed moved easier in the knee-deep snow than the 254th infantrymen weighted down with heavy gear, rifles, and ammunition. Alerted by fallen 254th patrolmen's bodies, Ed and the men with him avoided land mines. Struggling behind Ed, soldiers waited until their leader spotted German fortifications. Working together, they won out over German troops on Hill 216, Jebsheim, Bois de la Hardt, and moved eastward until the Colmar Pocket crumbled.

In February, Ed reported to field headquarters, where he received orders for the most dangerous assignment he'd ever undertaken and a letter waiting for him from Helen.

> My dearest,
>
> We miss you very much and want you to know things are going well with us. Thad and Penny adapted well to their new schedule and continue to stay with Natalie on school nights. I pick them up after school on Friday, and they stay with me until after the Sunday tea. Thad has excellent school grades, looks forward to weekends at Adalia Hall, and brings along the football you gave him for Christmas. Saturdays, he plays football in the dorm's side yard with the ROTC sailors you and he met at Middleton. Girls in the dorm taught Penny cheers. She has become an official cheerleader at the football skirmishes. We attend Sunday school at First Baptist, and Thad sits with his sailor friends during the worship service. At Sunday-afternoon tea, sailors sit Penny on top of the parlor piano, and Penny sings her heart out, and Thad belts out, "Don't sit under the apple tree, with anyone else but me," with the sailors and Adalia girls. I hate to tell you, but I believe Thad will always be a navy man. The weekend rests work well for Natalie, and she looks great. Lieutenant Wiley asked Susan Sanders to marry him and shipped out. For now, Susan stays busy with Lucinda. We keep up with the war news, and the Allies appear on the road to victory. We

look forward to your homecoming, no one more than I, the luckiest girl in the world. I yearn to wrap my arms about you and tell you how very much I love you. You are in my heart and prayers every second.

With all my love, Helen

Ed pulled out two pieces of paper enclosed with Helen's letter. Penny's drawing of male stick figures playing football included an offside girl stick figure with red hair in a skirt. The artist signed the picture with a heart.

The letter from Thad brought tears to his eyes. "Dear Daddy. I miss you. I play football with sailors. We sing songs. Love, Thad." Ed could not believe his son was old enough to write letters.

Pulling two sheets of crumpled paper from his back pocket, he split the one sheet into halves. On one half, he drew a tall, skirted stick figure and boy and girl stick figures. He signed his letter to Penny with a male stick figure and a heart.

On the other half sheet of the paper, he printed a note to Thad: "Mom wrote about your excellent grades and how well you play football. I am proud of you. While I am away, you are the man of the house. Take care of Penny, Mom, and Grandmother. I love you. Dad."

Ed swiped his wet eyes with the back of his hand. He did not have the heart to write, "Thad, when I get home, we will play football, fish, and hunt."

Ed stared at the second crumpled sheet of paper, the last of his stationery, and wrote his heart out to Helen.

My darling wife,

We married without my telling you over and over how much I love you. In our wedding ceremony, Rev. Wells said what I knew from the moment I saw you, "Divine Providence brought us together." You have enriched my life and the lives of our children beyond my capacity to understand. You are always in my heart. The agony of leaving you blesses me each day with the hope the war will end soon. You are my life, my all. At night, I long to hold you in my arms and hear your sweet voice whisper, "I love

you." Remember, the Lord brought us together. Nothing
is impossible for Him. I pray we'll be together again soon.

With unbearable pain and all my love, Ed

He wanted to write more, but the uncertainties he faced forced him to
fold the letter and slip the drawing for Penny and the note to Thad in the
envelope addressed to Helen. Whirlybird sounds alerted him. He shoved
the envelope into his coat pocket and ran toward a landing helicopter.

"Climb aboard, Colonel!"

"Thanks for the lift."

"We will land in about thirty minutes. A plane is waiting for you."

"Thanks. Where is the best place at headquarters to drop off outgoing
mail?"

"In the hangar office. I have a letter to mail. If you have a letter ready,
I can mail it with mine."

"I do have something ready to mail." He fished the envelope from his
pocket and handed it to the pilot.

"Before I check in, I'll mail my letter and yours, Colonel. A letter I
mailed to my wife arrived in two weeks."

"That's good. I hope the letter to my wife gets there that fast."

"Sir, I see your plane on the ground, revved up and ready to take off. I'll
put this chopper down as close to your aircraft as I can get it," said the pilot.

Ed ran to the waiting plane and closed the door behind him. Sometimes
on night flights, they dropped supplies to freedom fighters. Unfortunately,
that wasn't why he jumped tonight. He would parachute alone into enemy
territory, destroy anything he found that was useful to the enemy, and
uncover intelligence necessary for impending Allied troop advancement.

A sergeant on board handed him a change of clothes and a package
sealed in plastic and said, "I'll take your uniform, sir."

The pilot announced, "We're near the target, Colonel."

The sergeant tapped him on the shoulder and opened the plane door.
The frigid wind struck Ed in the face. Shivering, he leaped from the aircraft
into the moonless night and plummeted through icy air until he pulled the
ripcord. The open parachute slowed his descent.

OSS command reasoned a small field where a battle raged a few days
ago the safest spot for landing. The stench of death hit Ed's nostrils before
he touched down at the edge of battle-scarred trees. He landed, stood,

rolled up his chute, and, dragging it behind him, crawled on his stomach over dead bodies. At the tree line, he listened for sounds in the forest. He heard only the wind. Animals had departed, and birds had ceased singing during the battle.

Easing his hand forward, he touched a rigid body and rolled over it. Unfastening a short- handle shovel at his side, Ed dug into the ground and buried the chute. After kicking and shoveling dirt into the hole, he covered the parachute grave with the stiff body.

Rigor mortis had not set in on several bodies he rolled over. Hoping he could render first aid, he felt for a pulse and flashed a penlight into the blue or brown eyes of each limp body. He found no heartbeats and gently closed the eyelids on two American bodies and one German. If he'd parachuted sooner, would the unattended men have lived? Nauseated but trained to operate in all environments, he edged toward the tree line.

He crawled by German trenches and concrete bunkers, optimistic the enemy had departed the battlefield with the forest animals. When he reached the edge of the forest, he pounded on the hard earth with the shovel until he dug into softer ground. Peeling off all of his clothes, Ed dropped them into the burrowed hole and masked the gap with loose dirt and frozen vegetation. Shuddering, he pulled on clean underclothes, wool pants, a shirt, and a jacket over his quivering body and silently thanked whoever packed the warm clothes, thick knee socks, and stout boots that fit perfectly. Disguised as a German farmer, he walked downhill and heard cattle lowing in the distance. Squatting behind a tree, he pulled out a silk map from a side pocket, located the German town he sought, and hiked toward it.

As secretly as Hans Schiller entered the US for sabotage and destruction, Ed Matthews slipped into Germany for a different mission— protect soldiers and civilians from a crazed government at war.

Calm nerves, good physical condition, and the ability to act under pressure served the colonel well. He was not a brave man, but the American counterintelligence agent's fundamental moral values far outweighed Germany's saboteurs. He'd never kill an innocent German citizen.

* * *

During the bitter days of 1945, winter weather canceled out exercising in the prison yard, and the prison librarian sent a full cart of books, including a Gideon Bible, to Hans's cell. Hans exercised, updated his wall calendar, and, chagrined by the lack of war news, read out-of-date magazines and newspapers. He thumbed through the Bible and began reading scripture, once familiar to him.

On the first cold and sunny February day, guards led the prisoner to the outside exercise area. Hans smirked at the enclosure, a steel cage. "No chance for escape from a coop strong enough to repel zoo elephants," he mumbled.

From the exercise yard, Hans looked up at a multistoried building and watched an American flag flap freely in the breeze. He said in disgust, "I spend my last days on Earth caged like an animal."

CHAPTER 46

More Fighting and Mourning

March–April 1945

Ed gathered counterintelligence for American soldiers fighting their way from France into Germany. In early April, he parachuted behind lines into the Ruhr area. The Allies captured 317 German soldiers along with twenty-four generals, but the ten thousand American casualties, killed or missing, depressed the US agent. He read, over and over, the last lines in his latest letter from Helen.

> Darling, we miss you and pray for you and the end of the war. When you come home, you'll be surprised how much Thad and Penny have grown. We're blessed to have each other and will be together soon. And the peace of God, which passeth all understanding, shall keep your heart and mind through Christ Jesus (Philippians 4:7). Love always, Helen.

The scripture lifted his faith in God, boosted his spirits, and sharpened his mind for counterintelligence. Ed folded and slipped the letter inside a holder made from a scrap of rubber that he kept over his heart.

* * *

Cut off from the outside world, Hans Schiller depended on his cement-wall calendar. At daybreak, he pulled another button off his shirt and scratched "12" on his April calendar. Hans worried prison laundry guards would discover the missing buttons and tip off the OSS. But they hadn't yet, so he continued to keep track of days spent in the dreary cell. What could they do to him anyway? Nothing would be worse than facing the firing squad. Hans looked at the sun's reflection on the wall and presumed battles continued in Europe and the Pacific.

In the exercise yard, he heard church bells tolling and noticed the American flag flew at half-mast. Guards continued not to speak to him or speak to one another in his presence. Not knowing why the American flag was at half-staff puzzled him. He scratched his head before squatting to do more push-ups. Exercise kept him sane.

The following week, exercising outside, he watched the wind-whipped stars-and-stripes flag still flying at half-staff. Why? He surmised the longer the flag flew at half-staff, the more sorrowful the event. Had the Allies lost the war?

* * *

On the morning of April 12, 1945, WACs gathered in Lucinda's room, listening to radio reports. President Roosevelt's death. That evening, Americans sorrowfully celebrated the White House inauguration of Harry S. Truman, president and commander in chief of the United States military forces.

Later in April, WACs gathered again in Lucinda's room to hear radio reports. A firing squad executed Mussolini, the Italian Fascist Party leader, and his mistress and in dishonor hung them upside down in the village square. Lucinda didn't understand why people beat their hanging bodies with hammers. On the last day of April, Lucinda and Susan listened to radio reports. Hitler and his wife committed suicide with cyanide, and in his last moments, Hitler shot himself.

The end of the war in Europe was uppermost in people's minds. Lucinda constantly prayed for David's safety in the Pacific.

CHAPTER 47

V-E Day

May 1945

*A*mericans celebrated Germany's unconditional surrender on May 7, and throughout the day, WACs screamed and danced about the barracks, but Lucinda Reed didn't join in the merriment.

Casting her eyes on the American flag, Lucinda grieved for David. The flag continued to fly at half-mast, the full thirty days in respect and mourning of President Roosevelt. Emotionally, Lucinda was at half-mast. She grieved over David. She went to her room and closed the door but could not block out the sound of horns honking and church bells ringing out Allied victory.

Sunny May days boosted Lucinda's thoughts of David, alive and well. She'd finished the last correspondence lesson, and on her way to give the lesson to Susan, she met the lieutenant in the hall.

"Hi!" said Susan with sparkling eyes and a wide smile. "I have wonderful news for you. With the war over Europe over, the OSS released you. Pack up! You are going home!"

Lucinda stared at Susan and then burst into tears, tears she'd held back over David. Her guardian-turned-friend laughed. "Dry your tears. I have more great news. Phil works with Colonel Matthews in Germany, and orders came through assigning me to the colonel. Phil and I will be married overseas. I wish you could be a bridesmaid at our wedding."

Lucinda dried her cheeks on her sleeve and took her friend's hands. "Oh, Susan. I am so happy for you."

Susan danced Lucinda around in a circle. "I am delirious! I can't wait to see Phil."

* * *

Tom Cunningham met Lucinda at camp headquarters and drove her home. Happy to see her grandfather, Lucinda was quieter than usual. At home, she followed Colonel Matthews's orders and didn't say a word about her top secret encounter with Jim Waters.

Louisa Reed prepared for Lucinda's homecoming and cooked her daughter's favorite foods. At the dinner table, Lucinda found it hard to relax and celebrate the reunion with her family, but she helped her mother wash, dry, and put the dishes away. They hung their aprons on pegs inside the pantry door, and Lucinda said, "Mother, it's been a long day for me. I'm going to my room."

Louisa followed Lucinda to her room and said, "What is the matter, darling?"

Lucinda fell in her mother's arms and burst into tears. "Oh, Mother, I've wanted to talk to you. I'm in love with David Atherton, a sailor I met at Middleton. I don't even know where he is. I know David loves me, but he hasn't written one word since before he shipped out. The war is over for soldiers in Europe but not for sailors in the Pacific. After David received his commission, I believe he shipped out to the Pacific. I am so worried." Tears streamed down Lucinda's face, and she sat on her bed. Louisa handed Lucinda a box of Kleenex.

"Not knowing about David is enough to make you sick. No wonder you feel wretched. I know the feeling, with your father stationed in England and flying in planes over Germany.

"I thought Daddy trained pilots. I didn't know he flew over Germany. Is he okay?"

"Yes, he's fine and on his way home. He didn't want his children to know he flew with young pilots on dangerous missions.

"You've been under a burden, not knowing about David. But that doesn't have to be. Remember, God is everywhere, and He is with David wherever he is. We'll pray for David together, and I'll ask my WMU group to pray for David as well."

"Mother, I missed you. Telling you about David and knowing you are praying for him makes me feel better."

"I missed you, Lucinda, more than you know, but your grandfather assured me you were in good hands."

"I can't talk about it, Mother."

"I know, and I'll never ask."

"I'm glad you understand."

"Mail came for you today, dear. It's on your dresser." Lucinda jumped up, grabbed a manila envelope, and pulled out two letters.

"Letters from David?"

Lucinda sighed. "No. I wish. One letter is from the university, and the other is from Dean Wright, uh, Matthews. Did you know Dean Wright married the colonel we met at the camp? I attended their wedding."

"You did? How wonderful they're together."

Lucinda opened the letter from the university. Her eyes widened. "Good news, Mom. The university accepted my application for admission for the fall semester. Dean Matthews recommended me."

"I'm not surprised, Lucinda. Your father and grandfather will be pleased. See you in the morning, love." Louisa kissed Lucinda's forehead.

"Thank you, Mother, and thanks for the wonderful dinner."

Lucinda tossed the acceptance letter aside and ripped open Dean Matthews's envelope.

Dear Lucinda,

Colonel Matthews reports for work in Washington, but he has a postwar assignment in Europe. Colonel Matthews is taking the children and me with him to Europe. While the colonel is in Washington, I'll be home and will shop and pack for an indefinite stay in London. I'll need a babysitter off and on during the summer, and you are the first person who came to my mind. Before we leave for England, we plan a week at the beach. Will you join us in Jackson and at the beach to help with the children? Please drop me a note with your answer, and we will arrange for you to come to Jackson.

Sincerely,
Helen Matthews

Lucinda jumped from her bed, threw her door open, and yelled, "Mother!" Louisa rushed to her room, and Lucinda shoved the letter into her hands. "Read this!"

* * *

Louisa drove Lucinda to McComb for a direct train to Jackson, and Dean Matthews, Thad, and Penny met her at the train station.

"Lucinda!" Penny squealed and ran to her. Thad followed and extended his hand for a manly handshake.

"Hello, Lucinda. Are you hungry? We're on our way to Primo's for lunch."

"My favorite restaurant," said Lucinda, and they walked to the ground level of the station and the car.

Dean Matthews placed the luggage in the trunk. "When Colonel Matthews returns from Washington, we have reservations at the Edgewater Gulf Hotel in Biloxi. The hotel has air-conditioning."

"Air-conditioning? I am surprised. I haven't been to many air-conditioned buildings."

"Yes, isn't that wonderful? There is a glass-enclosed pool for Penny, who sunburns easily. The grounds are beautiful. The children can play, and you can relax while watching them. There are also tennis courts and a golf course. Ed plans to give me golf lessons. We'll see how that goes," said Helen, laughing. " Ed wants to go deep-sea fishing one day and eat out at seafood restaurants. We need you for babysitting, and we'll pay you for helping us out."

"Dean Matthews, you do not have to pay me to stay in a luxury hotel and help you in Jackson."

"Of course, we will pay you, Lucinda. It is unthinkable any other way. And I am no longer the dean of women. We need to settle on an appropriate name for you to call me." Helen shifted the car into gear.

Lucinda frowned. "I am not sure what else to call you. Maybe Dean Matthews?"

Helen shook her head with a smirk then laughed. "No, goodness. Not that."

"How about Miss Helen?"

"Let's go with Miss Helen for now. Someday, when you are older, we will be Lucinda and Helen to each other."

Lucinda liked that idea, amazed the most formidable people in her life turned out to be the most personable. Helen Matthews's kindness overwhelmed her, and Lucinda thanked the Lord for blessing her with the tremendous woman who one day would be her friend Helen.

CHAPTER 48

Summertime

July–August 1945

Enrolled in the first summer semester at the university, Lucinda studied and listened to news of the battles in the Pacific and heard Premier Suzuki announce Japan would keep fighting and *never* accept unconditional surrender. Her heart yearned to know about David. Was the love of her life alive and well?

In late July, Lucinda joined the Matthews in Biloxi and took Thad and Penny to the beach early in the morning and late in the evening. After a week of fun, the family returned home.

While Miss Helen and the colonel shopped in Jackson for their stay in London, Lucinda babysat the children. On August 6, the Matthews rushed in from shopping, and Ed said, "An American B-29 dropped an atomic bomb in Japan."

Ed turned on the radio, and they heard, "Seventy to eighty thousand people killed in Hiroshima."

For three days, Ed hovered over the radio and said, "Thousands will die from the radiation of the world's first nuclear bomb. Why hasn't Japan surrendered?"

On August 9, the Matthews and Lucinda heard another radio report, "The US dropped a more powerful atomic bomb on Nagasaki."

"Japan will unconditionally surrender now," the colonel said and drew his eyebrows together. "A quick end to the war spares the lives of thousands of Americans and Japanese on Japan's mainland. Let us thank God the war is over. Thad, hand me the family Bible."

Ed turned to Psalm 66, verse 7, and read: "'He ruleth by his power for ever; his eyes behold the nations: let not the rebellious exalt themselves. Selah.'

"Children, many men and women and little children died and suffered in this war. The war began because evil men wanted power and glory for themselves. Power and glory belong only to God, our Father, His Son, and the Holy Spirit. Let us pray."

* * *

In Japan, Emperor Hirohito announced unconditional surrender on August 15. Two days later, Natalie and Lucinda said goodbye to the Matthews at the train station in Jackson.

With her short legs, Penny attempted to board the train. Lucinda laughed, and Ed reached to pick her up, but Penny said, "I can do it by myself." Her father shook his head and stood behind his daughter. Half-crawling, Penny boarded the train by herself.

The children blew kisses from a compartment window. To their delight, Lucinda caught the kisses midair and blew them back. Wiping a tear away, she whispered, "The war's over. Will I hear from David?"

As the train rolled away, Natalie said, "I am happy for Edward and Helen, but it is hard to see my babies leave. I will be by myself in that big house. Any weekend you can get away from your studies, please come and stay with me."

Lucinda locked her arm into the weeping grandmother's and said, "Thank you. It's three hundred miles from Myrtle to the university; Jackson is nearer for me. I'd love visiting you."

* * *

A military plane assigned to OSS landed at an airbase near London, taxied down the long runway, and stopped before US Army Air Force headquarters. Ed Matthews and his family exited the plane and walked to a car waiting for them.

"Colonel Matthews," the driver said as he saluted and presented his credentials, "I'm your OSS chauffeur in London."

Ed returned his salute. "Thank you, Sergeant. Here are the directions. If you have any questions, please ask my wife. She is familiar with London." Helen opened her purse and handed Ed the keys to her house in London.

Ed turned in the front seat and said, "Thad and Penny, we're on our way to your mom's house, where we'll live in London. During the week, I'll be at work across the English Channel, but most weekends I'll be in London with you."

"Why can't we go with you?" Thad wrinkled his eyebrows.

"France and Germany have food and housing shortages. I'll live in army barracks. And you don't speak French and German. You'll speak English at school in London.

"On the way to your mother's house, we'll pass by buildings bombed during the war. Don't be frightened. The war is over, and London is safe," he said, reassuring Thad and Penny. "Mom's house escaped severe damage when German planes and rockets hit London. Britain rations food, but you won't go hungry."

"Will you eat where you are?" said Penny.

Ed laughed. "Yes, Penny. I will eat but no sweets."

Penny pouted. "Where we live, can we eat ice cream and cake?"

"Not often, but you will eat well. During the war, the British people planted gardens with vegetables, and their food is more nutritious than before the war." Troubled by her father's words, Penny frowned. "Nutritious means better food, Penny. Your mother's house in London is the best place to live."

Helen rolled her eyes at her husband. "Children, your dad and I have two houses, one in Jackson and one in London."

Ed lifted his eyebrows and shrugged. "What's mine is yours, what's yours is yours."

Helen reached across the back of the front seat and lightly punched Ed's shoulder. "That's not the way it works, my darling. What's mine is ours."

"Where will you live when you are not living in *our* house in London?" said Thad.

"Difficult to say, son, except on army posts in France and Germany."

The driver pulled the car up to the curb. "Here's our house," said Helen.

Penny and Thad looked wide-eyed at the home where they would live.

"There's no grass. The steps to the house are on the sidewalk, different from our house in Jackson," said Thad.

"We have a garden in back of the house," said Helen.

"Garden?"

"Yes, flowers and vegetables and with grass for you," said Helen.

Ed unlocked the door, and Penny dashed by him and ran around the elegant rooms in her new home.

"Things are dusty, Ed," said Helen.

"I'll be here a couple of days to help you clean."

Helen removed her gloves. "Look. The caretaker left mail on the foyer table. There's a letter for me from someone named David Atherton." She tipped her head. "The name is familiar."

Ed looked over Helen's shoulder and raised an eyebrow at the envelope addressed to Dean Wright.

"Do you know him?"

Ed did not answer her.

"I should know better than to ask."

"Yes, it is better not to ask," he said grimly to his wife and kissed her cheek before removing his coat.

"I'm sorry," said Helen.

Ed walked away from Helen. *David Atherton is alive.* The OSS held POW Hans Schiller, and after Schiller's army transfer, David Atherton would testify in person for prosecutors in a military trial.

* * *

In the still, hot August air, Hans stretched, limbered up his back and leg muscles, and looked at the droopy American flying at full-mast. The American flag antagonized him. Why the flag flew at half-mast for thirty days in April and May still puzzled him. In moments, he heard cars honking, whistles blowing, and church bells ringing. The constant sounds proclaimed celebration, and cathedral bells pealed out Allied victory. The war was over. How long now before his trial?

Concentrating on German physical and mental toughness, the captured saboteur pushed up and down on the blistering concrete, sweated until exhausted, and whispered, "I'll stand without a blindfold before the firing squad.

Limp from exercising and the heat, Hans sat on his bed, closed his eyes, and randomly reached for one of the books provided by the prison librarian. Gripping a book in his hands, he opened his eyes and read, *Holy Bible, placed by The Gideons.*

CHAPTER 49

V-J Day, WWII Victory

*H*ans didn't understand why he heard car horns, whistles, and church bells in May and August and again on September 2, but when noise went on hour after hour, he realized the war was over. The Allies won.

He leaned across the prison cell bed and scratched off the second of September 1945 on his wall calendar, then pressed his fingers against his temples. The calendar screamed defeat, and the echoes of celebration disheartened him. *My life has no meaning; execution ends the misery.*

Hans sat with his head in his hands and remembered the first two years of the war when an extraordinary German fighting force achieved astonishing success. Jumping from his bed, he threw his head and shoulders back in a proud German military stance and pictured himself standing before a firing squad.

* * *

In West Texas, Dave and Molly Atherton listened to the September 2 radio broadcast of Japan's formal surrender aboard the USS *Missouri*, anchored in Tokyo Bay.

"I know David is alive, and we'll hear from him soon," Molly said from the couch. She continued listening to the surrender ceremony and added another row to the throw she was knitting for her son's homecoming.

Dave didn't share his wife's hope for their son. A second telegram from a navy chaplain reported their son missing from a hospital ship, bombed by a Japanese suicide pilot. The explosion killed patients, doctors, and nurses.

Dave stared at the Philco. In the late thirties, he'd humored Molly and bought the lowboy model radio, mounted on legs, for their living room. Over the years, they enjoyed tuning in and listening to Lum and Abner, Jack Benny, and Bob Hope. He never dreamed they'd sit and listen to programs like "How to Do Business with Hitler," war news from Europe and Japan. Finally, they heard the September 2 broadcast of the end of the war.

Morbid over the fate of his son, Dave slumped and burrowed deep into his high-back, upholstered chair by the radio, turning his face away from Molly. The phone ringing broke into his dark thoughts. He expected the hospital call. "Hello, this is Doctor—"

"Dad?"

"David? David!" His heart raced. "Molly, come quick. It's David!" Dave cradled the phone between Molly's ear and his head.

"Dad, Mother?"

"Oh, son. Are you all right? You sound far off. They reported you missing," said his mother.

"I'm not missing. The navy rescued me twice in the Pacific, transferred me from the bombed hospital ship, the US *Comfort*, that limped in for dry dock and repairs at Guam to Pearl Harbor. From Pearl, the navy flew me to Los Angeles and then to the navy hospital in San Diego. Dad, Colonel Walters, my orthopedic surgeon, wants to speak with you. Doctor Walters, my father."

Dave waved Molly away and put the phone closer to his ear and said, "I understand, Doctor Wallace. We want to be with David. We'll be ready when you call."

Dave hung the phone on the wall box hook and returned to the living room. Molly stared at him from the couch. "What's wrong with our boy?"

Her husband sat beside Molly and wrapped his arms around her. "David has severe injuries to his legs. The doctor has tough decisions for David, and we need to be with him. We'll never make it to San Diego on time by train, but Dr. Walters can get us on a plane within hours. He'll call with the exact time in a few minutes."

Molly looked down at her hands and then back at her husband. "Dave, will they amputate his legs?"

"I don't know, but we are flying out there. I have to find a surgeon to cover for me. Go upstairs and pack for the trip." Sobbing, Molly rushed upstairs.

Dr. Atherton clicked the phone. "Operator, this is Doctor Atherton. Please ring my nurse at 3390."

* * *

September 20, 1945

In Berlin, Colonel Ed Matthews interrogated liberated victims of concentration camps for the upcoming international military tribunals of war criminals. After his last interview, he rubbed his neck and cleared his desk for Friday's work.

The phone on his desk rang, and Ed grimaced at the jarring sound. A late-day call on the last workday of the week raised a red flag. He looked forward to the weekend with Helen and the children, and he didn't want to miss his flight to London. He paused with his hand on the receiver before he said, "Colonel Matthews."

"Ed, Mike Ward. How are things going over there?"

"We're getting enormous evidence from concentration camp victims for the upcoming international law trials."

"Are you ready for the latest information from Washington?"

"What's up?" said Ed.

"The termination of OSS."

"The government's closing out the OSS?"

"Yes. And OSS work is being reassigned to the State and War Departments and other agencies. Shutting down the OSS brought about Hans Schiller's transfer to federal prison until a trial by an army tribunal or military commission."

"Interesting."

"And you'll be interested to know, as Schiller's case officer, your responsibility transferred with Schiller. The army requested a meeting between you and the prison warden in Washington."

"I'm on call with whatever happens to Schiller?"

"That's right. You're booked on a flight from Berlin to DC tomorrow."

"Hans Schiller's an albatross around my neck. I thought I left my Schiller burden with you. What else is new?"

"Schiller confessed only the names of men under his command. Our investigation of Schiller, his team, and the restaurant led to a New Orleans banker and an older man, Arnold Kellet, both German agents.

We arrested the banker. When we confronted Keller, he died from a heart attack."

"I'm not surprised your investigation uncovered a support system for Schiller."

"We weren't surprised either. You've heard about Koch?" said Mike.

"Yeah. Bernie Koch's name popped up in the latest intelligence report," said Ed.

"Schiller's right-hand man escaped our dragnet. In a letter to Schiller from his mother, we discovered Koch visited Schiller's mother in Berlin. Another letter from Schiller's mother revealed the mother and sister moved from a bombed-out Berlin apartment to a country house in the American sector where Koch routinely visited them."

"American intelligence keeps an eye on Koch, our wayward saboteur?"

"So it appears, but the war is over."

"Not for me," said Ed. "I'll be in Europe with the army of occupation for a while. Is my flight tomorrow to Washington out of Berlin or London?"

"Berlin."

CHAPTER 50

Postwar Days

March 1946

ucinda determined she'd never love anyone but David Atherton and grieved for her sailor sweetheart. In a spinster role, she dressed plainly, never wore makeup, brushed her hair straight back, and twisted it into a bun.

Lucinda's primness didn't curb the interest of veterans enrolled in the university under the GI Bill with paid tuition and expenses. She ignored the flirtations of war-weary young men who asked her for dates.

One insistent veteran eyed the pretty, gloomy-looking girl and said, "Hi, Lucinda. I'm Ray. We're in the same English class. How about going out for dinner with me?"

"I don't date."

"You're young and pretty. Why not?"

"I just don't. That's why."

"No, there's a reason. I bet you're pining for someone lost in the war. If your lost love were the right kind of guy, he'd want you to date."

"Thank you. I can't go out with you."

"That's it."

"Yes, that's the way it is."

At home, Louisa attempted to help Lucinda overcome her sorrow for David. "Lucinda, you're wearing skirts and blouses we bought before the war. You have interviews coming up for a job, and you need new clothes. Let's go shopping."

"I don't want to shop, Mother."

"You never wear makeup or lipstick and pull your hair straight back. You look sad."

"I'm fine, neat, and clean. Employers are interested in an employee's ability, not their clothes." Louisa sighed and said no more.

* * *

In her new job at the university medical school hospital and library, Lucinda kept her dowdy hairdo and worked in dreary-looking clothes. Attracted by Lucinda's beauty, medical students ignored her appearance and asked Lucinda for dates, but she never accepted.

On a bright March day, the would-be spinster assembled research notes and references she'd written on cards in the library and walked to her office to type up the information. A swift breeze blew a scarf off her head. She chased the scarf and brushed tendrils of hair from her eyes, and almost ran into a med student walking ahead of her. The lanky figure disappeared inside her office building, and she followed. Inside, the David lookalike walked down the long corridor, stopped, and propped himself against the wall.

Lucinda walked closer to the tall figure. Was she hallucinating? *No.* David stood with his head down, reading a letter written on fancy blue stationery.

Stunned, Lucinda said, "Hi." David never looked up from the letter. Her face flushed, and she walked with quick steps away from him.

Lucinda couldn't believe she'd seen David in the corridor, but she had. He hadn't changed, not one bit. He was as good-looking as the first time she saw him. Absorbed in the letter, he hadn't acknowledged her. She didn't exist for him, never had and never would. His silence provoked a wave of burning anger within her, not to mention disappointment. She had waited for him, pined over him, prayed, and remained faithful to him through the war.

Thoughts stifled for two years exploded in her head. David had seen her behind the hedge and revealed her name, or the OSS team would never have discovered her footprints and locked her up for six months. It had to be his fault. Who else would have reported her?

Now David courted someone who wrote letters to him on fancy stationery. Hot tears covered Lucinda's face, and she said, "If ever see David Atherton again, I won't speak to him."

In her apartment, she examined herself in a long mirror. *I'll never be a plain Jane again. Free of David, I'm no longer committed to single life forever.* She unpinned the bun on the back of her head and called a hairstylist for an appointment early the next morning.

In an adrenaline-induced frenzy, she pulled everything out of her closet, scrutinized her clothes, and packed her spinster outfits in a box for Goodwill. On other garments, she nipped hanging threads, sewed on loose or missing buttons, and took a tuck here and there for a tighter fit.

She checked her watch and rushed out before shops closed for a pretty new dress or two. Exhausted after trying on and buying three new outfits, she lathered her face with Pond's cold cream, showered, and gave herself a manicure and pedicure.

The second she put her head on her pillow, thoughts of David sounded like a Chinese gong in her head. The spinster mode was her creation, not God's. She thanked the Lord for bringing David home safely. "He is all yours, for whatever, Lord. I accept Your decision. I saw him reading a letter from a girl he loves, and you did too, Lord. I pray David will be happy. At twenty-two, I am no longer content to be an unmarried woman. If there is a Christian man out there You want for me, please do not keep me waiting. Let me know real soon. In Your will, I pray. In Jesus's name. Amen."

Lucinda's alarm sounded two hours early. She dressed and hurried for her appointment at the hair salon. The sleepy-eyed beautician washed, styled, and combed Lucinda's reddish-brown hair. "Do you always have your hair done at this hour?"

"Not always," said Lucinda, looking in the mirror at her new image. "I've never looked better in my life."

The now wide-awake stylist agreed. "Lucinda, would you consent to be my model at an upcoming stylist show?"

"Of course, I will. I love my hair," said a smiling Lucinda. She paid the stylist and rushed out for work. *I have no worries. The Lord provides, and He'll find a sweetheart for me.* At the library, she picked up an armload of books, walked to her office building, and stepped off the elevator across from her office.

"Lucinda?"

Startled, she whirled around, and there stood David, tall and handsome as ever. She pledged never to speak to him again, but her feet wouldn't move.

"Lucinda, you look fantastic. It's wonderful to see you again."

"We met yesterday. I spoke to you, and you never looked up." She tipped her chin up and pursed her lips.

David narrowed his eyes. "What are you talking about?"

"I walked right by you, spoke to you, and you never looked up."

He looked confused. "You walked right by me, spoke, and I didn't speak to you? Where were you? Where was I?"

"You were leaning against the first-floor corridor wall. I spoke, but you were too absorbed in a piece of blue stationery to look up." The amused look that crossed David's face infuriated her.

"So the letter was a problem."

"No, your reading it."

"You were jealous?" said David with a twinkle in his eye.

"No, indeed. How could I be jealous? You don't know I exist."

"Oh, no. I know you exist," said David, laughing at her anger.

"Don't laugh at me. I've prayed for you every night for two years."

David's eyes gleamed. "Mm-mm, I see. You prayed for me every night for two years. What did you pray last night?"

"I thanked God you were alive."

"Is that all?" said David, grinning.

She tightened her arms around the books and hugged them to her chest. "That's between the Lord and me."

"When praying about me, that's three. You, the Lord, and me," said David and stepped toward her.

Lucinda stepped back, but her eyes never left his. "Prayers are private."

"The Lord works in strange and mysterious ways." David reached into his pocket and held up the letter. "Would you like to read the letter?"

"Why would I want to read a letter from some girl you love?" *Some girl who's not me.*

"Come with me for a Coke, and I'll tell you all about the girl I love," said David.

Lucinda shook her head. "You are impossible. You came up here to tell me you are in love with whoever wrote that letter and want to talk about her over a Coke with me? How dare you insult me?"

"The letter is not from the girl I love, but I confess the letter is about the girl I love with all my heart. Don't be angry, Lucinda."

Standing her ground, Lucinda said, "I am not angry."

David reached out and tucked a loose strand of Lucinda's hair behind her ear, sending shivers down her spine. "The letter is from Dean Helen Wright, now Helen Matthews."

How did Dean Matthews know how to get in touch with him? And why hadn't Helen Matthews told her? The dean knew how she felt about David and how she worried about him.

"The letter is from Miss Helen?"

"That's right. I want to tell you all about it. Let's get out of this hallway." David reached for Lucinda's books.

"No. I have other plans." *Don't I, Lord?*

"What plans?" quizzed David.

"Now who's jealous?" Lucinda smiled coyly.

He pulled the letter from his back pocket and held it up. "This letter is from Mrs. Matthews in response to a letter I wrote to her. I will not tell you what's in the letter unless you come with me. Please," he said. He placed his free hand on her shoulder and looked intently into her eyes.

"Give me those books and go with me to the snack shop." His demand shocked her.

After he'd ignored her for two years—and yesterday she wasn't about to let David Atherton tell her what to do, she gave in and said, "I will go with you. There is no need for you to carry my books. We're standing in front of my office."

Weak in the knees, she handed him the books and unlocked the door. "You may put the books on my desk." She adjusted the time on a Will Be Back sign and hung it on the office door.

David tucked the mysterious letter back into his pocket. "Do you come to work this early every morning?" he said and grasped her hand in his.

"No." *Oh, Lord, don't put me through this. It is too much to feel his strong hand gripping mine again. He loves someone else.*

David walked toward the exit.

"You are limping. Were you hurt?"

He shrugged. "Yeah, kinda banged up."

"What happened?" She put her hand on his upper arm, then removed it. "Tell me."

"I will, but first, I'm hungry. I plan to order bacon, eggs, grits, biscuits, and coffee. Will you join me for breakfast?"

"Yes." The David she loved was back. Maybe he had fallen in love with a nurse. She wanted him to take her in his arms. *Lord, give me the strength and grace to hear him out.*

David ushered her into a booth at the popular snack shop. She waited until he ordered and said, "David, tell me what happened to you."

"I was blown off my first ship and put aboard the *Comfort*, a hospital ship. Next, a kamikaze pilot hit the *Comfort*. The explosion severely injured my right leg and threw me into the sea."

"I remember hearing about that. You were on the *Comfort?*"

"Yep. I was strapped out on a gurney and rolled right out to sea, but sailors rescued me. The USS *Comfort* limped into Guam for repairs. Months later, the navy shipped me to Pearl Harbor, Los Angeles, and finally to the navy hospital in San Diego for surgery. Encouraged by my surgeon, I applied for medical school and was accepted. The navy arranged for follow-up treatment at the university orthopedic clinic, and here I am. Look at this." David thrust out his right leg and exposed a prosthesis attached to his knee.

Lucinda cringed. "Oh, David, you lost your leg."

"The lower right limb," said David.

"I am so sorry."

"I have been blessed with the best orthopedic care in the world." David pulled out his wallet. "I have something that kept me alive. I read it on my ship, on the *Comfort*, when I lost my leg and throughout rehab." Carefully unfolding onion paper, he said, "Some days, I read it every hour."

Lucinda's hand went to her mouth. "My letter to you! But you never answered it."

"I read it, wrapped it in a waterproof scrap I found, and put it in my wallet. Seconds later, the Japanese bombed my ship."

Tears streamed down Lucinda's face.

"Hey, don't cry. I'm okay. A month ago, I called Dean Wright's office, trying to locate you, and found out she'd married. The college gave me the dean's address in Jackson, and her mother-in-law gave me her address in London."

"This is unbelievable." Lucinda wiped her tears with a napkin.

David took her hand from across the table. "I didn't want to contact you until I walked again." He dropped his gaze to their hands and ran his thumb over the top of hers. "I want to know one thing. Is there anyone else? What other plans were you talking about earlier?"

"My plans are whatever the Lord wills for me," she said calmly but tingled all over from the look in David's eyes and his husky voice.

"Lucinda, I am here and can walk by the grace of God. I've loved you since the day we met. I love you with all my heart. You saw the prosthesis. I don't want you to martyr yourself. I want you to think before you answer. Will you marry me?"

Lucinda's breath caught in her throat, and she looked into David's eyes. "For two years, I've thought about marrying you. I don't need to think about it, David Atherton. Yes. Yes!"

"I have a prosthesis. I am not the same guy who sang, 'I don't want to sit under the apple tree with anyone but you.'"

"You are the same to me, darling," said Lucinda. David reached across the table, squeezed her hand, and kissed it. He wrinkled his face. "I don't want to want to make a public spectacle."

"Always one to abide by protocol," teased Lucinda.

"My protocol is to kiss you again and again and ask you to marry me on bended knee. Let's get out of here." David tossed cash on the table, gripped Lucinda's hand tightly, and led her out of the snack shop. "I have waited so long to take you in my arms, kiss you, and tell you how much I love you."

Lucinda said demurely, "There's a hedge."

David pulled Lucinda behind the hedge, took her face in his hands, kissed her, and dropped down on his good knee. "I love you with all my heart, sweetheart. Will you marry me?"

"Yes, yes, and yes again. You've asked me twice; I answered twice. It's official."

"Not yet," said David. He reached in his pocket, pulled out a box, and slipped a diamond ring on Lucinda's finger. "Now it's official." He tugged on his prosthesis, stood up, and hugged her.

"It's beautiful," said Lucinda, admiring the gorgeous diamond on her finger. "You didn't know until yesterday where I was, and you bought this ring?" she said, twirling the stunning platinum ring around her finger.

"My grandmother left her engagement ring to me. My parents had it. When I told them about you, they gave me the ring. My parents are here, and now that you've accepted my proposal, you get to eat dinner with them tonight."

"I can't wait to meet them."

"I'm still curious to hear what you prayed last night," taunted David.

"I told you. I thanked the Lord for keeping you safe."

"After seeing me in the hall and not speaking, I can't believe you love me as much as you say, and that's all you prayed."

"I thought you loved someone else."

"You prayed for someone else?"

Lucinda laughed. "Only the Lord knows the truth. Oh, David, I love you." She snuggled in his arms. "It's between the Lord and me."

"No, now we're three, the Lord, you, and me. No secrets."

"I haven't seen the blue letter yet," joked Lucinda.

David smiled and handed her the letter. "After I read Dean Wright's letter yesterday, I called your folks and told them about the prosthesis, gave your father a rundown on my finances, and told him, if you'd have me, I planned to marry you. Incidentally, my paycheck went into savings while I was in the hospital, and I am still in the navy on disability. The government's GI Bill is paying for med school."

"David, I can't believe this. You called my parents before you asked me?"

"It is the proper way. Your father was a little hesitant. They want to meet me, of course."

"I can believe that. After you left Middleton, I mentioned you to my mother, and the Woman's Missionary Union, WMU, prayed for your safety during the war."

"The Lord kept me afloat and brought me back to you. One of these days soon, I want to thank your mother's friends for their prayers." He placed a hand on her cheek. "Lucinda, I prayed for you every day after I left Middleton. I told your father I loved you before I left Middleton. I told my parents about you in San Diego, and they said if the good Lord was willing to save me at sea, He saved you for me." He kissed her again. "I wanted to call from San Diego but couldn't until I could walk. I thought about marrying you before we shipped out, but honestly, Lucinda, you needed time to grow up."

She stiffened. "I was grown-up."

"Not quite," David said with a sly grin on his face. "Seriously, I was in no position to bind you to me until the end of the war. By the way, why did you leave Middleton?"

"I will tell you. Not now." Tears welled in her eyes, despite her struggle to keep them back. Someday she'd tell her sweetheart about the German spy, Colonel Matthews, and her life in the barracks.

"Why are you crying, sweetheart? I wondered; that's all." He reached over and brushed her hair from her cheek. "Forget it. Let's talk about the wedding date. We will marry at the end of the quarter."

"I can't believe you made all these plans. You didn't even know where I was until yesterday," Lucinda said.

"I work on the Lord's timetable, not mine."

"Since you've made so many plans, I have one request. I never saw you all *grown-up* in your officer's uniform. Will you wear the uniform on our wedding day?"

David laughed. "I can handle that if you can share what you prayed about last night."

Lucinda smiled. "The Lord's timetable."

CHAPTER 51

A Decision

June 11, 1946

*H*ans Schiller marked through June 11 on his cell wall. It had been nine months since the church bells rang, car horns beeped for hours, and he knew the Allied forces had defeated Nazi Germany.

Late in September 1945, guards shackled him and put a change of clothes and his articles into a clean laundry bag. Except for the Gideon Bible, the guards packed up all of the books and magazines on loan from the prison library. Hans watched one guard place the Bible in the laundry bag and waited for the blindfold and hood routine. Without covering his head, guards ushered him outside the building and loaded him onto a bus. The driver pulled the vehicle into heavy city traffic. Hans peered out the bus window and gasped at well-known sites in Washington, DC, the city unknown to him for months.

The OSS transferred him to the US Army and placed him in isolation at a federal prison. Stressed out more and more each month, Hans waited for his trial. His prison keepers kept him supplied with paper and pen for writing to his family, but writing the letters was difficult. He balanced the writing tablet on his knees but suffered from writer's block. Did he dare write the truth? "Mutter, you don't know the US imprisoned your son for sabotage and a military trial, with execution a foregone conclusion. I pray you and my sister never know."

He could not write his mother the truth and scribbled, "I have a good place to sleep and plenty to eat. Hope to see you soon. Love to you and Schwester."

Censors combed his letters and those from his mother for information. Mutter was smart. He omitted German friends' names in letters to his mother, and his mother did the same. Hans wondered if his mother or sister shared his letters with Ulla, his long-ago sweetheart. Thinking about his family and Ulla disheartened him. "I'm a Nazi saboteur. How much longer before I face the military tribunal?" he muttered.

Reading the Bible and exercising kept his mind off the inevitable. Lowering his body to the floor, he pushed up and down and counted, "Fifty-one, fifty-two," and on and on until he collapsed on the floor.

Half-asleep in a pool of sweat, he heard the door to his cell open and looked up. A guard and an army lieutenant stood inside his cell.

"Agent Schiller, come with me," said the officer. The lieutenant's command jolted him, but Hans pulled himself up and saluted.

The guard said, "You will shower before we take you to the warden's office."

In the shower, as usual, the guard handed Hans bar soap and a towel. The word *warden* echoed in his ears. Hans took his time lathering and rinsing off his body, until the guard shouted, "Your clothes are in the garment bag hanging on the wall, and shoes are in the sack by the chair."

Hans slowly wiped his body dry, but beads of water formed on his upper lip. He opened the garment bag and found a German officer uniform. His moment had come—*trial time*. Hans scowled at the sinister black SS officer's uniform. Facing an American military tribunal, he'd preferred the less intimidating, well-tailored, field-gray Wehrmacht (Nazi troops) uniform. Hans shoved his feet into American-made Florsheim shoes and stood. The American-made shoes fit perfectly. Standing in the Florsheims before a firing squad, his feet wouldn't hurt.

Hans dragged his fingers through his wet hair. A guard handed him a comb, and Hans smoothed out his tangled hair.

"Ready?" said the officer.

"Yes." *I've waited long, miserable months for this day.*

Hans's taut leg muscles served him well on his walk to the warden's office, and his German heritage and robust health gave him the courage to face his captors. A personal victory—but was it? *Oh, God, I repent of my sins. Have mercy on me. Give me eternal life.*

* * *

Hans, shocked to see Colonel Matthews in the warden's office, saluted the colonel calmly. *Payback time. You and I are equivalents, Colonel, trained to be spies, saboteurs, and killers. If I were free, revenge would be mine. But the revenge is yours—my execution.*

The colonel spoke first. "Agent Schiller, under an order for American and German prisoners of war exchange, the United States Army will fly you to the American sector of Berlin where you will be released, repatriated."

Hans's legs buckled beneath him. The guard put his hand on Hans's back and steadied him. Hans straightened up and said weakly, "Thank you." The American sector of Berlin? How had the Allies divided his country?

A correctional officer entered and handed him a small bag. The colonel said, "Personal belongings from your cell. You will be transported directly to the airport for the flight to Berlin."

Hans paled, said thank you again, and saluted.

* * *

Accompanied by Colonel Matthews, Hans entered an army air force plane for the long flight to his homeland. At daybreak, from the air, he stared at the unbelievable mass destruction of Berlin apartments and buildings. The plane jolted on landing and rolled to a stop away from terminal buildings. An army sedan pulled close to the plane for Colonel Matthews and Hans's trip to the US Army headquarters in Berlin.

In a darkened room, Hans watched documentaries of Nazi destruction in German-occupied countries and concentration camps. After viewing the films, a US sergeant escorted Hans to an office labeled Repatriations. Surprised to find himself seated before Colonel Matthews again, Hans relaxed as the colonel said, "Allied nations transfer some repatriated POWs for labor in France and England. Because OSS, American Intelligence, held you, pending a military trial until transfer to a US federal prison, your repatriation was different.

"Under the Geneva Convention, POWs may work with pay. Held in maximum security, you did not have the choice of working, and there is no stipend on discharge." The colonel pointed to a box near the door. "The army boxed up your personal belongings from The Café and The Willow." Hans glanced over his shoulder and saw the laundry bag packed by prison guards in DC.

"The army provides transportation to your mother's home in the country. The driver is waiting in the front office for you. Repatriation completed. You may leave."

Schiller said thank you and saluted, and the colonel returned the salute.

CHAPTER 52

Fifty Years Later

*A*t the famous New York hotel, an attendant recognized the elderly gentlemen approaching the front desk and hit a buzzer for the manager, who appeared and greeted the distinguished guest.

"Mr. Schiller. It's good to see you. We were saddened to hear about Mrs. Schiller."

"Thank you for your kind words. Mrs. Schiller's death was a shock. We planned the trip together. I intend to fulfill the purpose of our journey to the US. I reserved a suite for several weeks, but I'll be in and out of the city during that time."

"We'll have a limo and the concierge available for you at any time."

"Thank you very much. I'll call the concierge this afternoon," said Hans.

The manager signaled an operator and said, "Hold an elevator."

A porter appeared with a baggage cart and reached for Hans's briefcase. Hans waved his hand over his luggage and said, "I'll hold onto the case," and gripped it tighter. The manager smiled and accompanied Hans and the porter to the elevator.

In a luxury suite, a butler adjusted drapes and turned on lamps. The manager examined the bedroom and living room and handed Hans the keys. "Welcome. Your suite appears in perfect order." He placed his card and a newspaper on the handsome desk in the living room and said, "If you need anything, call me anytime, twenty-four seven."

"Thank you," Hans said and tipped the porter, who closed the suite door.

Hans opened his briefcase and arranged documents on the desk. Loneliness, the same bleak feeling he experienced in prison, swept over the successful businessman. He missed Ulla and had to accomplish alone what he and his sweetheart planned to do together. Swiping his brow, Hans slipped off his shoes and stretched out on the sofa. He'd glanced over at the papers signed by Ulla and him on the desk. His wife's death changed the game plan. Without Ulla, where would his sweetheart's visionary idea lead him?

The canceled US trip began when he and Ulla joined former POWs and their spouses on a memory trip to Camp Clinton.

"Hans, I want to see what you saw, go where you went, get a sense of your experiences during the war while I prayed and waited for you to come home."

He and his Ulla strolled about the Middleton campus, sat on the chapel steps, and stood at the site that led to his capture. At the football field, he jumped at the hedge and startled his wife. "Hans!" Ulla shrieked.

"Now you know. A leap at the hedge led to my capture and sent me home to my sweetheart," he'd said and hugged his wife.

Glancing at the documents legalized before Ulla's death, he mulled over carrying out Ulla's dream on his own. He could tap out on two fingers the people who knew the details of his capture. The colonel and Bernie Koch. He'd considered asking Bernie Koch to help him carry out Ulla's mission in the US. It wasn't too late to get Bernie's help, but out of respect for his darling Ulla, Hans decided against including Bernie on Ulla's mission, a mission for the man she loved. *I never deserved the love you gave me, Ulla.*

Until his repatriation, he didn't know what happened to Bernie, but one day Bernie showed up at his mother's house, the house inherited from her brother, his uncle Ernst.

In Berlin, Bernie confided, "After the camp escape for you failed, Hans, I drove back country roads to the Baton Rouge apartment and stayed there until the food ran out. I settled up with the apartment manager, hung around the docks for a couple of days, stowed away on a freighter to Brazil, and worked my way back to Germany." Bernie patted his stomach. "I have starved here now for months."

Hans remembered asking Bernie about job prospects. "None, except construction, but very little building with money scarce," said Bernie.

Hans's mother overheard the conversation. After Bernie left, his mother said, "Hans, my brother left money in a bank in Switzerland, and what's mine is yours," He partnered with his mother and founded a tool company that grew worldwide.

From the start of Schiller International, Inc., his espionage partner had been on the payroll, and Bernie's culinary ambitions materialized into an upscale restaurant in Paris, one of Schiller International's holdings. Bernie laughed as his Parisian patrons savored the food made from Mettie's Mississippi recipes.

War secrets bonded Hans and Bernie's friendship for life. Once a year, the Koch and Schiller families enjoyed vacations at the beach or a skiing trip. When Hans and Bernie were alone, they discussed their sabotage days and the emotions that surfaced while they worked undercover. Hans admitted his attraction for the college girl to Bernie and divulged that living as a sleeper in Myrtle continued to bother him.

"I never get rid of a hangover from the deception with friends I made in Myrtle. They were genuine people, Americans who knew what they were fighting for, and I didn't have a clue why I was fighting against them. I'd like to know how my Myrtle friends are, the direction of their lives after the war."

"Why don't we subscribe to the *Myrtle Gazette* and keep up with them?"

"That would have to be top secret between the two of us."

"We're old hands at that. We can make it work."

Bernie subscribed to the small-town, weekly newspaper under a fabricated name. The weekly paper arrived at a post office box in New York and was forwarded to a Paris box for Bernie. Bernie forwarded the newspaper in a fictitiously addressed manila envelope to a mailbox in Berlin known only to Hans. Keeping up with the people he once knew eased Hans's pain over the broken friendships.

From an article about the Gilead Baptist WMU and the women who prayed for David Atherton's safe return from the war, Hans learned Atherton spoke to the group about his war experiences, injuries, and amputation. WMU members from throughout the state came to the luncheon to hear the wounded veteran speak. The *Myrtle Gazette* printed Atherton's speech, a full account of the V-12 seaman/commissioned lieutenant's miraculous recovery, his homecoming, and his marriage to Lucinda Reed.

David and Lucinda Atherton lived in the Washington, DC, area, and accounts of their children's births and vacations in Myrtle appeared on the social page of the *Myrtle Gazette*, and Hans read of Tom Cunningham's and Louisa's deaths. From reading Myrtle's local news, he learned Colonel Matthews's son, Thad, married Lucinda Reed Atherton's daughter.

Hans slipped his hand into the top pocket of the briefcase, pulled out a copy of the *Myrtle Gazette,* and turned to David Atherton's obituary. Shifting his shoulders about and pushing his arms straight out, he rubbed his palms together and squelched thoughts of the girl who attracted him long ago.

Hans thought a moment before he picked up the phone. "This is Hans Schiller. Please book a flight for me to DC tonight at about six or seven o'clock. Thank you." He was glad he didn't bring Bernie along. His mission was too personal. Feelings he suppressed years ago kept surfacing. He closed his eyes and took a deep breath. Ulla had an appointment for her mission with a New York attorney, but he had an appointment with a man who once threatened to kill him.

* * *

Hans walked into the law office of Edward Matthews and Associates and introduced himself to the receptionist. "I'm James Smith. I have an appointment with Mr. Matthews."

"Yes, sir. He is expecting you, Mr. Smith." She buzzed her boss and walked Mr. Smith to the door.

Edward Matthews walked from behind his desk and extended his hand. "Mr. Smith." He dropped his hand, and the smile vanished from his face. "Hans Schiller."

"I felt an assumed name ensured an appointment for a matter of importance to me," said Hans, smiling.

The colonel wasn't amused. "A new client named Smith red-flagged the appointment for me. It occurred to me the name was fictitious. James and Smith are common names in America."

Hans looked at the stern expression on the colonel's face and continued. "If you'll forgive the alias and not throw me out, I'll get right to the point."

Ed remained standing and said, "I'll give you about two minutes of my time."

"Schiller International, Inc., my company, has lawyers in the US, but I need an attorney for a personal matter. Researching, I found your name and knew you would be the best attorney in America for my wife's mission."

At the mention of his wife, Ed said, "The firm is exacting about clients we take on." He pointed to the leather chairs placed before his massive desk.

Relieved Matthews would hear him out, Hans sat and faced the grim attorney rigidly seated in a tall swivel chair. Ed reached for a yellow legal pad and pen and looked at him. "Mr. Schiller, a few words from you will tell me if our firm is the right choice for you and your wife."

"I'll be brief. Nothing had more impact on my life than my capture and your threat to kill me, except what happened at the Middleton campus hedge. You know that, but you do not know the rest of the story."

Ed glared at him and looked at his watch.

"The war changed my life," Hans said. "Hiding out on Middleton's historic chapel steps cracked my sinister role in life. The student voices brought on poignant memories of collegiate life at the Universität Heidelberg, and thoughts of Ulla, my sweetheart, raced through my heart. At the parade field, the sight of the girl reminded me of Ulla and flooded my mind with desire, but the college girl could identify me, and in a saboteur frame of mind, I had to liquidate her."

Hans kept talking to the unreadable man on the other side of the desk. Edward, well trained in counterintelligence, sat with his back straight, his arms stiff at his side, and didn't move a muscle.

"Capture was a blessing. Being isolated in prison, expecting a trial with a certain death sentence, I read a lot. The prison library reading material included a Bible, a source of comfort during those many months. In prison, I confessed, repented of my sins. I asked the Lord for forgiveness for my many years in espionage and sabotage.

"Colonel, I've had a beautiful life. Ulla and I married, not long after my release in Berlin. We had a happy marriage, blessed with four devoted children. Ulla and I grew spiritually. Last year, we traveled with other ex-POWs and their wives to Camp Clinton.

"The yellow tulips planted by POWs at Camp Clinton intrigued Ulla. She said the color yellow represented joy, happiness, and honor. We walked around flowerbeds of yellow tulips on the Middleton campus and sat on the chapel steps, my hideout on spying trips to Middleton.

"At the chapel, Ulla reminded me the color yellow also stood for cowardliness and deceit, my life in espionage. We discussed how God's purpose for me unfolded. After years of treachery, followed by my capture and months of isolation, the Bible led me from spiritual blindness to spiritual recovery, no longer an agent of the devil. I surrendered my life to Christ in prison."

Ed Matthews's grim expression faded, and he relaxed in his chair.

"The trip to Middleton sparked Ulla's idea of a gift to Middleton, the place that led to my capture. That is the purpose of my appointment today."

"But your wife is not with you?"

"Several months after we made arrangements for a donation to Middleton, Ulla died of a heart attack."

Edward leaned forward for the first time and said, "I am sorry for your loss and offer you my sympathy."

Hans knitted his eyebrows. "Thank you. Ulla will always be with me. I want to thank you for not blowing my head off on December 15, 1944. I would have deserved it. I believe what a man thinks, he is. Even though I did not follow through on my thoughts of killing the girl, I sinned. The Lord saved me from the act of murdering her, and I asked for His forgiveness, and now, Colonel Matthews, I ask you to forgive me."

Convinced of Hans's sincerity, Ed held up a hand. "You asked for the Lord's forgiveness. That is enough for me. We are all sinners."

"The Lord defused an explosive situation. It is hard for me to believe I ever believed in the Nazi leaders' evil power. I grew up in the Lutheran Church and was a Christian but turned my back on what I knew to be true. Now, I am far from a perfect man, but I try to live up to His commandments and to be obedient. My cup runneth over. Psalm 23:5. The good Lord blessed me with a Godly wife and children and bestowed His heavenly blessings over every facet of my life.

"I come here humbly, asking you to handle an anonymous gift to Middleton College." Hans handed a check to the distinguished attorney for the establishment of an endowment at Middleton College.

Ed Matthews's eyes popped at the sizeable amount of the certified check drawn on a bank in England, payable to Middleton College. "Mr. Schiller, I am overwhelmed with the amount on this check and believe it to be the largest endowment ever bestowed on Middleton College."

"The Cold War and the Berlin Wall never dampened the growth of Schiller International, Inc. The corporation prospered beyond my wildest dreams. We have offices all over the world." Hans placed some papers on Ed's desk. "A few months before Ulla died, we finalized the endowment for Middleton. Funds routed through several banks ultimately deposit in a coded Swiss bank account, almost impossible to trace to Ulla and me."

Ed carefully read the documents before he spoke. "The documents confirm what you are telling me. It would be tough locating the source of this magnificent gift to Middleton College."

"My wife was an amazing woman. As the sole administrator of Schiller International's endowment funds, she made charitable gifts under her maiden name. The Middleton endowment was her idea. On her death, the account reverted to Schiller International, Inc. As CEO of Schiller, Inc., I am the legal donor." Hans leaned forward and looked Ed in the eyes. "I want you to run an intelligence report on me from the time OSS released me until now. I believe I will qualify as an acceptable *anonymous* donor. Will you administer the Middleton endowment for me?"

Edward moved his fingers across the folder containing the endowment documents. "The firm handles the legalities for clients with similar requests and portfolios that conform to each client's specific demands. We can manage the anonymous endowment from you for Middleton College. With proper management, the funds allotted to Middleton College appear never ending."

Ed paused. "But before I accept, I have one stipulation. It is not wise for one person to be in charge of an endowment. I don't have retirement in mind, but at my age, nothing is certain. I want another lawyer, a partner who understands the purpose, donor anonymity, and conservative investments, to work with me on the endowment. We need to formulate a legal document for the perpetual management of the invested funds."

Acknowledging Ed's request, Hans nodded several times in approval and said, "I agree." Edward Matthews's exactness and grasp of the college endowment pleased him. "I assume we are about the same age and in good health, but a second attorney is the best advice."

"I'm a few years older than you, Mr. Schiller, and have an attorney in mind to work with me on the fund. Thad Matthews, my son. Thad is an experienced lawyer and an alumnus of Middleton. I trust him. You can trust him. His wife is an alumna of Middleton."

Hans looked down and folded his hands in his lap. Ed Matthews didn't need to know he read about the Matthews-Reed marriage in the *Myrtle Gazette.*

Hans looked up and said, "Your son would be the best choice."

"Thad is in his office. Would you like me to call him? We can work out a few details while you are here."

"That would be great, and I'll be around for a few days to sign the necessary paperwork."

"Good." Ed buzzed his secretary. "Ask Thad to come to my office."

Excited by Ed Matthews's acceptance of him for a client, Hans handed a card across the desk. "Colonel, you may invoice your professional services at the address on this card."

Ed looked at the card and chuckled. "Mr. Schiller, the title of colonel ended with the war. In light of your generosity and the magnitude of your gift, the firm will absorb all our costs. Each month, you'll receive a financial statement with full disclosure of the investment fund and expenditures, and each semester, an update from Middleton with the names of students who receive scholarships.

"There will be the usual investment fees, but we'll do our best to keep the percentage as low as possible."

"Mr. Matthews, I do not expect you to handle the fund for nothing. I came here prepared to pay for legal expertise and advice."

"No, no. We service other charitable funds at no cost to the firm. In honesty, we have nothing comparable to your donation. We are grateful for the opportunity to administer the fund for the benefit of Middleton College. Should investment reports and the Middleton report be mailed to the address on this card?"

"Yes. It will be fun looking over investment statements and reading about students who benefit from the fund. I thank you, but you do not have to forego your charges for the fund. If any cost comes up, please send a bill to the address on the card."

"You'll never receive an invoice from this firm, Mr. Schiller." A rap sounded at the door, and Thad walked in.

"Thad, this is Mr. Schiller, a new client. Mr. Schiller enlisted our help for a top secret endowment for Middleton. We are ready to go to work on it. Can you clear your schedule so we can get started on this now?"

"No problem. If you give me a moment, I'll have my secretary take care of my schedule. My wife dropped by my office, and I suggested lunch. She'll understand."

"Good. Have your secretary send lunch trays in here for us."

Hans spoke up. "Excuse me, Thad. If you don't mind, and I'll yield to your father's advice, I'd like to meet your wife." Thad looked to his father for approval.

"Mr. Schiller made an appointment under an assumed name, Smith. He seeks anonymity for the endowment fund, and we need to keep it that way."

"Mrs. Schiller and I went to a lot of trouble to keep our charitable contributions anonymous. I'm CEO of Schiller International, Inc., and it's a challenge for me to live undercover." Han's eyes twinkled, and he looked with amusement at Ed Matthews. "For now, I prefer Smith."

Ed ignored Hans's sly reference to the past. "I'm not sure Smith will cut it, but we'll go with Smith for now," said Ed.

"I'm good at new names," said Hans with a grin. Ed frowned.

Puzzled at the expressions of the new client and his father, Thad said, "I'll be back in a few seconds, Dad."

"Bring Lucy with you," said Ed.

After Thad left, Hans looked at the stoic man he engaged for his attorney. "Mr. Matthews, I'm a different man from the man you first met, but I don't take life too seriously."

"You've always been an intelligent, clever, talented man. I'm impressed with your humbleness and spiritual sincerity."

"Only by the grace of God," said Hans.

"How far do you want to go—anonymous?"

"Ulla and I planned to keep Schiller International's name anonymous. It worked under her given name. I haven't had any part of Schiller International, Inc. charitable funds until now, and it's new and exciting for me. I'd like to keep the corporation name and my name anonymous."

Thad entered the office with his wife. "Lucy, this is Mr. Smith, a new client who wanted to meet you."

Hans caught his breath, and his eyes widened. Lucy Atherton-Matthews was the image of her mother. He stood and offered his hand. "I am delighted to meet you, Mrs. Matthews, and apologies for disrupting lunch with your husband."

Lucy Matthews shook his hand. "Please don't apologize. I came into town to meet my mother at the airport and need to be on my way. It's great meeting you, Mr. Smith."

Thad followed his wife to the door and said, "Dad, lunch trays are on the way, and I'll get the coffee."

The news Lucinda Reed was in town electrified Hans. He was a widower. Lucinda Reed Atherton, a widow. Would it be possible to see Lucinda again? Would she recognize him?

Out of the corner of his eye, Hans saw Ed Matthews gazing at him with amazement.

Hans looked his old enemy in the eye and said, "With God, all things are possible."

* * *

And other sheep I have which are not of this fold:
them also I must bring, and they shall hear my voice;
and there shall be one fold, and one shepherd.
—John 10:16

CPSIA information can be obtained
at www.ICGtesting.com
Printed in the USA
BVHW070709100720
583333BV00001B/71